Francis William Lauderdale Adams

Australian Essays

Francis William Lauderdale Adams

Australian Essays

ISBN/EAN: 9783337312732

Printed in Europe, USA, Canada, Australia, Japan

Cover: Foto ©Andreas Hilbeck / pixelio.de

More available books at **www.hansebooks.com**

BY

FRANCIS W. L. ADAMS.

AUTHOR OF

"LEICESTER, AN AUTOBIOGRAPHY."

Melbourne :

WILLIAM INGLIS & CO., FLINDERS STREET EAST.

LONDON PUBLISHERS: GRIFFITH, FARRAN & CO.

———

MDCCCLXXXVI.

MELBOURNE :
WILLIAM INGLIS AND CO., PRINTERS,
FLINDERS STREET EAST.

TO

MATTHEW ARNOLD

IN ENGLAND.

' *Master, with this I send you, as a boy*
that watches from below some cross-bow bird
swoop on his quarry carried up aloft,
and cries a cry of victory to his flight
with sheer joy of achievement—So to you
I send my voice across the sundering sea,
weak, lost within the winds and surfy waves,
but with all glad acknowledgment fulfilled
and honour to you and to sovran Truth!'

January, 1886.

CONTENTS.

— ✦━━━✦ —

PREFACE.

—◆◆◆—

I T would be absurd to suppose that it will not seem clear, to whatever readers this little book may find here, that one of the principal characters of the Dialogue is a man for whom we all, I think, feel more interest, admiration, and respect than any other among us. That this is so in reality, I must beg to deny, and I hope that, when I state that I neither have myself, nor know anyone who has, the honour of his acquaintance— nay, that I have never even *seen* him—I hope that I shall stand acquitted of all charges of personality. As for the other characters, there will too, I daresay, be found people ready to declare who are the originals, and to explain everything which is inconsistent with their theory by ascribing it to designed mystification on the part of the Author. For this, it seems, is an occupation like another. The Author believes that so much of a man's life as is public belongs to the public, and is at the fair use of the public's literary analysts, *videlicet* the critics, and that it is by no means an unfair use, to take such a life and freely present it in that individual form which it actually has to us in our moments of imagination and reflection. It seems, then, to him foolish, in considering, (to take it in the form of a well-known example), a book like D'Israeli's "Lothair" or "Endymion," to be trying to identify the characters with actual men. D'Israeli simply uses as much of actual men and actual events as he requires for his criticism of the time he is portraying, and is careless of the rest. I see here no attempt at mystification. I simply see an artist picking out the choicest materials he has to hand.

As regards both the Dialogue and the Essays, I would like to point out that they are professedly didactic, and, as such, are of course cast into the form which I believe most calculated to achieve their object. I am sure that I have neither the intention nor the wish to impugn the competency of the australian Press to deal with things australian. I am myself

a member, a very humble member of it, and am quite ready to
do myself the sincere pleasure of praising it.   At the same
time I cannot blind myself to the fact that its criticism is not
(let us say) ideal.   The "business of criticism," says the first
of living critics, " is simply *to know the best that is known and
thought in the world, and by in its turn making this known, to
create a current of true and fresh ideas.*"   Well now, I cannot,
I say, look upon this australian Press, of which I am so humble
a member, as the creator of such a current; and, (I will make
a clean breast of it at once!), bright and charming as I have
always found him in the " Echoes of the Week" and places of
like resort, I have viewed the triumphal approach of Mr. Sala
to us, and his even more triumphal progress among us, with
(as someone will presently be saying of me)—"with a jaundiced
eye."   And why?   The truth, the real truth, is, (May I be
forgiven for saying so?), that I do not believe that even Mr. Sala
can help us australian pressmen, (since I dare to place myself
in a company which includes such stupendous personages as
"The Vagabond" and the Editor of the Melbourne *Herald*),
to create that "current of true and fresh ideas" to which we
have alluded.   Truth, alas, is the private property of no man
—not even of Mr. George Augustus Sala.   And I confess to
finding myself at the point of wishing that, even for mere
variety's sake, we should hear more than we do of the ideas of
such personages as Goethe, Emerson, Renan, Arnold, and so
on: writers, of course, familiar to us all, and whom I, at any rate
must still continue to consider as not wholly exhausted.   They
may not have the depth of thought, the accuracy of detail,
the exquisite tact of expression which distinguish the genial
littérateur, and make his work, as one of my fellow pressmen
said the other day, "epoch-making," but I really do still
continue—I *must* still continue—to think that, despite all
these disadvantages, they are still capable of helping us a little
to that critical haven where our souls would be—to the source
of "a current of true and fresh ideas."

September, 1885.

AUSTRALIAN ESSAYS.

MELBOURNE, AND HER CIVILIZATION,

AS THEY STRIKE AN ENGLISHMAN.

Iт is difficult to speak of Melbourne fitly. The judgment of neither native nor foreigner can escape the influence of the phenomenal aspect of the city. Not fifty years ago its first child, Batman's, was born; not forty, it was a city; a little over thirty, it was the metropolis of a colony; and now (as the inscription on Batman's grave tells us) "*Circumspice!*" To natives their Melbourne is, and is only, "the magnificent city, classed by Sir George Bowen as the ninth in the world," "one of the wonders of the world." They cannot criticise, they can only praise it. To a foreigner, however, who, with all respect and admiration for the excellencies of the Melbourne of to-day as compared with the Melbourne of half-a-century ago, has travelled and seen and read, and cares very little for glorifying the *amour-propre* of this class or of that, and very much for really arriving at some more or less accurate idea of the significance of this city and its civilization ; to such a man, I say, the native melodies in the style of "Rule Britannia" which he hears everywhere and at all times are distasteful. Nay, he may possibly have at last to guard himself against the opposite extreme, and hold off depreciation with the one hand as he does laudation with the other !

The first thing, I think, that strikes a man who knows the three great modern cities of the world—London, Paris, New York—and is walking observingly about Melbourne is, that

Melbourne is made up of curious elements. There is something of London in her, something of Paris, something of New York, and something of her own. Here is an attraction to start with. Melbourne has, what might be called, the *metropolitan tone*. The look on the faces of her inhabitants is the *metropolitan look*. These people live quickly : such as life presents itself to them, they know it: as far as they can see, they have no prejudices. "I was born in Melbourne," said the wife of a small bootmaker to me once, "I was born in Melbourne, and I went to Tasmania for a bit, but I soon came back again. *I like to be in a place where they go ahead.*" The wife of a small bootmaker, you see, has the *metropolitan tone*, the *metropolitan look* about her ; she sees that there is a greater pleasure in life than sitting under your vine and your fig-tree ; she likes to be in a place where they go ahead. And she is a type of her city. Melbourne likes to "go ahead." Look at her public buildings, her New Law Courts not finished yet, her Town Hall, her Hospital, her Library, her Houses of Parliament, and above all her Banks! Nay, and she has become desirous of a fleet and has established a "Naval Torpedo Corps" with seven electricians. All this is well, very well. Melbourne, I say, lives quickly: such as life presents itself to her, she knows it : as far as she can see, she has no prejudices.

As far as she can see.—The limitation is important. The real question is, *how* far can she see ? how far does her civilization answer the requirements of a really fine civilization? what scope in it is there (as Mr. Arnold would say) for the satisfaction of the claims of conduct, of intellect and knowledge, of beauty and manners? Now in order the better to answer this question, let us think for a moment what are the chief elements that have operated and are still operating in this Melbourne and her civilization.

This is an English colony: it springs, as its poet Gordon (of whom there will presently be something to be remarked) says, in large capitals, it springs from "*the Anglo-Saxon race* . . . *the Norman blood.*" Well, if there is one quality which distinguishes this race, this blood, it is its determined strength. Wherever we have gone, whatever we have done, we have gone and we have done with all our heart and soul. We have made small, if any, attempt to conciliate others. Either they have had to give way before, or adapt themselves to us. India, America, Australia, they all bear witness to our determined, our pitiless

strength. What is the state of the weaker nations that opposed
us there? In America and Australia they are perishing off the
face of the earth; even in New Zealand, where the aborigines
are a really fine and noble race, we are, it seems, swiftly destroying them. In India, whose climate is too extreme for us ever to
make it a colony in the sense that America and Australia are
colonies; in India, since we could neither make the aborigines
give way, nor make them adapt themselves to us, we have simply
let them alone. They do not understand us, nor we them.
Of late, it is true, an interest in them, in their religion and
literature, has been springing up, but what a strange aspect do
we, the lords of India for some hundred and thirty years,
present! "In my own experience among Englishmen," says
an Indian scholar writing to the *Times* in 1874, "I have found
no general indifference to India, but I have found a Cimmerian
darkness about the manners and habits of my countrymen, an
almost poetical description of our customs, and a conception
no less wild and startling than the vagaries of Mandeville and
Marco Polo concerning our religion." Do we want any further
testimony than this to the determined, the pitiless strength of
"the Anglo-Saxon race . . . the Norman blood?"

Well, and how does all this concern Australia in general and
Melbourne in particular? It concerns them in this way, that
the civilization of Australia, of Melbourne, is an Anglo-Saxon
civilization, a civilization of the Norman blood, and that, with
all the good attendant on such a civilization, there is also all
the evil. All? Well, I will not say all, for that would be to
contradict one of the first and chief statements I made about
her, namely that "as far as she can see Melbourne has no
prejudices," a statement which I could not make of England.
" *This our native or adopted land,*" says an intelligent Australian critic, the late Mr. Marcus Clarke, "*has no past, no
story. No poet speaks to us.*" "*No,*" we might add, "*and
(thus far happily for you) neither, as far as you can see, does
any direct preacher of prejudice.*" And here, as I take it, we
have put our finger upon what is at once the strength and the
weakness of this civilization.

Let us consider it for a moment. The Australians have no
prejudice about an endowed Church, as we English have, and
hence they have, what we have not, religious liberty. As far
as I can make out, there is no reason why the wife of a clergyman of the Church of England should in this colony look

down upon the wife of a dissenting minister as her social inferior, and this is, on the whole, I think, well, for it tends to break up the notion of caste that exists between the two sects ; it tends, I mean, to their mutual benefit, to the interchange of the church's sense of "the beauty of holiness" with the chapel's sense of the passion of holiness.   Here, then, you are better off than we.   On the other hand, you have no prejudice, as we at last have, against Protection, and consequently you go on benefiting a class at the expense of the community in a manner that can only, I think, be defined as short-sighted and foolish.   Here we are better off than you.   Again, however, you have not the prejudice that we have against the interven-tion of the State.   You have nationalized your railways, and are attempting, as much as possible, to nationalize your land.*   You are beginning to see that a land tax, at any given rate of annual value, would be (as Mr. Fawcett puts it) "a valuable national resource, which might be utilized in rendering unnecessary the imposition of many taxes which will otherwise have to be imposed."   Here you are better off than we, better off both in fortune and general speculation.   Again, you have not yet arrived at Federalism, and what a waste of time and all time's products is implied in the want of central unity !   Now the first and third of these instances show the strength that is in this civilization, and the second shows a portion of the weakness, at present only a small portion, but, unless vigorous measures are resorted to and soon, this Protection will become the great evil that it is in America.   There is just the same cry there as here: " Protect the native industries until they are strong enough to stand alone"—as if an industry that has once been protected will ever care to stand alone again until it is compelled to ! as if a class benefited at the expense of the community will ever give up its benefit until the community takes it away again !

On one of the first afternoons I spent in Melbourne, I remember strolling into a well-known book-mart, the book-mart "at the sign of the rainbow."   I was interested both in the books and the people who were looking at or buying them. Here I found, almost at the London prices (for we get our twopence or threepence in the shilling on books now in London), all, or almost all, of the average London books of the day.   The popular scientific, theological, and even literary

* The remark is, of course, general.   Most of Victoria, as we all know, is unfortunately definitely sold.

books were to hand, somewhat cast into the shade, it is true, by a profusion of cheap English novels and journals, but still they were to hand. And who were the people that were buying them? The people of the dominant class, the middle-class. I began to enquire at what rate the popular, scientific, and even literary books were selling. Fairly, was the answer. "And how do Gordon's poems sell?" "*Oh they sell well,*" was the answer, "*he's the only poet we've turned out.*"

This pleased me, it made me think that the " go-ahead " element in Victorian and Melbourne life had gone ahead in this direction also. If, in a similar book-mart in Falmouth (say), I had asked how the poems of Charles Kingsley were sell-ing, it is a question whether much more than the name would have been recognized. And yet the middle-class here is as, and perhaps more, badly—more appallingly badly—off for a higher education than the English provincial middle class is. Whence comes it, then, that a poet like Gordon with the cheer and charge of our chivalry in him, with his sad "trust and only trust," and his

> " weary longings and yearnings
> for the mystical better things : "

Whence comes it that he is a popular poet here? Let him answer us English for himself and Melbourne :

> " You are slow, very slow, in discerning
> that book-lore and wisdom are twain:"

Yes, indeed, to Melbourne, such as life presents itself to her, she knows it, and, what is more, she knows that she knows it, and her self-knowledge gives her a contempt for the pedantry of the old world. Walk about in her streets, look at her private build-ings, these banks of hers, for instance, and you will see this. They *mean* something, they *express* something : they do not (as Mr. Arnold said of our British Belgravian architecture) "only express the impotence of the artist to express anything." They express a certain sense of movement, of progress, of conscious power. They say: "Some thirty years ago the first gold nuggets made their entry into William Street. Well, many more nuggets have followed, and wealth of other sorts has followed the nuggets, and we express that wealth—we express movement, progress, conscious power.—*Is that, now, what your English banks express?*" And we can only say that it is not, that our English banks express something quite different ; something, if deeper, slower ; if stronger, more clumsy.

But the matter does not end here. When we took the instance of the books and the people "at the sign of the rainbow," we took also the abode itself of the rainbow ; when we took the best of the private buildings, we took also the others. Many of them are hideous enough, we know ; this is what Americans, English, and Australians have in common, this inevitable brand of their civilization, of their determined, their pitiless strength. The same horrible "pot hat," "frock coat," and the rest, are to be found in London, in Calcutta, in New York, in Melbourne.

Let us sum up. "The Anglo-Saxon race, the Norman blood:" a colony made of this : a city into whose hands wealth and its power is suddenly phenomenally cast : a general sense of movement, of progress, of conscious power. This, I say, is Melbourne—Melbourne with its fine public buildings and tendency towards banality, with its hideous houses and tendency towards anarchy. And Melbourne is, after all, the Melbournians. Alas, then, how will this city and its civilization stand the test of a really fine city and fine civilization ? how far will they answer the requirements of such a civilization ? what scope is there in them for the satisfaction of the claims of conduct, of intellect and knowledge, of beauty, and manners ?

Of the first I have only to say that, so far as I can see, its claims are satisfied, satisfied as well as in a large city, and in a city of the above-mentioned composition, they can be. But of the second, of the claims of intellect and knowledge, what enormous room for improvement there is ! What a splendid field for culture lies in this middle-class that makes a popular poet of Adam Lindsay Gordon ! It tempts one to prophesy that, given a higher education for this middle-class, and fifty—forty—thirty years to work it through a generation, and it will leave the English middle-class as far behind in intellect and knowledge as, at the present moment, it is left behind by the middle-class, or rather the one great educated upper-class, of France.

There is still the other claim, that of beauty and manners. And it is here that your Australian, your Melbourne civilization is, I think, most wanting, is most weak ; it is here that one feels the terrible need of "a past, a story, a poet to speak to you." With the Library are a sculpture gallery and a picture gallery. What an arrangement in them both ! In the sculpture gallery "are to be seen," we are told, "admirably executed casts of ancient and modern sculpture, from the best European sources, copies of the Elgin marbles from the British Museum, and other productions from the European Continent." Yes, and Summers stands side by side with Michaelangelo! And poor busts of Moore and Goethe come between Antinous and the Louvre Apollo the Lizard slayer! But this, it may be said, is after all only an affair of an individual, the arranger. Not altogether so. If an audience thinks that a thing is done badly, they express their opinion, and the failure has to vanish. And how large a portion of the audience of Melbourne city, pray, is of opinion that quite half of its architecture is a failure, is hideous, is worthy only, as architecture, of abhorrence? how many are shocked by the atrocity of the Medical College building at the University? how many feel that Bourke Street, taken as a whole, is simply an insult to good taste?

"Yes, all this," it is said, "may be true, as abstract theory, but it is at present quite out of the sphere of practical application. You would talk of Federalism, and here is our good ex-Premier of New South Wales, Sir Henry Parkes, making it the subject of a farewell denunciation. 'I venture to say now,' says Sir Henry Parkes, 'here amongst you what I said when I had an opportunity in London, what I ventured to say to Lord Derby himself, that this federation scheme must prove a failure.' You talk of Free-trade and here is what an intelligent writer in the *Argus* says *apropos* of 'the promised tariff negotiations with Tasmania.' 'In America,' he says, 'there is no difficulty in inducing the States to see that, whatever may be their policy as regards the outside world, they should interchange as between each other in order that they may stand on as broad a base as possible, but we can only speculate on the existence of such a national spirit here.' —These facts, my good sir," it is said, "as indicative of the amount of opposition that the nation feels to the ideas of Free-trade and Federalism, are not encouraging."—They are not, let us admit it at once, but there are others which are; others, some of which we have been considering, and, above and beyond everything, there is one invaluable and in the end irresistible ally of these ideas : there is *the Tendency of the Age —the Time-Spirit*, as Goethe calls it. Things move more quickly now than they used to do : ideas, the modern ideas, are permeating the masses swiftly and thoroughly and universally.

We cannot tell, we can only speculate as to what another fifty
—forty—thirty years will actually bring forth.

Free-trade--Federalism — Higher Education, they all go
together.   The necessities of life are cheap here, wonderfully
cheap ; a man can get a dinner here for sixpence that he could
not get in England for twice or thrice the amount.   "There are
not," says the *Australasian Schoolmaster*, the organ of the State
Schools, "there are not many under-fed children in the Australian [as there are in the English] schools."   But the luxuries
of life (and let us remember that what we call the luxuries of
life are, after all, necessities ; they are the things which go to
make up our civilization, the things which make us feel that
there is a greater pleasure in life than sitting under your vine
and your fig-tree, whatever Mr. George may have to say to the
contrary)—the luxuries of life, I say, are dear here, very dear,
owing to, what I must be permitted to call, an exorbitant tariff,
and, consequently, the money that would be spent in fostering
a higher ideal of life, in preparing the way for a national higher
education, is spent on these luxuries, and the claims of intellect
and knowledge, and of beauty and manners, have to suffer for
it.   Here is your Mr. Marcus Clarke, for instance, talking
grimly, not to say bitterly, of " the capacity of this city to foster
poetic instinct," of his "astonishment that such work" as
Gordon's "was ever produced here."   He is astonished, you
see, that the claims of intellect and knowledge, and of beauty
and manners are enough satisfied in this city to produce a
talent of this sort ; he is astonished, because he does not see
that there is an element in this city which, in its way, is making
for at any rate the intellect and knowledge—an element which
is a product, not of England but of Australia ; a general sense
of movement, of progress, of conscious power.

Free-trade—Federalism—Higher Education, they all, I say,
go together ; but if one is more important than the other, then
it is the last.   Improvement, real improvement, must always be
from within outwards, not from without inwards.   All abiding
good comes, as it has been well said, by evolution not by
revolution.   "Our chief, our gravest want in this country at
present," says Arnold, "our *unum necessarium*, is a middle-
class, homogeneous, intelligent, civilized, brought up in good
public schools, and on the first plane."   How true is this of
Australia too, of Melbourne !   There are State schools for the
lower-class, but what is there for the great upper educated

class of the nation ? The voluntary schools, the "private adventure schools." And what sort of education do *they* supply either in England or here ? "The voluntary schools," says a happy shallow man in some Publishers' circular I lit on the other day, "the voluntary schools of the country" [of England] "have reached the highest degree of efficiency." This, to those who have taken the trouble to study the question, not to say to have considerable absolute experience in the English voluntary schools—this is intelligence as surprising as it ought to be gratifying. To such men, the idea they had arrived at of the English voluntary schools was somewhat different ; their idea being that these schools were, both socially and intellectually, the most inadequate that fall to the lot of any middle class among the civilized nations of Europe. "Comprehend," says Arnold to us Englishmen, and he might as well be saying it to you Australians, "comprehend that middle-class education—the higher education, as we have put it, of the great upper educated class—is a great democratic reform, of the truest, surest, safest description."

"But there are many difficulties to be overcome—so many, that we doubt these abstract theories to be at present within the sphere of practical application. There is such a mass of opposition to the idea of Federalism. And, as for the idea of Free-trade, we can only speculate on the existence of a national spirit here. The thinking public is quite content with its State schools for the lower class, and cares little or nothing about State schools and a higher education for the upper class. They are much more interested in the religious questions of the day—the Catholic attitude, the conflict between Mr. Strong and his Presbytery on the subject of Religious Liberalism or Latitudinarianism, as you may please to call it, etcetera, etcerera, etcetera."—All this is so, let us admit it at once, but it does not discourage us. We know, or think we know (which is, after all, almost the same thing), that these three questions—Free-trade, Federalism, Higher Education—are the three great, the three vital questions for Australia, for Melbourne. We know that, sooner or later, they will have to be properly considered and decided upon, and that, if Melbourne is to keep the place which she now holds as the leading city, intellectually and commercially, of Australia, they will have to be decided upon in that way which conforms with "the intelligible law of things," with the *Tendency of the Age*, with the *Time-Spirit.* For this is the one invaluable and, in the end, irresistible ally of Progress—of Progress onward and upward.

December, 1884.

NOTE.—No one, speaking of Free-trade and Federalism in Australia, can omit a tribute of thanks to the *Argus* and the *Federal Australian* for what they have respectively done for the two causes. The cause of Higher Education, however, still waits for a champion in the Press.

THE POETRY OF ADAM LINDSAY GORDON.

"In the whole range of English literature," says an Australian critic reviewing the complete edition of Gordon's poems, " in the whole range of English literature there have been few poets possessed of a finer lyrical faculty than Adam Lindsay Gordon. . . . 'Ashtaroth,'" continues our critic now warm at his work, "'Ashtaroth' is worthy to rank with any of Tennyson's songs, and is far more musical than the best of Browning's." Then there is "the beauty of his ballad poetry, such as 'Fauconshawe' and 'Rippling Water,' which are perfect of their style;" and so on in the same strain, more or less, until the reader is surprised that our critic ends up with no further claim for his poet than that he "deserves to be ranked with the genuine poets of his generation." One does not propose to criticise, verbally, criticism of this sort: it would be unkind to do so, and, above all, it would be useless. This is a native melody in the style of "Rule Britannia:" "Australia, and especially Victoria, is great and therefore her poet must be great also. Let us say that Melbourne is the equal of any English city save London, and Gordon the equal of any English poet save Shakspere and Milton!"

Now let us hear what another Australian critic, one who cares more about finding out the real deep true significance of Gordon and his poetry than of glorifying the *amour-propre* of this class or of that: let us hear what Mr. Marcus Clarke has to say. "Written as they were" (as Gordon's poems were) "at odd times in leisure moments of a stirring and adventurous life, it is not to be wondered at if they are unequal and unfinished. The astonishment of those who knew the man, and can gauge the capacity of this city to foster poetic instinct, is, that such work was ever produced here at all."—What a different tone is this from that of our first and enthusiastic critic! "*Unequal and unfinished*"—"*astonishment that such work was ever produced here at all!*" But this is not all that Mr. Clarke has to say about Gordon's poetry: he has also to notice what influence was at work in it, and (most important of all!) what is its real deep true significance. He talks of Gordon "owning nothing but a love for horsemanship and a head full of Browning and Shelley," and follows this up by saying that "the influence of Browning and of Swinburne" (who, as we all know, has been, creatively and demonstratively, the chief prophet in his generation of the poet who, he likes to think, is 'beloved above all other poets, being beyond all other poets— in one word, and the only proper word,—divine')—" the influence of Browning and of Swinburne upon the writer's taste is plain. There is plainly visible also, however, a keen sense of natural beauty and a manly admiration for healthy living." Well, and the conclusion of the whole matter? "The student of these unpretending volumes will be repaid for his labour. *He will find in them something very like the beginnings of a national school of Australian poetry.*"

Let us hasten to offer up our small tribute of praise and thanks to Mr. Clarke for his critical sagacity here, and let us venture to hope that the "Poems of Adam Lindsay Gordon" may go down to posterity accompanied always by this small "Preface" of Mr. Clarke, who both "knew the man" and was yet the first to appreciate this aspect of his work.

What, however, Mr. Clarke has to say about the facts of Gordon's life is, at best, inaccurate. It is Mr. Sutherland to whom our gratitude is due here, gratitude for having discovered for us all the details of the poet's life which it is necessary for us to know.*

What, then, remains for any other critic to do? There remains to him, as it seems to me, the task of doing what Mr. Clarke tells us he did not propose to do, "of criticising these volumes," and also of trying, as befits one who comes later, and to whom, therefore, the events of the past have fallen into that symmetry and proper porportion that the events of the present can scarcely ever fall into : of trying, I say, to bring out more clearly (one aspect of which he has done little more than indicate), the real, deep, true significance of the poet's work ; in a word, of trying to understand, instead of being " astonished " at it.

The first thing to notice about Gordon's poetry is, that it is almost all in regular and rymed rhythms. There is not a line

---

of blank verse in it.   Now, a " fine faculty" for regular and
rymed rhythms is by no means a synonym for a " fine lyrical
faculty."   Shelley, our greatest master in poetry of pure
melody, has a "fine faculty" for regular and rymed rhythms,
but has also a fine faculty for irregular rhythms : lines in
which the regular rhythm is broken, in order that a more
subtle melody may be expressed, are frequent in him.   In Mr.
Swinburne such lines are rare—he has a fine faculty for regular
and rymed rhythms, but his faculty for irregular rhythms is (let
us say) less fine.   Gordon, who is the disciple of this first side
of Mr. Swinburne's technical talent, who, in his turn, is a
disciple of the first side of Shelley's—Gordon, I say, is in this
respect to Mr. Swinburne what Mr. Swinburne is to Shelley.

Mr. Hammersley, one of the few survivors of that peculiar
phase of colonial and Victorian feeling which produced the
poetry of Gordon, and who " may say he knew him intimately"
—tells us* how he " was often amused to hear him quote from
the poets, and his recitations used to make me laugh outright.
One day I said, ' Hang it, Gordon, you can write good poetry,
but you can't read.' "   What was the matter with his " reading,"
then?   He used to "read" in "a sing-song fashion."   Mr.
Woods, too, tells us† that " Gordon had an odd way of
reciting poetry, and his delivery was monotonous ; but," he
adds, " his way of emphasising the beautiful portions of what
he recited was charming from its earnestness."   Gordon's
criticism on his own verses was : "'They don't *ring* so badly
after all, old fellow, do they ?"   He had no faculty for
irregular rhythms.   He cannot, then, be said to possess a
"fine lyrical faculty ;" he possessed a fine faculty for regular
and rymed rhythms.   (As for his rymes, as rymes, they are
as a rule excellent, although there is often too little of the
"poet or prophet," as he says, in them, and too much of the
"jingler of rymes," the dealer in " verse-jingle chimes.")
Since, however, this faculty of his is a fine faculty, it must not
be described as (in the usual and bad sense of the word)
imitative.   There are, I think, passages in him that Byron
might have written ("To my Sister"), that Lord Tennyson
might have written ("The Road to Avernus," scene x.), that
Mr. Swinburne might have written ("A Dedication"), and
the latter are frequent.   In no other poets, save Wordsworth
and the earlier works of Mr. Arnold, do I find precisely this

---

* *Victorian Review*, May, 1884. (No. 55).   †*Melbourne Review*, April, 1884. (No. 34).

same sort of (shall I say) parallelism of feeling and expression
on certain subjects that I do in Mr. Swinburne and Gordon.
But it is, I think, very open to question whether Gordon
would have grown, as Mr. Arnold has, into a purely distinctive
style of his own. Gordon is terribly lacking in variety ; to live
with a close study of him for several days is one of the most
trying of critical tasks. " My rymes," he asks—

> " My rymes, are they stale ? If my metre
>   is varied, one chime rings through all ;
> one chime—though I sing more or sing less,
>   I have but one string to my lute."

I doubt, I say, whether under any circumstances Gordon
would have produced, as Mr. Hammersley thought, " poems
worthy to be ranked with some of the masterpieces of the
English language." He had not patience enough, he had not
clear-sightedness enough ! " A more dare-devil rider," says
Mr. Hammersley, " never crossed a horse. . . As a steeple-
chase rider he was, of course, in the very first rank, and his
name is indelibly associated with many of the most famous
chases run in Victoria, although in my opinion, and I think in
that of many good judges too, he was deficient in what is
termed 'good hands,' and when it came to a finish was far
behind a Mount or a Watson." (And, considering his short-
sightedness, which Mr. Woods designates as "painful," this is
not to be wondered at). It is the same with his poetry. All
in his poetry that is good has been done at a rush ; the rest is
inferior, poor, and sometimes quite worthless. He has little, if
any, sense of real artistic workmanship either in whole or in
parts : " he is deficient in what is termed 'good hands.'"
Take, for instance, his dramatic lyric, " Ashtaroth." It is
worth reading. There are two beautiful songs in it, " On
the Current," and "Oh ! days and years departed." There
are a few fine passages, a few fine dramatic touches, in it, and
one splendid outburst of Orion's (" I hate thee not, thy grievous
plight "), but the poem, taken as a whole is, I say, worth
reading. Many of the speeches are weak, and some are
not poetry at all, but rymed prose, and bad at that. A sus-
tained effort, such as a piece like this requires, was impossible
to him. I say nothing of the ludicrous attempt at an adapta-
tion of Faust, Mephistopheles and Margarete, which is the
basis of the poem : I merely remark that, judged by its own
poor standard of judgment, it is quite a failure. Perhaps

some day we shall have a selection from the poet's work, from
which what is worthless will be eliminated, in order that all
our attention may be fixed on what is good, and perhaps the
selector will have the courage to dismiss all this poem, save
some dozen or so of extracts, into the gulf of oblivion or
an appendix. Encumbered as Gordon at present is with such
an amount of worthless work, there is a danger that much of
what is good may perish also.

All his poetry that is good, I say, has been done at a rush.
The dramatic touches in it are as frequent as they are fine.
Take, for instance, this from the "Rhyme of Joyous Guard."
—Lancelot, old, worn-out, feeling that "there is nothing good
for him under the sun but to perish as" (his bright past) "has
perished," is thinking of the close of his career and Arthur's:
of the discovery of his amour with Guinevere, his siege in
Joyous Guard, his encounters with "brave Gawain," whom he
virtually slew, and then "the crime of Modred," and "the
king by the knave's hand stricken"—

> " And the once-loved knight, was he there to save
>   that knightly king who that knighthood gave?
> *Ah, Christ! will he greet me as knight or knave*
>   *in the day when the dust shall quicken!"*

This is splendid! And, as I have said, it by no means
stands alone. As a set-off against this excellence of his, is the
defect of prolixity. Byron had it, but Byron was an unsur-
passed improviser, not an artist. Like, too, his technical
master of the "Poems and Ballads" when he gets hold of a
regular or rymed rhythm that pleases him, Gordon will go on
making it "ring," listening as the "verse-jingle chimes,"
till we are all quite weary of it. He is regardless of what Goethe
calls "the æsthetic whole." Indeed, it may justly be said that
few, very few, of his poems are "æsthetic wholes" at all, but
only passages.

So much, then, for the outward form of his poetry. We
have now to consider what is the significance to us of his life
and work, of his personality, and of his "criticism of life."

In the first place, let us begin by stating that Gordon *has* a
personality. Mr. Hammersley tells us how "at times Gordon
was the strangest, most weird, mysterious man I ever saw, and
I could not help feeling almost afraid of him, and yet there
was a fascination about him that made me like to see him."
There was the fascination of his converse. "He was one of

the few men I have known in the colonies," asseverates Mr. Hammersley, "that never made me tire of listening to him." And there was the fascination of his individuality : " His wild haunting eye," "a look something like what is termed the evil eye." (This reminds one of what Mr. Clarke has to say about "the dominant note of Australian scenery: Weird Melancholy.") Mr. Woods' whole article bears witness to this personal fascination of Gordon's. Well, it is the same in his poetry : I mean, that it is the same as Mr. Hammersley *means*. There is attraction in Gordon. We want to go to see anything that he has had to do with. We seek out his grave and brood over it.* He is the Australian fellow to Baudelaire and James Thomson, the last martyrs, let us hope, to our terrible period of transition from the Old World into the New, from Mediævalism into Modernity. There is attraction in Gordon. We should like to have seen and known the original of Laurence Raby, of Maurice, of the man of the "Sea-spray and Smoke-Drift," and " Bush Ballads and Galloping Rhymes." He is an individuality, and a modern and a colonial individuality. He looks at life as it is, not as it is represented.

> " In thy grandeur, oh sea ! we acknowledge,
>   in thy fairness, oh earth ! we confess,
>   hidden truths that are taught in no college,
>   hidden songs that no parchment express."

And, as for the pedants of the Old World, why ! (as we know)

> " They are slow, very slow, in discerning
>   that book-lore and wisdom are twain."

Here, then, is the first charm in Gordon, and his work ; they are modern, they represent the main-current of the age, not some side-water or back-water, that are perhaps nice enough in their way, but still—side-waters or back-waters, and *only* side-waters or back-waters.

Gordon and his work are modern, but not wholly modern ; he belongs, as I have said, to a period of transition. Like

---

* I may parenthetically remark that the idea that Gordon is buried in St. Kilda Cemetery is incorrect, as my doing so may perhaps save others from the trouble of a fruitless pilgrimage there, not to say an examination of all the Cemetery books. He is buried in Brighton Cemetery. The tombstone is a block of blue-stone, topped with a shattered column crowned with a laurel-wreath. The four sides of the block have marble tablets let into them, on which are severally written : "The Poet Gordon. Died June 24, 1870, aged 37 years ;" " Sea-Spray and Smoke-Drift ;" " Bush Ballads and Galloping Rhymes ;" " Ashtaroth." The Cemetery is wooded and wild, the vegetation, including the grave-flowers, stragglingly luxuriant. Not altogether an unfitting " sleeping place " for him.

Mary Magdalene, he feels that "they have taken away my Lord, and I know not where they have laid Him." He has lost the Old, and he has not won the New Faith. He is a poet of the twilight and the dawn. "On this earth so rough," he says,

> " on this earth so rough, we know quite enough,
>   and, I sometimes fancy, a little too much,"

and so, we have to suffer! Burns, Byron, Leopardi, Heine, Musset, Baudelaire, Clough, Thomson—greater and lesser, this is true of them all! Their early life is embittered by it, their later life made desperate. "Years back," says Gordon,

> " Years back I believed a little,
>   and as I believed I spoke."

Years back he could utter prayer, years back when he was a child He cannot utter it now : " For prayer must die since hope is dead." *Now* he can only wonder

> " Is there nothing real but confusion ?
>   is nothing certain but death ?
> is nothing fair, save illusion ?
>   is nothing good that has breath ? . ."

" I can hardly vouch," he says, again,

> " I can hardly vouch
> for the truth of what little I see. . . .
> On earth there's little worth a sigh,
>   and nothing worth a tear."

But ah,

> " the restless throbbings and burnings
>   that hope unsatisfied brings,
> the weary longings and yearnings
>   for the mystical better things. . . .
> There are others toiling and straining
>   'neath burdens graver than mine—
> They are weary, yet uncomplaining—
>   I know it, yet I repine.
> I know it, how time will ravage,
>   how time will level, and yet
> I long with a longing savage,
>   I regret with a fierce regret. . . ."

We are sorely tired, "we, with our bodies thus weakly, with hearts hard and dangerous."

> " We have suffered and striven
> till we have grown reckless of pain,
> though feeble of heart, and of brain."

C

Who has expressed the malady of our time better? "Our burdens are heavy, our natures weak," he says again. We cannot escape from them :

> " Round about one fiery centre
>   wayward thoughts like moths revolve ;"

We cannot write a description of a horse-race without letting them come in, without calling our description by a name expressive of them—"*Ex fumo dare lucem :*"

> " *Till the good is brought forth from evil,*
>   *as day is brought forth from night.*—
> Vain dreams ! for our fathers cherished
>   high hopes in the days that were ;
> and these men wondered and perished,
>   nor better than these we fare ;
> And our due at least is their due,
>   they fought against odds and fell ;
> " *En avant les enfants perdus !*"
> We fight against odds as well."

Enfant perdu : so the dying Heine calls himself. *Enfants perdus,* that is what they were ! The storms of our terrible period of transition raged about them : "they could not wait their passing," as Arnold says—

> " they could not wait their passing, they are dead."

" I am slow," says Gordon,

> " I am slow in learning, and swift in
>   forgetting, and I have grown
> so weary with long sand-sifting !
>   T'wards the mist, where the breakers moan
> the rudderless bark is drifting,
> through the shoals of the quick-sands shifting--
> In the end shall the night-rack lifting,
>   discover the shores unknown?"

The idea of killing himself seems to have been with him from almost the first. It was not "bitter" to him : "man in his blindness" taught so ; but, to him that

> " mystic hour
> when the wings of the shadowy angel lower,"

was not without its charm. "When I first heard the sad news," Mr. Hammersley tells us, "I was not the least surprised. I really expected that what did happen would happen." We all know Gordon's poem, "De Te." The last two verses of it are the best criticism that we have to offer "of

him," "found dead in the heather, near his home, with a bullet
from his own rifle in his brain :"

> " No man may shirk the allotted work,
>   the deed to do, the death to die ;
> at least I think so—neither Turk,
>   nor Jew, nor infidel am I—
> And yet I wonder when I try
>   to solve one question, may or must,
> and shall I solve it by-and-bye,
>   beyond the dark, beneath the dust ?
> *I trust so, and I only trust.*

> " Aye what they will, such trifles kill.
>   Comrade, for one good deed of yours,
> your history shall not help to fill
>   the mouths of many brainless boors.
> It may be death absolves or cures
>   the sin of life. 'Twere hazardous
> to assert so. If the sin endures,
>   say only, ' *God, who has judged him thus,
> be merciful to him, and us.*' "

And his work, his "criticism of life?" Is there nothing in
it but this "*trust and only trust?*" There is more, much
more ! "There is plainly visible," says Mr. Clarke, "a keen
sense of natural beauty, and a manly admiration for healthy
living. . . a very clear perception of the loveliness of duty
and of labour." Let us see if this, too, is so, or if any
qualification of this remark is needed ; and, if so, what qualification.

Gordon's life and work were a failure. He himself would, I
am sure, have been the first to admit it and have assigned the
cause, and rightly, to bad luck in general and certain failings
in himself in particular. Is it not bad luck to be born into an
age that makes of its poets its martyrs? Gordon struggled
and schemed. He was a livery-stable keeper, a landowner, a
member of assembly, a keeper of racehorses, and a failure in
all. It was only as jockey and stockrider that he was a success
—that is to say, an object of admiration to others and of
happiness to himself. "He sometimes," says Mr. Woods,
" compared the lot of a bushman with that of other states of
mankind, saying that it was in many ways preferable to any
one," and for himself he was right. Let us not lament his
failure in what he was not meant to be a success. Gordon,
happy in life and love, might well have become at best a
dilettante, at worst a materialized blockhead, he has so little

patience, so little clear-sightedness! Perhaps it is, after all,
better as it is. The axe cuts down the sandal tree, and the
tree sheds forth its perfume.

> " Our sweetest songs are those which tell of saddest thought."

We love a poet more for what he has suffered than what he has
done, and yet ultimately, if we will only see it, what he suffers
and what he does are the same. As boys we love our Byron
and our Shelley ; as men our Goethe and our Shakspere.
Gordon, I say, as poet and failure is better than prose-man and
success. But see now what he has to say about this life in
which he failed so.

Firstly, there is all the doubt and bewilderment of a period
of transition :

> " We are children lost in the wood."

" Lord," prays this woman that loves Laurence Raby,

> " Lord, lead us out of this tangled wild,
> where the wise and the prudent have been beguiled,
> and only the babes have stood."

Meantime,

> " Onward ! onward ! still we wander,
> nearer draws the goal ;
> Half the riddle's read, we ponder
> vainly on the whole. . . . .
> Onward ! onward ! toiling ever,
> weary steps and slow ;
> doubting oft, despairing never,
> to the goal we go !"

To what goal ? Well,

> " The chances are I go where most men go."

Let us leave the rest with God—God whose " dealings with us "
are unfathomable, God who is " fathomless." Thus he achieves
his resignation. But he never blinds himself to things ; he
never answers " the painful riddle of the earth " by " stopping
up his mouth with a clod " (as Heine says). This world is a

> " world of rapine and wrong,
> where the weak and the timid seem lawful prey
> for the resolute and the strong."

Sometimes there rises in him the

> " wail of discordant sadness for the wrongs he never can right,"

for the brothers, and ah for the sisters, he cannot help. But
sometimes, also, he bursts forth into " a song of gladness, a
pæan of joyous might." Both are in him : the wail for the

lost Lord and the thanksgiving to God for his "GLORIOUS OXYGEN." (The capitals are his own.) With the first, we have done : let us look at the second and see what he has to show us of living and loving, of action and women, and then see what he has to show us of life as a whole, "the conclusion of the whole matter."

I have said elsewhere that there is in Gordon the cheer and charge of our chivalry. There is. He was well worthy of a place in the charge of our cavalry at Waterloo, or Balaclava. There is in him that "magnificence" which now, alas, as the Frenchman, truly said, "is not war." These men "glory in daring that dies or prevails." And when, as at Balaclava, they die, their poet exclaims (in capitals)—

> " not in vain,
> as a type of our chivalry ! "

What exclamations of rapture such a sight draws from him !

> " Oh ! the moments of yonder maddening ride,
>   long years of life outvie ! . . . .
> God send me an ending as fair as his,
>   who died in his stirrups there ! . . . ."

Here is a race :—

> " They came with the rush of the southern surf,
>   on the bar of the storm-girt bay ;
> and like muffled drums on the sounding turf
>   their hoof-strokes echo away."

I know no poetry that describes the rush of horsemen quite as Gordon does. Take this description of the Balaclava charge from his " Lay of the Last Charger."

> " Now we were close to them, every horse striding
>   madly ;—St. Luce pass't with never a groan ;—
> Sadly my master look'd round—he was riding—
>   on the boy's right, with a line of his own.

> " Thrusting his hand in his breast or breast-pocket,
>   while from his wrist the sword swung by a chain,
> swiftly he drew out some trinket or locket.
>   kiss't it (I think) and replaced it again.

> " Burst, while his fingers reclined on the haft,
>   jarring concussion and earth-shaking din,
> Horse counter'd horse, and I reel'd, *but he laugh't,*
>   *down went his man, cloven clean to the chin !*"

Lord Tennyson has watched his charge through Mr. Russell's field-glass, and we follow his view of it, but Gordon has ridden it and takes us with him. Old and miserable, the friend of the man who had ridden this " Last Charger," offers up the same prayer as the man who had " visioned it in the smoke : "

> " Would to God I had died with your master, old man,"

for—

> " he was never more happy in life than in death."

What I find so admirable in Gordon, and in almost all his characters is, that they are *men*, I mean *men* as opposed to dreamers or students. His Lancelot *is* Lancelot, the knight who has lived and loved largely. Tennyson's is not. I must confess that I really think that "The Rhyme of Joyous Guard" is worth all the other " Idylls of the King," save " Lancelot and Elaine," and " The Passing of Arthur," put together. I mean that I really think it has more real deep true significance. Take this conclusion, the last prayer of Lancelot, old and passed from the world :

> " If ever I smote as a man should smite,
>   if I struck one stroke that seem'd good in Thy sight,
>   by Thy loving mercy prevailing,
>   Lord ! let her stand in the light of Thy face,
>   cloth'd with Thy love, and crown'd with Thy grace,
>   when I gnash my teeth in the terrible place
>   that is fill'd with weeping and wailing."

This is splendid ! His men, I say, are *men*, men such as we find in Byron. Orion (Satan) says that

> " The angel Michael was once my foe ;
> *He had a little the best of our strife,*
>   *yet he never could deal so stark a blow."*

The lover in " No Name," thinking of meeting " the slayer of the soul " he loved, says :

> " And I know that if, here or there, alone,
>   I found him fairly, and face to face,
> *having slain his body, I would slay my own,*
>   *that my soul to Satan his soul might chase :*

a remark in the strain of Heathcliff. Most of his lovers love passionately and sensuously, and only passionately and sensuously : The poet " revels in the rosy whiteness of that golden-headed girl :" if one thing is harder to forgive to a successful rival than another it is that

> " he has held her long in his arms,
>   and has kissed her over and over again :"

his chief regret over a dear dead girl is

> " for the red that never was fairly kiss'd—
>   for the white that never was fairly press'd :"

and, when he leaves his love for ever, he is in anguish at the thought that

> " 'twill, doubtless, be another's lot
> those very lips to press :"

a remark in the more morbid strain of Keats to Fanny Brawne.

When Lancelot first kisses Guinevere, he, the mighty knight, " well nigh swoons." Love, with Gordon's lovers, " consumes their hearts with a fiery drought." " Laurence," says Estelle to her lover,

> " Laurence, you kiss me too hard :"

and the man of " Britomarte " is at hand with the appropriate criticism that

> " men at the bottom are merely brutes."

But we must not think that *all* Gordon's lovers love in this way, any more than that all his men merely charge and cheer. The battle is over.

> " And what then? The colours reversed, the drums muffled,
> the black nodding plumes, the dead march and the pall,
> the stern faces, soldier-like, silent, unruffled,
> the slow sacred music that floats over all."

This is beautiful, and no less beautiful is the tenderness of his love.

> " A grim grey coast, and a sea-board ghastly,
> and shores trod seldom by feet of men—
> where the batter'd hulk and the broken mast lie,
> they have lain embedded these long years ten.
> *Love! when we wandered here together,*
> *hand in hand through the sparkling weather,*
> *from the heights and hollows of fern and heather,*
> *God surely loved us a little then."*

Nor is it rare to find passages in him

> " with the song like the song of a maiden,
> with the scent like the scent of a flower."

For " dark and true and tender is the north" with all its storm and stress.

Poor " sick stock-rider " and poet, with his wild eyes and wild words, and that " shyness and reserve which kept him locked up, as it were, in himself!" Our proud, passionate heart " out-wore its breast " as " the sword outwears its sheath," and so we " took our rest," but not before we had won our resignation and known, or almost known, the truth, even as

Empedocles did, and yet died because " he was come too late"
—or too soon—

> " and the world hath the day, and must break thee,
> not thou the world."

Gordon won his resignation, and knew, or almost knew, the
truth. The "criticism of life" that we find in the first two
scenes of " The Road to Avernus " is almost ripe : pessimistic,
it is true, but almost ripe. Laurence has lost his love, (and
Laurence, let us remember, is the lover that " kisses too
hard !") Does he despair in the strain of "Rolla," or
" bluster," and take refuge in the breast of " the wondrous
mother age," and the " vision of the world " in the strain of the
man of " Locksley Hall?" No, he has lost his love, and the
loss is bitter, but

> " such has been, and such shall still be, here as there, in sun or star.
> These things are to be and will be ; those things were to be and are."

" As it was so," he says again,

> " as it was so in the beginning,
> it shall be so in the end."

There is the feeling here of a man who is striving to see things
as they are. He will not blind himself to things : he will not
answer " the painful riddle of the earth " by " stopping up his
mouth with a clod." He will have true faith, or no faith.
Fate rules us, he sees :

> " Man thinks, discarding the beaten track,
>   that the sins of his youth are slain,
> when he seeks fresh sins, but he soon comes back
>   to his old pet sins again . . . .
> Some flashes like faint sparks from heaven,
>   come rarely with rushing of wings ;
> We are conscious at times, we have striven,
>   though seldom, to grasp better things ;
> These pass, leaving hearts that have faltered,
>   good angels with faces estranged,
> and the skin of the Æthiop unalter'd,
>   and the spots of the leopard unchanged."

And yet life, life as life, independent of living and loving, of
activity and women, is not altogether hopeless :

> " Doubtless all are bad, yet few are
> cruel, false, and dissolute."

He never gets any farther than this. He sees, or almost
sees, truth, as Moses saw Canaan, and then he fails. He has

not had patience enough, not clear-sightedness enough! He cannot enter the Promised Land. "In defiance of pain and terror he has pressed resolutely across the howling deserts of Infidelity;" but he has not the strength left to do more than reach "the new, firm lands of Faith beyond." He has loved life, living and loving, activity and women, and he has not feared to look into the reality of things, man and Nature and God, their sunshine and their shadow, their life and their death, and there is no hesitation in his message to us— "Onward! Onward!"—But that is all. He knows nothing of *how* we are to go onward, or to *where*. He has had enough to do to get himself as far as he has got, to achieve what he has achieved. His life and work are a failure. We cannot for a moment think of calling him a great poet: his claim on our interest as a poet is that he is one of the poets, one of the martyrs, of our terrible period of transition, and that in him is to be found "something very like the beginnings of a national school of Australian poetry." Of this second aspect of him— of how he is representative of what I have taken to be the distinctive marks of this Australian, this Melbourne civilisation, its general sense of movement, of progress, of conscious power: of this aspect of him I have spoken elsewhere, too, and there seems no need to do more here than to repeat the assertion. But, for my part, I cannot lay the stress on either this aspect of him, or the other which makes him "the poet of Australian scenery," that I do on the first aspect of him. Gordon's life and work are a failure, but they are a failure with enough redeeming points to raise them from local, or even colonial, into general interest. As our first and enthusiastic critic puts it: "he deserves to be ranked with the genuine poets of his generation," and I feel sure that he ultimately will be. For he is representative not only of Australian, but of modern feeling: he tells not only of Australia from the fifties to the seventies, but of our terrible period of transition from the Old World into the New, from Mediævalism into Modernity.

Poor "sick stock-rider" and poet, with his wild eyes and wild words—Our proud, passionate heart "outwore its breast," as "the sword outwears its sheath," and so we "took our rest." "Sleep!" says Mr. Swinburne, in the most beautiful and satisfactory of his poems, "Ave atque Vale," the lament over another of the martyrs—the author of "Les Fleurs du Mal:"—

" Sleep ; and, if life were bitter to thee, pardon,
    if sweet, give thanks ; thou hast no more to live ;
    and to give thanks is good, and to forgive   .   .
Content thee, howsoe'er, whose days are done ;
    There lies not any troublous thing before,
    nor sight nor sound to war against thee more,
for whom all winds are quiet as the sun,
    all waters as the shore."

January, 1885.

THE SALVATION ARMY.

I.

WHEN a man speaks of Modern Europe, he is generally taken to mean the Europe of steam and electricity. As a matter of fact, Modern Europe really dates back to about the middle of the last century, when certain ideas which we call "modern" first began to be promulgated. And these ideas were not, as in this expression "Modern Europe" it is tacitly supposed, merely scientific; they were not only concerned with steam and electricity; they were social. And thus, when we use the expression, if we are to use it, in this particular sense, we should remember that it means, not only that the whole world is netted with railways and telegraphs, but also that, speaking generally, the European races are no longer governed by kings or aristocracies, but by middle-classes or, as some prefer to put it, by peoples. And this, as I take it, is far the more important fact of the two. I will go further, and say that it is the most important fact of our civilization—nay, that it *is* our civilization, and that, therefore, whoever would seek to understand the meaning of any movement, great or small, which is taking place in our civilization, must seek it here, and here only! Our civilization is our government by the Middle-class or, as some prefer to put it, by the People. But that these individuals who prefer to put it so are, let us say, if not mistaken, at any rate inaccurate, is precisely what I want in this little article to try to show, and in as striking a manner as I can, so that, not only may I try to do something towards making clear to us the real deep true significance of a much misunderstood movement, but also that of a much more misunderstood power—the Middle-class of the European races. I do not propose to go through my subject thoroughly: to do so would require more time and more space than any editor could afford me. I shall merely touch on one phase of the great spiritual movement which is at present permeating the European races, and then turn to consider another phase of it— a phase which is of peculiar interest to us of England, America, and Australia.

II.

In Europe there is but one country that still suffers the despotism of an aristocracy, and that country is Russia. The modern ideas, the modern social ideas, have taken all this time to pass from France, Germany, and England into Russia, and have seized on what, for lack of a better word, I might call, its nascent middle-class. The results have been, and still are, wonderful and terrible. A group of men (for they are little more) has suddenly realised that the immense mass of the People is being despotised over in the interest of a group in reality little larger than itself. All, I will not say freedom, but possibilities of freedom are resolutely withheld. Russia at present has not the guaranteed protection of its men's and women's liberties which the English of the fourteenth, the thirteenth, the twelfth, the eleventh, the tenth centuries had! This to-day is a state of things which cannot continue. The group of men who see and feel this, not clearly and quietly as we outsiders can, but intensely and passionately, is waging a duel to the death with the other group, with the despotism, for the bare principles of freedom. On the one hand are knowledge and light, on the other ignorance and darkness, the modern against the ancient spirit. But, thanks to the fact that there are men whose whole interest is to resist the one and support the other to the last, the light has become lightning and not only irradiates but strikes. It is considered by some a question whether this despotism, armed with all resources of wealth and military power, will be able to stamp out this group before the immense mass of the People is awakened to the meaning of it all. Others, however, merely consider whether the Russian government will be destroyed by a revolution or constitutionalized by a reform. We English, you see, consider it all clearly and quietly as mere outsiders, and so, as regards the *aspect* of the problem, we are ; but not, not as regards the problem itself! These modern ideas, these social ideas, are working not only in Russia, where the abuses which surround them make them burn so fiercely, but more or less all over Europe, and in England rather more than less. Ireland, we all see, smoulders with them. And why, pray? Because England and Ireland are always snarling at one another, "it being their nature to?" Not so. It is because that aspect of the problem which is presented to Great Britain generally is a little more pressing

in Ireland than in England or Scotland. The trouble in
Ireland is not national but social. The strife is not between
Irish and English: it is between peasants and landlords.
Unhappily many landlords are English: unhappily many
peasants believe that the English as a nation support the landlords as a class. Hence whatever Irish hatred of England
there may be : but the trouble is not, I repeat, national, it is
social. It is the People rising against the Middle-class.

Well, this movement, whether it be in Russia, in England, in
Germany, in France, in America, we are all pretty well agreed
to call the Socialistic movement. It represents the effort of
the People after social improvement. It took its rise not from
within the people, but from *without*. The French, English,
and German Socialists were originally groups of men who suddenly realized that the immense mass of the People was being
despotized over in the interest of the Middle-class. Each
country has its peculiar aspect of this fact, but the fact is the
same in each. In France the Middle-class made and supported the Empire, and, having stamped out the People's wild
attempt at power in '71, made and supports the Republic. In
Germany—dismembered Germany—the problem was pushed
back before the apparently greater one of national unity, but
now it arises again and demands solution. In England the
landed proprietors, and still more the capitalists, are beginning
to have qualms; but the real struggle does not lie between
them and the Socialists : they are but overgrown individuals of
a class. There will be no more Tories and no more Con-
servatives : the future lies in the struggle between Liberals and
Socialists, the Middle-class and the People.

This Socialistic movement, then, took its rise not from
within the People but from *without*, and not in connection
with Religion, the great ally of the powers that were, the
Middle-class, but on the whole antagonistic to it. This movement took its rise in men of intellect who had little or no care
for Religion, and its tendency is intellectual and careless of
Religion. The Middle-class has shown nothing but dislike to
this movement : the Middle-class has understood enough of the
ideas of this movement to know that they are subversive of its
own superiority. As for the People, they have understood
little or nothing. Socialists tell them, what is indeed the
truth, that they are the masters : that to-morrow, if they
pleased, they could send a parliament up to Westminster that

should dictate what terms they pleased to " their lords and
masters, the landowners and the capitalists." The People does
not happily believe it. They are so hopeless : they have been
deceived so often by those who said they would help them.
(Bill here, you see, with a wife and six children, all living in a
den that the Zoological people would consider unfit for a
hyena—Bill cannot be made to understand how the question
comes home to *him*.') Besides which, let us say it at once
and insist upon it, the People is the most long-suffering of all
things : it desires to despoil no man, it only desires the happiness which mere food, clothing, and a house will give it.

In this state of affairs—the powerlessness of the Socialists to
bring home to the People the great idea of social improvement—lie the causes of the religious movement whose best-
known and best representative is the Salvation Army.

III.

Consider it—first generally and then particularly.

In Russia the People has religion and no freedom. In
England the People has freedom and no religion. (In both,
let us add, the People has misery unspeakable). The one
question presses for solution in the one country, the other in
the other. The two most piteous spectacles in Europe are the
religious People of Russia, and the free People of England.
The Aristocracy which governs the one, the Middle-class
which governs the other, both are equally indifferent to the
People. Add to the fact of the utter want of religion of the
English People (it is understood that by People I mean the
masses), the fact of their utter want of, I will not say the com-
forts, but the necessities of life, and you have a field for revolution such as nowhere else, I believe, presents itself save in
Russia herself.—I speak in the present, as if the problem
presented itself to me to-day just as it did years ago, and I am
delighted to notice that at last the English Middle-class is
awakening to the fact of the misery of the People, and also of
the danger of letting that misery continue. But it is quite a
mistake to suppose that either the one or the other is mitigated,
not to say ended, or that it will be so for years to come.

Religion in England—and Religion has, inaptly enough,
become a synonym for Christianity, in which general sense of
the term I use it here—Religion in England, just like everything else, is conducted in the interest of the Middle-class. Go

into the London back-streets on a sunday morning. You will
find the men leaning against the walls, the women at the
doors, the children in the gutters. The public-houses, you
observe, are closed : the Middle-class does not like that the
People should be drinking beer and spirits while they themselves are indulging in religious worship. Enter the church or
the chapel. What are the services like? We all know them—
a performance on the part of the choir, or a discreet, sibilant,
half-articulate murmur on the part of the congregation. The
clergyman or minister reads out a portion of the wonderful and
beautiful history of Jesus in a fine meaningless monotone, and
"here endeth the second lesson." But of the passion and the
peace of the Galilean story, what does *he* know? He has
forgotten or never known Jesus, but he can tell you plenty
about Christ. Listen to the sermons. What do they treat of?
Matters that are likely to interest the men and women outside
there? The sermons are empty of Jesus and full of Christ—
empty of the truth of the Master and full of the dogmas of the
Pupils. Theology, theological dogmas, Catholic or Protestant, .
are perhaps interesting to men and women who are well to do,
and like to have something to argue about; but what does
poverty care for them? The man who has eaten a good
breakfast and is waiting for a good dinner may care to have it
shown to him, that he and his fellows are the one body of
Christians that is absolutely and entirely orthodox; but
the man with an empty belly, and little or no prospect of
filling it, may perhaps be forgiven for not caring a jot whether
these are blasts of true or false doctrine, or not. The matter
does not affect him : he stops outside. So should we.

Now, I would not for a moment imply that there are not
priests, clergymen, and ministers who have done, and are
doing, fine and noble work among the People. There are
many such. But what I do say is, that, speaking generally, the
church and the chapel have both utterly failed to seriously
affect the mass of the People, and that they have done so for the
reasons I have given above.—"In the year 1865," says Mr.
Booth in one of the Salvation Army pamphlets, "Mr. Booth
was led, by the Providence of God, by no plan or idea of his
own, to the East of London, where the appalling fact that the
enormous bulk of the population were totally ignorant and
deficient of real religion, and altogether uninfluenced by the
existing religious organizations, so impressed him that he

determined to devote his life to *making* these people *hear* and
know God, and thus save them from the abyss of misery in
which they were plunged, and rescue them from the damnation
that was before them. The Salvation Army is the result."
The Salvation Army is the result. He simply states the fact.
It was " by no plan or idea of his own." He has, so far as I
know, never explained more than the phenomena of it.* I
have talked with one of his sons on the subject, and all he has
to tell me in explanation of 859 corps or stations, 2041 paid
officials, and *War Cry* newspapers with a weekly circulation of
550,000, is *how*, as he takes it, the Salvationists "get at" the
People ; but he knows, and probably cares, absolutely nothing
about the *why*. " The grate was set," I say, " You were the
match, and behold the fire !" " It is the Lord," he says, and I
do not think of contradicting him. It is not natural that a
man who takes part in a movement should know more than the
how of it, should know the *why*. If he did, he would not be
as unhesitating as he is in his belief that his movement is so
good. To achieve little we must aim at much. He who lives
passionately in the present must leave the dead to bury their
dead and the babes unborn to consider their suckling : he must
create, he has not time to criticise. At the same time how
important it is that there should be not only doers but
watchers ; not only creators but critics ; not only those who
concern themselves with the *how* but also those who concern
themselves with the *why*, for the *why* unlocks the gates of both
the past and the future : it tells us not only the *whence* but also
the *whither*.

   Now, as I have said, in a certain state of affairs which we
have noticed lies *this why*, and there, if we can only look well
enough, we shall find it. The Salvation Army is, like everything else an organism. It has its seed, and all its stages of
development up to its maturity and down into its decay, when
it, too, like everything else, will go to form nutriment for other
organisms, just as others have for its own.

   Now, nothing will help us more in our search after this *why*
than a knowledge of the *how*, and, since this knowledge is, at
any rate among the governing classes, wonderfully limited, I propose giving a short account of how the Salvation Army and its
work has struck me personally. It seems almost needless to
state that I am an unprejudiced observer. The Salvation

---

* His little article on it in the *Contemporary Review* is a mere circular.

Army, as the Salvation Army, is literally nothing to me: my only
interest in it lies in the influence which it exerts, whether for
good or evil, on the People.   I have no cause to plead.   If
anyone can point out mistakes of mine, or even demonstrate
to me that my whole view of this matter is an illusion, no one,
I am sure, will be more pleased and grateful than myself.
Those are our real benefactors who demonstrate to us an
illusion and open the way to a better view of things.

<h2 style="text-align:center">IV.</h2>

I propose, I said, giving a short account of how the Salvation Army and its work has struck me personally.   When I
was in England I studied it, as I study all movements that are
going on around me, with more or less care.   Since I have
been in Australia I have done the same, and, as I have found
the differences between the English and Australian Salvation
Armies to be immaterial ones, and as I am now addressing an
Australian audience, I shall speak of the Salvation Army as I
have seen it here, so that he who cares may go and see for
himself whether I am correct or incorrect in my view of it.
This, too, will enable him more easily, if he desires it, to point
out my mistakes and even demonstrate to me that my whole
view is an illusion, and make me his pleased and grateful
debtor for life.   First, however, let me just notice what these
differences between the English and Australian Salvation
Armies are.   In one word the Australian is less exaggerative.
The People in Australia breathes free: it does not feel the
weight of the two great divisions of the Middle-class that is
above it, the well-to-do and the gentlemen.   Workmen here
do not go slouching down the streets, as they do in England,
crushed under the sense of their inferiority.   This is a true
republic, the truest, as I take it, in the world.   In England
the average man feels that he is an inferior: in America he
feels that he is a superior : in Australia he feels that he is an
equal.   This is indeed delightful.   It is the first thing that
strikes a new arrival in this country, and although Australia's
sins—sins against true civilization, I mean -are as many as they
are heinous, still a multitude of them, as it seems to me, is
covered by this—namely, that here the People is neither servile
nor insolent, but only shows its respect of itself by its respect
of others.   Nowhere else but in France is there, I think,
anything quite like it.

D

There is, then, naturally less exaggerativeness in the Australian than the English Salvation Army. When a man is, as they say, "saved" there, it is from a far deeper "abyss of misery" than it is here. The very atmosphere of England is heavy with the degradation of the People. For a man to become, no longer passively, but actively aware of this, is almost overwhelming, and so is his feeling when he believes that he has escaped from it. Hence those wild words and acts of the Salvationists which have offended so many. Add to this the excitement caused by a large gathering, religious emulation, etc., etc., and the matter is a simple one.

Now let us go to a Salvationist popular service, and see their manner of work there. The hall is crowded. The great bulk of the congregation is made up of the upper stratum of the People, servants, small shopkeepers, etc. There are also a not inconsiderable number of the lower stratum of the People, labourers. Many outsiders have come from curiosity. On the stage or platform are a certain number of the regular paid officials in their uniforms, and of "hallelujah lasses" in their straight dresses and poke-bonnets. Considering these men and women attentively, what most strikes us is that the generality are, as Jeffrey said lightly of Carlyle, "terribly in earnest." Some have the business-like air of all officials, religious or otherwise: some have a somewhat disgusted air, as if they were rather wearying of it all, now that the novelty has worn off. But the generality of them are, there is no doubt of it, "terribly in earnest." Presently the head officials enter, and the service is opened with a hymn. The Salvationists sing well: I remember that, at the first Salvationist service at which I was present, this singing of theirs was something like a revelation to me. It was not its "go," as we say, that affected me: it was its depth and sweetness. It comes from the heart and goes to the heart. This is the only language the People can either use or understand.

Just beside me a little boy of four or five, standing between his father's knees with shut eyes and waving arm, is shouting and bawling out the words of the hymn, so that he may attract attention and be an "edification." It is painful. (Later on during a prayer he lies along the floor on his stomach and eats a green apple and pinches a bigger boy's legs. Myself, I prefer him like that.) During the prayers there are frequent interruptions, chiefly from the platform, of "Hallelujah,"

" Praise God," and so on, for the most part in a business-like fashion, quite formal. A man cannot repeat the same words and acts for long with impunity.—These, and things like these, are the inevitable accompaniments of all services, religious or otherwise. We take them for granted, and pass on.

Presently a man is brought forward to give his testimony. He begins by saying that he never thought to address such a gathering as this, that he is a poor ignorant man, and so on, but that he trusts in Jesus to help him through alright. He tells his tale. It is a tale for ever old and for ever new. He was a drunkard, he was debauched, a blasphemer. He used his wife and children ill, he paid no heed to the clergyman and the minister. Then a Salvationist came to him and told him about Jesus. And that converted him, and now, etc., etc., etc. His excitement grows : his voice rises to a high-pitched monotone. He implores, he begs, he entreats, he abjures. "Come to Jesus, come to Jesus ! It's only him can make you happy ! You don't know how he loves you !—O dear people," he bursts out at length, "I could *die* for you, if you would only come to him !" In the end, it is painful : the high-pitched monotone oppresses us, and we are glad when he has ended.

Another follows, but with little or no variety. Then a girl speaks, "happy Janet" (say). She has just the same tale to tell : it is all Jesus, nothing but Jesus ! " 'To think," I heard one of these girls say, hushed and awed, "to think that the Son of God loved us so that he suffered all this for *us!* To think of the thorns wounding his beautiful brow !" and her voice broke.—Janet cannot say too much about the suffering of Jesus, because it was because he loved us all so, that he suffered. Then she tells how she had a brother, and the brother thought he was old enough to be by hisself, and do for hisself, and he went away, away to Mân-chester, and they were all very sad about it, e-specially mother. And the days and the weeks and the months went by, and they never heard anythink about him, and they went out and up and down the town, hoping he might come back and they might see him again, for he might be ashamed, they thought, to come into the house. And sometimes mother 'd come to wake her up early in the morning, and say : "Come, Janet, let's go out and look for Tom : maybe we'll find him *this* morning." And they used to go out and look for him in the early morning, and they couldn't find him. But at last he *did* come back, and O, dear people, how thin he was! Yes, he'd had enough of it! He found he couldn't do for hisself after all, so he came back to mother and us, and we loved him more than ever.—And O, dear people, that's the way with *us* and Jesus. We think we're old enough to be by ourselves and to do for ourselves. But we ar'n't : we're never old enough to do without Jesus! He's always loving us and strengthening us and giving us peace. So come to him; don't wait any longer but come to him! Don't think you're too wicked. No one's too wicked for Jesus : he suffered for us and he died for us, for *you* and *me*, and he loves us more than all the others do, and we can't tell how glad it makes him when we come to him!" Here, as in the singing, it is not the "go," the excitement, which affects us most, it is the depth and sweetness. It comes from the heart and goes to the heart. It is the only language the People can either use or understand.

Jesus!—It is always Jesus, I say, never or very rarely Christ. These Salvationists feel and know their Master. With them he lives : with us he exists. And Jesus is to them as some one dowered with all the possibilities of mortal happiness who yet renounced everything from his great love for the People, and suffered and died for them a cruel death. Herein is the secret of the sempiternal influence of Jesus : he is the great Lover. I do not for a moment think that these Salvationists have any connected scheme of the character or life of Jesus. They cannot argue about him, they would say : they know that he *lives*. They lay little or no stress on the risen Jesus, the Christ. Their concern is with the living Jesus, him who loved the flowers and the children and the publicans and the harlots, him who showed his love by his life and above all by his cruel death. This Jesus was not a philanthropist : he was better, he was a lover. "He, who might have been a great king, actually preferred to come and suffer and die a cruel death because he loved us so!" This love, this pity seems to them unique, godlike. "*To think of the thorns wounding his beautiful brow.*" Hence the power of Jesus to awaken in men a sense of sin, and, still more, a hope of salvation. "Why," they ask, "did this wonderful beautiful Jesus suffer all this?—*why?*" Then comes the answer. "*Because he saw that I was a sinner and he loved and pitied me so, that he suffered all this for my sake.*" It is an overwhelming fact. Once get a man to see it and his life is revolutionised : he believes in Love.

Napoleon, we remember, was puzzled by this sempiternal influence of Jesus. He remarked that he himself understood how to awaken in his own behalf the enthusiasm of men, but he was alive, whereas Jesus was dead. "*O Jerusalem, Jerusalem, thou that killest the prophets, and stonest them which are sent unto thee, how often would I have gathered thy children together, even as a hen gathereth her chickens under her wings, but ye would not!*" Yearning love like this was a mystery to our wonderful destructive Emperor: he would have called it foolish. And to many others beside him this sempiternal influence of Jesus has been, is, and will be the same. Here is our good Man of Science, the immortal dunce who dates knowledge from "Social Statics" and the "Origin of Species," who thinks Jesus was a very fine character, you know, but full of superstition and delusion. And here is our most irrational of Rationalists who has a pathetic faith in the method of the late lamented Bishop Colenso, a method which consists in the profound consideration of the geometry of the empyrean and the colour of mathematical figures. And lastly, here is our dear blatant Secularist whose discourse so pleasantly shows us how a man who was a blockhead as a Christian can be doubly a blockhead as a Secularist.—Here, I say, are these three types, or let us take them as individuals. Here is our good friend Mr. Caffyn, who was writing such brilliant letters to the *Argus* the other day, letters which show a nice acquaintance with the books of Dr. Maudsley and the rudiments of modern physiology; and here is the late lamented Sir Richard Hanson of Adelaide, whose mantle is just now descending on Mr. Justice Williams; and, lastly, here is our loquacious friend at the Hall of Science, Mr. Joseph Symes. All these gather around the poor ignorant labourer who is "saved," and demonstrate to him his foolishness in believing in such an outworn piece of nonsense as Christianity. "As for this Jesus of yours, my good man," they say after their several fashions, "he was a very fine character, you know, but—*he was only a man just like you or me!*" To whom the poor ignorant labourer answers with a smile: "Whether he be a fine character or not, I know not: one thing I know, that, *whereas I was blind, now I see.*" Come away, Mr. Caffyn: come away, ghost of Sir Richard: come away, Mr. Symes. It is quite useless to talk with a besotted Christo-maniac like this. Why, he absolutely believes that he has a spiritual experience of which you are ignorant, and can afford to smile at you! After this, the deluge!—Gentlemen, hadn't you better go home to dinner, and leave the poor devil alone?

To return to the meeting, which is not yet concluded.— When the testimonies are all given, those who feel that they have been leading a life of sin are exhorted to come forward and profess. The hall empties. Ten or twelve, men and women, young men and girls, come forward and kneel down at a bench in front of the platform. Some are inclined to be hysterical. The Salvationists, men and women, come and talk to them, leaning against them, their arms round their shoulders, exhorting and encouraging. This, you see, is Religious Socialism. No one can love Jesus, "the divine Communist" (as Heine calls him), with impunity. If you love, and to love is to know, Jesus, you must get others to love and to know him, and your desire to get others fills you with the same yearning love for them that Jesus has for you: "*O dear people, I could die for you, if you would only come to him!*"

Then, when no more will come forward, the service concludes with each of those who is "saved," speaking before them all—saying what has come to him to make him repent, and expressing his firm determination to lead a better life. The first step has now been taken—the man by his public confession is compromised. He cannot now so easily fall back. He is known to his fellows, who will exhort and encourage him. He has every incentive to date a new life from to-day, not to put it off over and over again to "to-morrow."

What, is all this, then, a trap? Yes, if you care to call it so. Men, to whom the "saved" and the "unsaved" life, the bliss of heaven and the anguish of hell, is a passionate reality, speak of it passionately to the ignorant or the careless, and then (like true guilefully guileless religionists) take advantage of the moment of realization which they have aroused in a soul, to compromise that soul before the world to lead a new life of continual realization. You see, these Salvationists are of the men and women of the People and they know the men and women, not only of the People, but of each and every class of us: they know how frail is unaided resolution, and they act on their knowledge. Do not think, though, that they believe that

weakness of will is to be found only among the People. Far
from it! They attack Respectability, they attack the hypocrisy
of the Middle-class, as fearlessly as they attack the open sin of
the People. Our good clergymen and ministers, for whom I
have, in many respects, so much admiration, are afraid to
attack the Middle-class : the Middle-class is the payer of pew-
rents. Alas, alas, ye cannot serve God and Mammon ! It is
really a great nuisance ; but ye cannot! Now these Salvationists do not happen to have pews : so they need not stand
hat in hand before Respectability. They can say boldly that
the Publican is as good as the Pharisee : that hypocrisy is no
better, if it is not far worse, than open sin. Look to it, my in-
so-many-respects-admirable clergymen and ministers, you are
not masters here but pupils !

V.

I am not going to discuss the question of Salvationist ritual.
Brass bands and concertinas give but a poor idea of "the
beauty of holiness : " a dissenting chapel does the same.
Banners and handkerchiefs and so on are apt to be tawdry : so
are dressed statues, standards, incense, and the rest. But who,
considering the hideousness of Protestantism and the tawdri-
ness of Catholicism, would therefore call Protestantism hideous
and Catholicism tawdry ? Certainly not I who am so sincere
an admirer of them both. Neither, then, considering what we
hear called the Christy-Minstrelism and Music-Hallism of the
Salvation Army, must we think that, when we have called their
meetings Christy Minstrels or Music Halls, we have quite disposed of them. Alas, my dear Middle-class, cannot you see
that the People is what you, who govern the People, have
made it ? Might I, a humble unit of your millions, suggest to
you that it is just because, what you call, your Upper Ten
Thousand is hideous that you are more hideous ? and that it
is just because you, my dear Middle-class, are more hideous
that the People is most hideous ? Will it be many ages, I
wonder, before you can be got to see this?—to see that you
had better take the mote out of your own eye before you are
so enthusiastic about taking the beams out of the eyes of your
neighbours ?

If, however, anyone wants to see what Mr. Booth himself
has to say in defence of his "Colours, Bands of Music, Processions, and other sensational methods employed " (as he

says), I would refer him to a little penny pamphlet called "All about the Salvation Army," which can be got at the Salvation Army Head-quarters in Russell Street. For myself, I have nothing to do with this side of the question: I profess that I consider most church-bells are as bad as most brass-bands, and am profoundly indifferent as to whether they are, as Mr. Booth would like to know, "unscriptural" or not. I am of opinion that the admirers of church-bells and brass-bands had better fight it out among themselves.

I have as good as said that what makes the outer strength of the Salvationists is their realization of Jesus as liver and lover. Love, yearning love, is undoubtedly the chief characteristic of Jesus. But, just as the sun gives forth not only heat but light, so did he. His life was love: his death was peace. "*My peace I leave with you.*" And it is just here, just in their realization of "the mildness and sweet reasonableness" of Jesus that the Salvationists are apt to be lacking: and it is just here that the Church of England more than any other Christian sect is, as it seems to me, so strong. The *Hymns Ancient and Modern* are, on the whole, the best song-book extant of this "mildness and sweet reasonableness." We must not, however, think that this demand for the peace as well as the love of Jesus is not recognised by the Salvationists: it is, but I cannot think that it is recognised adequately. As soon as a man is "saved" and has "professed," there are open to him, what they call, the Holiness Meetings. These are the answer to the demand for peace. But they differ only particularly from the other meetings. They are smaller, and hence quieter, than the others; but there is, so to speak, too much heat and too little light in them. Here is the weak point in the Salvationist movement, just as it is the strong point in (I always take the best example our Christianity can give us) the Church of England. Here it is the turn of the Salvationists to be not masters, but pupils. Let us hope that they will see this, and not only teach, but also (which is so much more difficult) be ready to learn from, us.

VI.

There are still two parts of the work of the Salvationists to consider—their work with the inmates of the prisons, and their work with the inmates of the brothels. Here again we have everything to learn from them, from them the true disciples of "the divine Communist." The former work they have made a speciality of, and they are rapidly making the latter. I doubt very much that our churches and chapels (I am not speaking now of the Catholics, whose work is almost exclusively among the Irish, and the Irish are of a race that, save in the matter of agrarian crime and a curious cruelty to dumb animals, is truly admirable for the honesty of its men and the chastity of its women) : I doubt very much, I say, that our churches and chapels will ever get much at either the criminals or the prostitutes. Our clergymen, who are so gentlemanly, and our ministers who are so respectable, can neither speak nor understand much the language of the People, the language of the heart. The clergymen are shocked by the foulness, the ministers by the ferocity, of the People. Both feel that they are condescending—the one from the height of refinement, the other from the height of righteousness. The people has no love for condescension of this sort. There are few words that stink more in its nostrils than that of charity, and indeed charity, when it means a gift from a superior to an inferior, is hateful enough. It is a popular delusion with the "charitable" that street beggars and the inmates of the workhouses are the People. Far otherwise is it, O "charitable" ones: these are not independent animals, they are parasites : they are (if you will pardon me saying so) your spiritual lice : so please make the best of them, since it is not only on account of, but *on*, you that they live.

Well, now, wherein is it that these fanatical ignorant Salvationists *do* get at the People? One of them answers us at once : "*No one's too wicked for Jesus, and so no one's too wicked for me who am the simple follower of Jesus. If he could do with publicans and harlots, why cannot I?*" They say, as Walt Whitman says to "a common prostitute,"

"Not till the sun excludes you do I exclude you,
    Not till the waters refuse to glisten for you and the leaves to rustle for
        you, do my words refuse to glisten and rustle for you."

This, you see, is Religious Socialism. It proclaims the spiritual equality of all men. The *spiritual* equality, let us notice ; it will have nothing to do with the social equality. "*My king dom is not of this world. . . . Give unto Cæsar the things which be Cæsar's, and to God the things which be God's.*" "Honour all men," says Peter, "love the brotherhood, fear God, honour the king." And more : Religious Socialism has a tendency to be careless of the dogmas of the creeds. " Is the Army hostile," asks Mr. Booth, " to the existing evangelical denominations ? Just the contrary. Numbers of its converts go to swell the membership of the churches. More than 400 persons, converted and trained in its ranks, have been engaged by other different religious organisations as Evangelists, Ministers," etc., etc., etc. We notice that he says "*evangelical* denominations ? " The Catholics, of course, from (who shall I say ?) Augustine to Pascal and Newman, are poor belated idolaters, only slightly better than the heathen. This, you see, is where Mr. Booth, like Mr. Spurgeon and the rest, so pleasantly shows us what nonsense an earnest short-sighted man is capable of believing and brandishing about the world with a godless blatancy. Personally, I cannot make myself angry with any of them for it. For what would an earnest man be without his faults ? without, as D'Israeli puts it, a single redeeming vice ?

In Melbourne there is a tendency now to let the Salvation Army have its own way unmolested with the criminals and the prostitutes. "It can't do any harm," people say, "and it may do good, and really, you know, the—the Social Evil wants looking to." Nay, more: having made this nice expression " Social Evil," we are at last plucking up courage to acknowledge that it exists, and that it is not necessarily a sign of filthy-mindedness to wish to discuss it. We speak of it now in papers which come under the eye of those dear creatures about whose stainless purity of mind we are all so anxious (even that Puritanic print, the *Melbourne Bulletin* is anxious, and the *Sydney Bulletin*, also, for all I know to the contrary)—"our wives and daughters." Why, possibly there are those among us who will live to see the day when the expression "fearful sinner," as applied to some poor girl driven out into the miseries of the streets, will be confined to the utterance of our good friends of the Scotch Presbytery, and other few such like. Then, it will be amusing : at present, it is only detestable.

VII.

Now let us go to the Barracks of the Prison Brigade, and see what has to be seen there. The officials (all, I believe, old criminals) and the men that they have just got hold of, are gathered for a sort of home service. Man after man, boy after boy, rises to give his "experience." The "experiences" can be pretty easily imagined. Then there are hymns, choruses, addresses by the higher officials present. All, or almost all here, there is no doubt of it, are "terribly in earnest." The interruptions, "Hallelujah," "Praise God," and so on, are all earnest. One boy with a maimed face gets up and says: "I was miserable in the streets, I'm very happy now. God bless the Major," and sits down again. For me, I confess that, over and over again, I have not known whether to answer the word and acts of these men, or shall I say children, with smiles or tears. Now and then I have answered them with both.

Afterwards we are shown the bedrooms, observing that we do not want to see them. I have seen many bedrooms that were delightful, and many keepers thereof whose hearts were as clean and hard as the floors. Also I have seen bedrooms that were poor and crowded, and the keepers thereof whose hearts were as rich as love and as soft as pity. I prefer the latter, myself, if I must choose between them, but tastes of course are different. Then the boy with the maimed face is brought in, to tell his tale and show his wounded leg. The People like you to look at their wounds and sores and casualties generally. It is painful. It is like the young ladies of the Middle-class who like you to look at their drawings and paintings, or listen to their playing and singing. I do not know which habit is the more painful of the two—perhaps, on the whole, the latter. The first only hurts my senses: the second hurts my soul. It makes me lose hope in my ideas for the future of the Middle-class: it makes me think it is doomed to the hideousness of clap-trap for ever. It is like a visit to the sculpture at the Melbourne Public Library.

They show us the rooms and bring us the boy, you notice, in that practical English spirit which is intent on making it clear that their cry is proportionate to their wool, a fact of which we are not altogether ignorant. Hence our carelessness about more than a glance at the rooms, or a short talk with the boy with the maimed face. I think I could tell him as much about himself as he can tell me. I have known him many times before.

It is pleasing to notice here how much they insist on the new life, how comparatively little stress they lay on the "conversion," on the being "saved." Also, that the Salvationists know how to laugh. It is only men who keep their religion for a fine heavy diet on sunday who cannot pray at one moment and laugh at another. If my religion is a part of *me*, it is also clearly a part of my laughter.

Now let us go the rounds of the opium dens and brothels round about Little Bourke Street. We walk, my Salvationist and I, into any house that we wish. No one opposes us : only once in the whole evening are we spoken to other than respectfully. " *You see*," says the mistress of the most facially contorted Chinee I have yet seen, " *You see, the Salvationists helps the girls, that's why we likes 'em !*" Here we are in a den, a girl lying on one side of the bed (the Chinese beds are like large alcoves. In the middle is the opium-tray, containing the pipe, a lamp, etc.), a Chinee on the other, getting her pipe ready for her. We sit and chat with her. She tells us about herself simply enough, showing no signs of wishing to alter her condition. Then the other girl comes in, and we chat with her. My Salvationist recognises her : she was at Bella's funeral. (Bella was a girl who fell down dead in the brothel opposite, and the Army buried her. All "the girls" about clubbed together, hired cabs, and went to the funeral.) "O yes," says the girl to him, "you said the service for Bella." She too tells us about herself simply enough. Her mother is at Ballarat.—"Does she know you're here ?"—"O yes, she knows."—"Does she think you're in service ?"—"O no, *she* knows what I'm doing ;" and so on. Presently I go into the other room and talk pigeon English with the remarkable spectacled Chinee, who is like a venerable old ape. Why will the English girls come and live with the Chinese? The answer is simple : the Chinese both pay them well and are kind to them. These girls are not bruised on the face and arms as most of the others are.

You perceive now how the Salvationists work here ? They are the " friends " of the girls : they "help" them. Find out from a girl if she is miserable : find out if she would sooner go back to a respectable life. Go everywhere fearlessly : Find out if any girl is being detained against her wishes. Be gentle with them as with equals. Make them feel that you care for them for their own sakes. Work upon their feelings —speak of their home, their mother, their father, their brothers, their sisters. Offer them a new start. Then, the moment that of their own free will they are ready to come, put them into a cab and drive straight away with them to the Home. Here they come under the influence of the women officials of the Army,

(some of whom, however, also do visiting work), the same
system being pursued with them as with the men. They are
not made to feel that they are dealing with people more loftily
refined or more loftily righteous than themselves. They are not
made to feel that they are "fearful sinners." They are made
to feel that sin is fearful and that they have sinned fearfully,
but that they have every hope before them, hope of a new life
before God and man. As for the women officials of the Salvation Army, I will say this, that in no body of female religionists, except the Catholic Sisters, have I found so many
sweet true women. I have also known Anglican Sisters who
were well worthy of a place beside them. Such women are
the essence of Christianity. They are the true children of
Mary Magdalene and Monica, of the love and of the affection
of the soul. Preference for any one of these three classes,
there can be none. I cannot exalt true love above true affection any more than I can exalt heat above light : their joy is
equal. But in one respect the Salvationist women have an
advantage over the others, just as the Salvationist men have
over the celibate priests—in just that, in the fact that they need
not be celibates. Many of these Salvationist girls and women
are the sweethearts or wives of their fellow-workers. This, I
think, is as it should be. He who neglects or despises that
great law of Nature and God, passion, will be assuredly
punished for it. To make a large body of men and women
celibates is to put a premium on immorality and hypocrisy.
This great rock the Salvation Army has avoided, and herein it
has done most wisely. Here, where Rome is weak, it is
strong. We must not, however, think that there is nothing to
be said in behalf of celibacy : there is much, very much. If
we were all men like Francis of Assissi or Vincent de Paul, it
would be perfect ; but unfortunately we are not. At the same
time, he who has seen the work of Catholic priests and of
Protestant clergymen or ministers in times of plague and pest
must feel how great a clog to perfect courage are those
hostages a man has given to fate in wife and children. On the
other hand, observe that times of pest and plague are comparatively rare, and that every great idea when put into
practice is but a mixed good. What we have to do is to
choose that which has least evil, or shall we say most good,
and this can, we feel sure, be only chosen in conformity with
all of those few great primeval laws which are the guides of life,
which are the direct words of Nature and of God.

VIII.

So much, then, for the *how* of the Salvation Army. Let us now consider if it has helped us to the *why*—nay, if it has not absolutely told us the *why!* Did we not instinctively catch at something we saw two or three times rising before us as with small but teleological significance in it ? Did we not feel, as we uttered that expression with which this something inspired us, that here was the *why* in propria persona? *Religious Socialism.*

In this state of affairs—the powerlessness of the Socialists to bring home to the People the great idea of social improvement : in the misery unspeakable of the People ; in the atmosphere heavy with the degradation of the People—what is it that the People has done? *It has evolved a movement, no longer from* without, *but from* within *itself. It has sought for consolation for its unspeakable wretchedness in the perennial spring of Religion, of the yearning love of Jesus. It has, at the touch of the first match that came to it, blazed up into the flaming fire of Religious Socialism.*

In the early part of the thirteenth century the People did the same, the People of Italy. But what a heaven lies between the man who led *that* movement and the man that is leading this ! O my eloquent Rationalists, O my loquacious Secularists, both of you whom I esteem so much—how ready are you to talk of the degradation which that gigantic superstition and delusion, Christianity, wrought upon the People ! Whenever are you tired of brandishing " starry Galileo " and scattering the scattered dust of poor old Copernicus in the face of Catholicism, making it to tremble and sneeze fearfully ? Does it never occur to you that that divine Goddess Scientia, whom you worship with such noble devotion, has wrought a far deeper degradation on the people than Catholicism ever did ?   Have you never seen, crouching under the shadow of your railways and your telegraphs and all your improved machinery, the unspeakable wretchedness of London, of Birmingham, of Manchester, of Glasgow ? And now that this People, whose lives your Goddess has made of such a sort that they will not stand too favourable a comparison with those of dogs—now that this People, in its passionate searching after some consolation, however slight, of whatever sort, seizes on this creature of superstition and delusion, this Jesus who is *only a man, just like you or me,* and whom you have so triumphantly

proved so, and makes him the text for this flaming fire of
Religious Socialism—has it never struck you, O my eloquent
Rationalists, O my loquacious Secularists, what an appalling
difference there is between Salvation Army banners, handkerchiefs, brass-bands, and concertinas, and the "green boughs,
flags, music, and songs of gladness" that came forth from the
Umbrian towns and villages to welcome Francis of Assissi?
have you never felt that there is any essential difference
between the perpetual Revivalist hymn of "My Jesus to know
and to feel his blood flow," and the "Canticle of the
Creatures?" But, above all, have you never felt that it is
more to that divine Goddess Scientia, whom you worship with
such noble devotion, than to anything else that this appalling
difference is due?

And you, O my Middle-class, of whom I am so humble a
unit, did it ever occur to you that it is rather a foolish thing to
paint a boy's face black and then be shocked at it? If the
People, its foulness and its ferocity, makes you shiver and
shudder, who pray made it foul and fierce but you who govern
it?—What do you say? "It was no business of yours?"
That was what Cain said, but respectable Christians like you
are not surely going to take that eminent casuist as your
mouth-piece? If you were Atheists or Agnostics, now, worshippers of "the struggle for existence and survival of the
fittest," of course that would be another matter, but you are
Christians, respectable Christians who always wear black coats
on sundays, and object to having the Library and Picture-
Gallery open.

Well, there! I cannot make myself angry with you, my dear
Middle-class. I admire your good qualities too much for that
—too much indeed, as I often tell myself; for who shall say
but that my belief in your ultimate regeneration and new birth
unto a really glorious place in a true civilization be not, after
all, but infatuation? Here is Carlyle, whom we all love and
admire so, trying to be our benefactor by demonstrating to us
our illusions on this matter, and telling us, ever since 1830, of
the "steady approach of democracy with revolution (probably
explosive) and a finis incomputable to man; steady decay of
all morality, political, social, individual; this once noble
England getting more and more ignoble, and untrue in every
fibre of it, till the gold (Goethe's composite king) will all be
eaten out, and noble England will have to collapse in shapeless

ruin, whether for ever or not none of us can know." Really there are hours when I am made quite to suffer by thinking of what is going to happen to my dear Middle-class when the People rise unanimously against it, —"roaring million-headed unreflecting, darkly suffering, darkly sinning 'Demos'" (as Carlyle says again), "come to call its old superiors to account at its maddest of tribunals." It will, I fear, be little good for the Mr. Caffyns of those times to write letters to the *Argus* of those times, explaining the physiological aspects of the movement. On such an occasion in Paris, in 1793, Mr. Caffyns went up into the arms of La Guillotine for much less heinous offences than that, and who would be left capable of recording whether, in this case, they went up "with a tripping movement" (as Mr. Caffyn tells us the fanatical "Hallelujah lasses" go), or whether they marched, as perhaps Mr. Caffyn himself marches to church or chapel every sunday morning, to the edification of all beholders? But let us not think of such an appalling spectacle. Mr. Caffyn is still with us, and the *Argus* is still with us, and perhaps some morning we shall have some more brilliant letters on the physiological aspects of Mr. Caffyn's friends, the hallelujah lasses.

I cannot, I say, make myself angry with you, my dear Middle-class of England (and you might plausibly suggest that it would not matter much if I did), and how then shall I even frown at this Middle-class of Victoria, about whom (if Carlyle is right) I am more infatuate still? Does not the People breathe free in Australia? Are we not liberated here from that charming "Upper Ten Thousand" which monopolises the best of the bad education England has to offer, the Public Schools and the Universities? Is there not a hope that, now that the primary education of the People is progressing so satisfactorily, some of our young rising politicians, (or even some of the old ones), may bring home to us the fact that we want equally—nay, far more!—a secondary education for the Middle-class? so that Victoria may step forward as a competitor with the most universally civilized nation in the world, France, and teach England the unspeakable glory and advantage of (we should call it) an Upper-class, "homogeneous, intelligent, civilized, brought up in good public schools" (and not, as now, in more or less good, or more or less bad, denominational, and "private adventure" schools) " and on the first plane."

If only this Upper-class of Victoria and of Australia generally could be brought to see it! If only it would confess its sins, many and heinous, against true civilization and be "converted" and lead a new life! Nothing, I think, strikes an Englishman more, coming out here, than the brightness and intelligence of the Victorian girls! ("Our daughters," you know.) And how heart-rending to discover that all this brightness and intelligence is wasted on the mere accidents and incidents of every-day existence! Two-shilling novels are her idea of literature: "Some day" and "Ehren on the Rhine" her idea of music: the coloured illustrations of the illustrated papers, her idea of art. And her brother is in a worse state! The tortoise English girl is, after all, better than the Australian hare, and the young male bull-dog than the kangaroo.

Everything crys out for the education, for the civilization, of the Upper-class, the ruling class. Educate it, civilize it, let it know what Truth is and what Beauty is, and abolish the bells and the brass-bands for ever! If the Upper-class is beautiful, its beauty will react on the Lower-class. Give us public schools for the Upper-class, as there are public schools for the Lower-class. Fight tooth and nail against any attempts after an "Upper Ten Thousand," whether it be of land or of wealth. Keep clearly before us the ideal of an Upper-class that is *homogeneous*. Let us have the man of business as cultured as the professional man, and the professional man as cultured as the man of means. Let us be a true Republic, offering every opportunity to the intelligence of the Lower-class to attain to the culture of the Upper. Let us not have ten thousand aristocrats, but ten hundred thousand, ever more and more, and never less and less! On the other hand, let us learn from the People the great lesson which they have to teach us—the lesson of the language of the heart. Let us learn from them the softness of pity, yea and the richness of love. Let us give them our *Social Socialism* and let us take their *Religious;* for, in the perfect marriage of light and heat, is the perfect day, the true civilization, the beauty of the truth of Nature and of God.

February, 1885.

E

SYDNEY AND HER CIVILIZATION,
AS THEY STRIKE AN ENGLISHMAN.

It was in 1770 that Cook entered the bay to which he gave
the name of Botany : in '88 that Philip landed in Port Jackson
with his convict settlement : in 1849 that the settlers refused
to receive any more convicts : and in '56 that the settlement
was acknowledged as a colony and dowered with a constitution. These few facts have a very different significance to
those which correspond to them in the history of Melbourne.
The epithet phenomenal cannot be applied to the former in
the same sense as to the latter ; nor yet, let us hasten to add,
the epithet premature. English people, who carry to a quite
quaint degree their modern representative poet's dislike of

> " Raw Haste, half-sister to Delay,"

find Melbourne "too American," as they say, and reserve all
their praise for "picturesque Sydney" and the harbour about
whose description Mr. Trollope went (as we are all never likely
to be able, at any rate in Sydney, to forget) into diffuse
despair. "The business thoroughfares," says a simple English
traveller, "as well as the shops themselves, have a far more
English appearance than those of the capital of Victoria," and
shuns all comment as superfluous. Let us not think of contradicting him. That elemental characteristic of the British
architect, "the impotence to express anything," is in no
danger of disappearing in Sydney, nor yet, let us again hasten
to add, in Melbourne : but, if it be possible to distinguish the
matter thus, I should say that in Sydney he had found his
happy hunting-grounds, whereas in Melbourne he was just
beginning to feel that there was a rival about.

No, it is just where Sydney is *un*-English that she has charm.
I do not now refer to her natural position, nor to her age—age
which will tone down, and perhaps some day almost mellow,
the masterpieces of even the British architect. I refer to those
buildings in the town, few and far between enough, it is true,

in which the Sydney perception of its individual life has striven
to express itself. The Sydney perception of its individual life
is not strong. As a local guide-book puts it more particularly,
"in the nomenclature of the streets Sydney shows intense
loyalty, and the lover of history will be delighted by the
associations which some of the names will summon to his
memory. For instance, his historical predilections will be
gratified in noticing that the principal street is named after
George the Third, during whose reign the colony was
founded." Of course, when the local guide-book tells us that a
thing is so, it *is* so; and when it says that our predilections,
historical or otherwise, will be gratified and delighted, they *are*
gratified and delighted. But these Sydney men and women,
with their intense loyalty, or rather what the writer in the local
guide-books means thereby, have not, what we called, the
metropolitan look—have not the metropolitan feeling. Mr.
Marcus Clarke, in the cleverest and also the most fantastic of
his clever but often fantastic criticisms, "The Future Australian Race," says boldly: "It is more than likely that what
should be the Australian Empire will be cut in half by a line
drawn through the centre of the continent. . . . All
beneath this line will be a Republic, having the mean climate,
and, in consequence, the development of Greece. The
intellectual capital of the Republic will be in Victoria; the
fashionable and luxurious capital on the shore of Sydney
Harbour." Then he adds that "the Australians will be a fret-
ful, clever, perverse, irritable race," showing us what, under all
their superficial differences, the people of Victoria and of New
South Wales have, he thinks, in common. I do not believe
that the whole secret of the matter is here laid open before us.
Mr. Marcus Clarke had an admirable acuteness of perception,
but he was apt, having swiftly perceived one aspect of a thing,
to write it down at once as *the* aspect without staying for a
second or third look at the thing itself. The consequence is
that he rarely reaches the whole secret of a thing: witness, for
instance, his view of Christianity, (but Mr. Arnold notices
how even a critic of Sainte-Beuve's calibre was capable of
illusion here), or of the significance of Gordon's poetry, which
I have spoken of elsewhere; and it is lamentable to think how
much of this false tendency in him was due to the circumstance
that he was a man of letters, and an Australian man of letters.
I do not believe, I say, that, when he tells us that the really

distinctive characteristic of Sydney is (for "will be" is only
"is" unmaterialized) fashion and luxury, and Melbourne
intellect, he has laid open before us the *whole* secret of the
present tendencies of these cities, or yet when he sees them
united with the common characteristics of fretfulness, cleverness, perverseness, irritability. But here, undoubtedly, is one
aspect of the matter expressed admirably. The men and
women of Sydney do not live so fast mentally as the men and
women of Melbourne : they give more free play to their
emotional passions. As we say, they "take things easier." They
cling to the past which Melbourne throws away : they consider
the present, which Melbourne has very little time for. Their
attachment to " the old country " is deeper ; they have intense
loyalty, as the writer in the local guide-book says. They are
much more possessed by the affairs of Melbourne than Melbourne is about theirs. The *Sydney Morning Herald* and the
Sydney Mail do not hold the same position in Melbourne as
the *Argus* and the *Australasian* do in Sydney. The Sydney
people are captious in their criticism on the younger capital,
just as Boston is on New York : they talk about being
" dragged at the chariot wheels of Victoria," and asseverate
that they will not endure it. Melbourne people criticise Sydney
good-humouredly, and justly so, since in that aspect of them
both, which people seem to think is alone worth criticising,
Melbourne is undoubtedly far superior. Intellect in the
modern world is the master : emotion is the handmaid.
Or, to put it in another way, our best average work at present
is being done in clear, nervous prose, while poetry is praised and
left to starve. Science is a better paymaster than Art, and
nearly all the best average intelligence of the world has turned
to the rising, and from the setting, sun. And Melbourne, I
say, Melbourne with her perception of movement, progress,
conscious power, has out-stripped this Sydney, whose perception of her individual life is so weak that all she has to point to
are her natural advantages, her age, and the meagre fact that
her " business thoroughfares, as well as the shops themselves,
have a far more English appearance than those of the capital of
Victoria." And yet, undoubtedly, Sydney has—or so it seems
to me—a rich and rare possession of her own, and one which
is worth as much as that of Melbourne, even as emotion is
worth as much as intellect, as poetry is worth as much as prose.
And there are, as we know, good judges who would change the

"as much" into "more." I, however, who have no pretentions to be a good judge, and am, as an acute English critic of mine so aptly put it once, only "Whitman and water:" I must still cling to the belief that perfection is to be found, and only to be found, in the *union* of these two qualities— of emotion and intellect, of poetry and prose. Or, as I said the other day,* true science (which is essentially intellectual) and true faith (which is essentially emotional) are to be, as they must be, harmonies, eternal harmonies, the "perfect music" and "noble words" of truth.

Well now, let us try and find out a little more definitely wherein these men and women of Sydney, these who have not the metropolitan look, the metropolitan feeling, show themselves, at any rate to the disinterested seeker after a really fine civilization, as the equals of our intellectual men and women of Melbourne. ("Intellectual," we are agreed, is here used as meaning that spiritual quality which is opposed to emotional). First of all, however, let us examine this phrase of ours, metropolitan look, metropolitan feeling, for fear it should be nothing but a phrase, a mere catchword, and, as such, worthy only the places where sawdust is stored.

Nothing is more certain than that our individual lives form, if not our faces, the expression of them. Our eyes and all the facial muscles are at the command of our natural inherited dispositions as modified by the circumstances of our lives. The average man who spends his days in the open air in companionship with the inanimate things about him, or in the settled intercourse of country life, married or single, will have a quite different look, a quite different *tone*, from the man whose days are passed in the brisk interchange of words and thoughts of the life of the city. And how much will this difference be accentuated by the fact that the city is a seat of large and intense ideas, that the very air is impregnated with the passionate thoughts, words, and acts of the whole civilized world! It is in such men that we find the metropolitan look, the metropolitan feeling. Their faces seem stripped of all useless flesh like the body of an athlete: their eyes are quick and clear, ready servants of the quick clear brain behind them. This is what we call the average intelligent man, the labourer of the past, the partner of

*Victorian Review, February, 1885, in a series of articles on contemporary English poets.

the present, the master of the future! Put this man, however, into a state of stress, intellectual or emotional, in his business or in his private life, and that fine nervous face of his will become lean and rigid, those quick clear eyes hard and naked. And, just as it is the pleasure of our civilization to see this man in the first stage, so is it the pain thereof to see him, alas too often, in the second. These are the most dread spectres that haunt metropolises : their anguish wrings the heart with an intensity, with an abidingness that the sight of mere misery brutal and degraded does not and cannot inspire us. London and New York swarm with such, and our miniature Australian intellectual capital, too, knows them only too well. They press the stamp of their struggle into the very brow of their city. It is they who bring home to us the lean and rigid, the hard and naked side of the best life of their city. While it is to their successful brothers that we owe what of us is phenomenal, it is to them, the unsuccessful, that we owe what of us is premature. They are the men who have formulated that exceeding bitter cry of " *Cruel London.*" Yes, London is cruel in this sense of the word, and so, to a less degree (In a hundred years shall we be able to say this?) is Melbourne. I do not think anyone would call Sydney cruel.

"Well," retorts the metropolitan, "perhaps not; but, on the other hand, the provincial look, the dull look of intellectual death, is far more common with such towns than with us. For me, I would sooner have heaven with hell than purgatory by itself.—Pah," he says, "Sydney is the city of smells and shopkeepers!" And I for my part, with all my admiration for the intellect of the average intelligent metropolitan in general and the Melbourne metropolitan in particular, should not think of contradicting him here. My only wish here is, as I have said, to find out wherein these people whom he calls, with such fine scorn, "provincials" and "shopkeepers," show themselves his equals, and whether they *do* show themselves his equals, or that I shall stand convicted of a delusion on the subject.

I believe much in first impressions (good ones, that is) provided only that we bring, what I have called, a second and third look to bear on the thing which has impressed us. And since I am graceless enough to speak of my own little private beliefs, let me add that I often find some difficulty in making my last impressions as good as my first, which is provoking to

anyone who has a dread and dislike of "impressionists" and
an attraction and affection towards "students." Hence I find
myself quite ready, when in the latter humour, to call my first
impressions shallow and careless, and when in the former, to
call my last impressions dead-dark and pedantic, so that Mr.
Marcus Clarke delights me not nor (some laborious scholar of
the Australasian future) neither, and all is vanity and vexation
of spirit! Let me, however, on this occasion retail my first
impressions with a trustful pen, for, as they were unself-
conscious and therefore unconnected with any theory on the
subject in hand, I believe they are really the best offering I
have to make on its altar.

The first thing, then, that struck me on walking about
Sydney one afternoon, looking at the place and the
people, was the appalling strength of the British civilization. In Melbourne, for reasons spoken of elsewhere,
this fact is not so striking. Melbourne, I have said, has
something of London, Paris, New York, and of its own.
The prevailing characteristic of Sydney is its British-
ness—the happy hunting grounds of the British architect with
his "impotence to express anything," the intense and gratifying
and delightful loyalty of the nomenclature of the streets, and
the rest. Everywhere are the thumb marks and the great toe
marks of the six-fingered six-toed giant, Mr. Arnold's life-long
foe, the British Philistine! I call this strength appalling ; for
observe that this is a country lying in a band of some five or
six degrees south of the tropic of Capricorn, whereas England
is a country lying in a band of some twenty-five or six degrees
north of the corresponding tropic of Cancer, and yet here are
the two peoples living lives almost identic! Rome changed
her Jupiter into Ammon when the Tiber flowed into the Nile :
Woden and the God of the Christians blended into one
another ; but the Jehovah (or shall we say the Moloch?) of
Puritanism, of Calvinism, is the same in Sydney as in London,
in Melbourne as in Edinburgh! There is nothing like it, save
in the history of that wonderful people which produced this
God that is "a jealous God." And further. These people in
Sydney have clung, not only to the faith but to the very
raiment of their giant. The same gloomy dresses, cumbrous
on the women, hideous on the men, that we see in England!
Now in Melbourne, where those dear "old-country" days,
wherein spring, summer, autumn, and winter alternate with a

fifth season excruciatingly peculiar to the place itself, are not infrequent; in Melbourne, I say, an attachment to the very tricks of one of the worst climates in the world might not be so unnatural; but in Sydney such an attachment becomes positively monstrous. The same food, the same overeating and overdrinking, and (observe how careful we are) at the same hours! If there is one thing, I believe, that the people of Sydney really grudge to Melbourne, it is her factories. If they could only make the atmosphere of Sydney (they do their best, however, with · their steamers for the harbour) as supremely filthy as that of London, Birmingham, Manchester, Glasgow, the people, the intensely loyal people of Sydney, would be happy. As it is, they have reluctantly to concede a point in favour of, what the newspapers call, " her younger rival." And yet how can I say this in the face of their eminently successful pollution of their harbour and their very streets with their drainage?

It is no wonder, then, we see, that, unlike Melbourne, Sydney's perception of her individual life is weak, miserably weak, all but imperceptible. She has to point to her natural advantages and her age. Now it is very nice to have a fine harbour, and Mr. Trollope is in his grave and we may safely say that he had a profuse literary talent, like many writers who lived before and many who will live after him ; but the chief point of interest in the harbour, at any rate to your disinterested enquirer into the present and future social state of the owners, is, *what effect does it, and the climate generally, have upon them?* not whether Mr. Trollope or anyone else " despairs of being able to convey to any reader his own idea of the beauty " of either. Now we all know what effect the " sabbath rest " has on the Middle class and People of England, and we all know how zealously all those " pious and simple-minded " people who, as Dr. Moorhouse puts it so well, live "entrenched in the old fortifications of unintelligent orthodoxy," are striving that that effect should not be in any way lessened—striving, not only in London but in Melbourne, and, so far, with considerable success in both. But here in Sydney, where, at first sight, one would least expect it, they are more liberal in these matters: their public institutions, Museums, Picture Gallery, and so on, are thrown open to the public on sundays.* No

---

It is gratifying to notice at the Technological Museum, where one would least expect it, the number of sunday visitors more than halves that of all the other days put together.

neighbouring town, so far as I know, partakes in the virtuous hatred of Geelong to sunday boats. The harbour is plied by a large number of small steamboats. The Middle-class and the People, thanks to the short hours of work (hence in large part Australia's excellence in sports) and the saturday half-holiday, can disport themselves on its banks or where they please. "Our harbour," then, and *our parks* too, are of more real use than merely, as they say, to blow about ; and so far, so good. Pleasure, that light fair Pleasure which should find its natural home in every fine climate, is undoubtedly drawing breath in the Sydney air. Mr. Marcus Clarke's acuteness of perception did not deceive him when he followed up this pallid plant into the full-grown tree with its flower and fruit of fashion and luxury. Yes, climate will ultimately work a transformation upon even the six-fingered six-toed giant. Moloch's fire will cease to burn and brand : Jehovah's jealousy will lose its harshness, and the sweet bright love of the White Christ will brood over and temper the hearts of this people to beauty and melody. Meantime, down there in Melbourne, Pleasure when it opens its mouth to breathe, will also open it to bite : the taint of cruelty will be upon it as it is upon all things purely intellectual, all things in which emotion has no part. "Melbourne," the wise man of Sydney will say then, "Melbourne is the city of stew-pans and stockbrokers. They know how to make money, but not how to spend it. If they have pleasure, it borders on pain as lust does on love. All the beauty they know is the beauty of light ; heat is a stranger to them. Their music lacks the minor keys. Years ago their one poet, Gordon, ran away from the city, and took refuge in the bush : if he were alive now, he would come to Sydney. No poet, no painter, no musician will be brought forth out of Melbourne.—You will make fine logicians, you Melbournians, and it does a man's heart good to think of your cog-wheels ; but believe me that you know no more of life than that it is an existence, or of death than that it is the stopping of a mouse-wheel." Thus our problematical "provincial," returning fine pity for the fine scorn of our problematical "metropolitan." Or, to drop the symbolism, thus my first impressions of the actual or inherent melody and beauty of the Sydney life, as evolved from my last impressions of the leanness and rigidness, the hardness and nakedness that is to be found so easily in life in Melbourne.

More than once that afternoon did this melody of beauty
come back to me wandering, like a sweet far-off chime.   It is
years since I heard that chime, the chime of Pleasure light and
fair, breathing around me—years ago, in its imperial haunt of
Paris.   Other chimes have their several melodies and beauties,
melodies and beauties perhaps above compare with this one,
but this one is pre-eminent for sweetness, and sweetness is a
rich and rare offering to the soul.   The afternoon was not a
fine one, and I had just been spending two months in peerless
weather by the Riverina.   I had, then, no meteorological
"pathetic fallacy," as Mr. Ruskin says, to help me to a
thoughtless faith in the actual or inherent melody of Sydney.
On the contrary, the rain rained, and the wind blew, and the
bursts of sunshine were few and far between, so that the
Genius of the place had to speak out if he wished to be heard.
And, as we have noticed, he did speak out, and was heard,
and was, and is, approved of.

Pass now from the outer public world into the inner : pass
from the parks and streets into the Picture Gallery, and think
of a similar passage in Melbourne.   It is quite useless to
murmur here, " *Melbourne — movement — progress — conscious
power;*" the words only pass into a dry tuneless jingle, like
Gordon at his worst, wherein nothing can be heard but, "*Leanness and rigidness—hardness and nakedness.*"   We see the
throng of the virtuous wives of the Bourke Street tradespeople
and of "our wealthy lower orders" moving about in that
badly constructed room, with its badly chosen and badly hung
pictures.   We think of the low, low ebb at which the intellect
of the metropolis has left its sense of melody and beauty.   We
wonder what Adelaide Ironsides, whom Mr. Brunton Stephens
has told us of in some charming verses,* would have made of
that people, of that city, whose capacity to foster poetic
instinct was "gauged" with such grimness by Mr. Clarke.†

---

* A volume of his, in which is included his "Miscellaneous Poems" and "Convict
Once," has lately appeared—at last another book, out of so much of this hopelessly
worthless colonial literature, which counts!

† Three of Miss Ironsides' pictures were, when I was in Sydney, housed in a sort of
shed behind the temporary Picture Gallery.   On one side of it the windows were open
to the dust and rain!   One of the pictures, the "Ars Longa, Vita Brevis," was much
spoiled ; another, the "Adoration of the Magi," a little.   I did what I could to alter
this state of affairs, but I could do nothing.   The Trustees do not know to whom the pictures belong, and there is not room enough in the Gallery, as it is, for even the purchased
pictures.   Perhaps when these three pictures are permanently spoiled, something will
be done.   For me, I must confine myself to pointing out the wonderful depth of quiet
feeling which is the chief characteristic of the work of this remarkable girl.   This is to
be noticed most in the "Marriage" picture and the "Ars Longa."   At the same time

And then we turn to this room, this people, and this city, and the fatuity of their intense loyalty seems a venial offence beside the arid barrenness of their intellectual neighbours. Such a construction (and, alas, not a merely temporary but a quite everlasting one) as the Melbourne Picture and Sculpture Galleries, such a choice, such an arrangement of pictures and statues, would not satisfy these men and women of Sydney, as it does the virtuous wives of the Bourke Street tradespeople and of "our wealthy lower orders." I do not say that the *Morning Herald* would burst out into correspondence on the subject, nor yet that that company of eminent men who legislate for an ungrateful country would speak with scorn or pity of these things. The chime of melody and beauty here is, if sweet, far off. Pleasure light and fair is as yet but drawing breath. The outer public life and the inner are but feeling their way to a perception of an individuality, to an individuality that seeks after that form of happiness whose chief expression is in melody and beauty. But in Melbourne there is nothing, or scarcely anything, of this. If no one would think of calling Sydney cruel, neither would anyone think of calling Melbourne sweet. The average intelligent man in Melbourne worships at the master-shrine alone: Intellect is his god, Intellect with its speech of clear nervous prose and its poetry of vigorous, if rather meretricious metres and "galloping rymes." He has no, or very little, care for Art as Art: that is an affair for women, and, as the only organised female public opinion is that of the virtuous tradeswoman and the wife of the wealthy lower orders, spiritual leanness and rigidness, hardness and nakedness are the popular product of the day.

Now there is, I will venture to say, not one social phenomenon, good or evil, in Victoria and New South Wales that cannot be traced to these their spiritual conditions which I have been trying to express. Let us take, what I have

there is something of passionate —of passion suppressed, but none the less existent and strong which adds a peculiar flavour and attraction to her work. The mother's face in the "Adoration" and the girl playing on the harp in the "Marriage" are really beautiful in thought and execution. For pure execution, however, I would direct attention to the drapery of the angel in the former picture, or, in a particular shape, the thorns in the "Ars Longa." I suppose that there is such a plethora of work like this of Miss Ironsides' in both Sydney and Melbourne that only one or two mentally impoverished people like myself can be expected to trouble about it, and it is in the hope of attracting the attention of one or two such that I write this. There are, however, three pictures by Mr. Folingsby in the Melbourne Gallery which would, I am sure, look quite nice in one of our new æsthetically furnished hotels, Mr. Hosie's (say) or the Grand, and then perhaps someone might put Miss Ironsides' in their places. This would be a gain for both the Hotels and the Gallery.

called, the three vital questions of the day—Free Trade—Federalism—Higher Education. New South Wales is in favour of Free Trade. Her perception of her individual life is weak : she clings to the past, she considers the present. Whereas Victoria—Victoria with her swarm of intelligent labourers and men of business—strong in her reliance on her intellect, resolutely turns to the future from which she thinks she will be able to carve out all her desires. Like America, she wants no help from without, she will brook no interference. She will not let her mineral products lie idle as New South Wales does. She is impatient of the true British characteristic, the slow patient evolution of things, the

> "broadening down
> From precedent to precedent."

She believes in the modern scientific spirit, and in none other. "Let us, then," she says, in her heart, "let us, then, by all means, move towards Federalism. Union is strength." But the eager grasping nature of her swarm of intelligent labourers will not let her see that the wisdom of her penny tariffs is but the foolishness of the pounds to come. New South Wales, on the other hand, is adverse to Federalism. She does not understand this modern scientific spirit—she dreads it, is jealous of it, and admires it ! It is so self-reliant, so self-confident ! And she, poor thing, is too much under the sway of the ancient historical spirit to perceive that there is also a modern historical spirit, and that it is good and at her doors. Hence her changeableness, hence her irresolution in the matter. Like her clever unscrupulous politician, Sir Henry Parkes, yesterday she wanted Federalism, to-day she does not : she will not be dragged at the chariot wheels of this dreadful modern scientific spirit which she does not understand, with Victoria shouting and cracking a stockwhip to urge on the horses faster and faster. Is she not the "Queen of the Pacific?" did not Governor Philip tell her she would be " the centre of the southern hemisphere—the brightest gem of the Southern Ocean ?" and who shall say he counted her chickens before they were hatched ?

To the disinterested seeker, then, after a really fine civilization, it is hard to say which is the more painful sight—Victoria, with her resolute pursuit of a purely intellectual future, which must end in arid barrenness, or New South

Wales with her fatuous attachment to the monstrous aspect of the past and present. Which, after all, is the better or the worse, illusion or delusion? Is Victoria never going to perceive that logicians and engineers are not the highest product of civilization? Will New South Wales never shake off the British architect, spiritual and material, and begin to evolve an individual life of her own? Is Mr. Marcus Clarke right when he tells us that "in another hundred years the average Australasian will be a tall, coarse, strong-jawed, greedy, pushing, talented man, excelling in swimming and horsemanship. His religion will be a form of Presbyterianism, his national policy a democracy tempered by the rate of exchange. His wife will be a thin, narrow woman, very fond of dress and idleness, caring little for her children, but without sufficient brain-power to sin with zest." Yes, this is indeed the future of the two tendencies, which are represented by the illuded progress of Victorian, the deluded stagnation of New South Wales. "*The virtuous tradeswoman and the wife of the wealthy lower orders, walking in the happy hunting-grounds of the British architect.*" What a picture! It is a satisfaction to think that, if it is to be, we shall never live to see it. But the question arises, "Is *it to be?*" Has not this acute perceiver of ours been once more writing down one aspect of the thing as *the* aspect, without staying for a second or third look at the thing itself? is not this a clever view of a part, but a fantastic view of the whole? has not Mr. Clarke, in a word, been leaving us this appalling picture of our future in much the same spirit as the world-wounded Hamlet left his cruel dowry to Ophelia? This, we are agreed, was indeed the future of the two tendencies, which are represented by the illuded progress of Victoria, the deluded stagnation of New South Wales; but we should add—*only if they are left to themselves.*

Only if they are left to themselves; and it is our hope, our trust that they will not be. We hope, we believe, that these two countries will learn from one another, each the lesson which the other will be competent to teach: that Victoria will awake to the vital importance of giving her Upper Class a Higher Education to correspond to the Elementary Education that she is giving her Lower Class, and that this Higher Education may be one filled with what we have called the modern historical spirit, with culture, with literary Culture: that New South Wales, leading and instructing Victoria here, having first learned from her example to have the courage to evolve an individual life of her own, will in her turn imbibe the modern scientific spirit, will imbibe what I may call scientific Culture ; and thus we shall be brought on to the day in which the people of Victoria and New South Wales shall, from their superficial differences, be united by common qualities better than those of fretfulness, cleverness, perverseness, irritability : For in this people lies the possibility of a really fine civilization, in the marriage in them of emotion and intellect, of poetry and prose.

> " Is the goal so far away?
> Far, how far no tongue can say.
> *Let us dream our dream to-day.*"

One last word on the last of the three vital questions of the day—Higher Education. When, on 1st April, Mr. Patterson, who presides over the Victorian Education Department, went down to Malmsbury to lay a foundation-stone for the Wesleyan denomination, and favoured us with his views on this question, or rather on the education system as it at present stands in Victoria, we had a hope (a faint hope) that he would do something more than sing the praises of the denominational schools in general, and the state schools ("those majestic monuments to enlightenment," as he says in his profuse political way, " that adorn and bless even the remotest portions of this colony ")— the state schools in particular. Our hope was destined to disappointment. Mr. Patterson had something to say about "the only legitimate checks on the abuse of political power when conferred upon the masses," and about "the unscrupulousness, as well as the boldness beyond reason " of that man who " would deny that the rising Australians, for sobriety and unassuming intelligence, would compare favourably with the old stock," so that he " was bound to record his conviction that the future of Australia would be quite safe in the hands of the Australians." He had also ready a defence of the secular character of the teaching in the state schools, and some nice little left-handed compliments for our good Wesleyans, *et hoc genus omne*, but not a word, and apparently not a thought, for the legitimate checks on "the abuses of *educational* power when conferred" on a middle-class as unprepared for rule as the worst education in the world can make it. "The Australian public," he says, "desires, above all things, to ensure good citizenship." The Australian public cares little that, in the state schools which it has founded for that especial purpose, dead dry intellectual knowledge is rampant—"that asinine feast of sow-thistles and brambles," as Milton disgustedly puts it, " which is commonly set before our youth as all the food and entertainment of their tenderest and most docile age"—" inanimate mechanical gerund-grinding," as Carlyle equally disgustedly called it—gerund-grinding and spiritual cockatoo screeching. Nor yet does it care that, in the denominational schools in which its own children are being brought up, the only supplement to the dead dry educational knowledge of the gerund and the cockatoo, is the merest flimsy smattering of Science caricatured and Literature misunderstood. Let us not, however, despair because our sucking colonial statesmen cannot see more than a few educational inches in front of their noses. Have we not got Dr. Moorhouse, our good Bishop of Melbourne, with us, "a mighty man with broad and sinewy hands?" And does he not, on every available opportunity, batter against the brazen walls of the gerund and the cockatoo, and bid them leave off grinding and screeching, and listen to reason? And here, too, is our good Roman Catholic Bishop of Sydney, Dr. Moran (whom we are all so sorry to think of losing), expressing his "fears that the atmosphere of the public schools is too chilly for a great many of our youth?" Perhaps one of these mornings the Victorian public will wake up, tired of listening to the chatter of the religious and secular dogmatists gathered together like eagles over the carcase of " Religion without Superstition," and there may arise a curiosity and a care for Higher Education and High Schools ; and we will hope, then, that no one will be foolish enough to say that they have been a very doubtful success in New South Wales and in Sydney—in Sydney, the home-elect of the six-fingered and six-toed giant of British Philistinism! And, perhaps, some day poor little Culture, putting off the cumbrous armour with which the gerund and the cockatoo want to load him, taking his sling in his hand and a few smooth stones from the brook, may smite great Goliath in the forehead, and cut off his head, and there be a signal rout of all the Philistines, even unto Gath and Gaza and the utmost borders of the land.

May, 1885.

[NOTE.—I am tempted to republish here a letter, which I sent lately to the *Sydney Morning Herald* wherein one aspect of the secondary education question was (more or less unconsciously) being discussed. No one, so far as I am aware, thought the letter worth serious consideration : at any rate no one thought it worth replying to, perhaps the reasons for its insertion were simply those which the "able Editor" assigned to me for the insertion of all his correspondence, namely that it be not either too illiterate or too offensive for publication. Well, I am sure that for my own part I am grateful for even so much toleration as this, and shall strive, as becomes my humble position in this great Australian press, to continue to deserve it.]

A RUGBY FOR NEW SOUTH WALES.
(*To the Editor of the Herald.*)

SIR,—In your issue of Saturday, May 9th, Mr. Edwin Bean, of All Saints' College, Bathurst, brought under serious consideration the suggestion made by your correspondent "A. N.," as regards what he called "A Rugby for New South Wales." Anything that a schoolmaster of Mr. Bean's talent and experience has to say must be interesting to those of us (alas, too few !) to whom the question of secondary education, whether in England or Australia, is a care. He will understand, then, that when I pass over, almost without notice, his criticisms on the individual aspects of the "reproduction" here "of that which is certainly best," as he says, "in the English Public schools, viz., what is called the Public school spirit"—that the only reason of my doing so is the fear of encroaching too much on your "valuable space." For, interesting as these criticisms are, the interest which lies in what I take to be the two real points at question here is, I must think, greater : these two points being *(1), the growing sense in all competent judges of discontent with the present condition of middle-class secondary education in Australia : (2), the means of ameliorating this condition.*

As regards the first point, I must here almost take it for granted, in the face of the fact that, so far as I am aware, there is not a single colonial politician who seems to realise that if the education of the People, the rulers of the future, is of vital importance to us all, the education of the Middle-, or, as we should say now, the Upper-class, the rulers of the present, is of importance at least quite as vital. The mass of intelligent men here, then, or, as we are wont to say, the intelligent public, naturally enough, holds the same opinion about upper-class secondary education that their political representatives do. "It is all right," they say. "What are you grumbling at in these 'private adventure schools,' as you call them? They do well enough, we think, for us upper-class people; and if you want your son to have a really first-rate education, why, are there not plenty of fine Denominational schools about—the King's School, Newington, and so on, and our splendid Grammar-school?" The only answer to "prophesyings" of this sort is, that the Upper-class, as a class, are, whatever they may think themselves, simply abominably educated : their education is, even when judged by its own miserable standard, superficial, incoherent, impalpable; and the sole necessary proof of this is, that a good three-quarters of the knowledge acquired by an average boy at an average private adventure school is of no subsequent use whatever to him, either in the culture of himself or in the prosecution of his business or trade. As for the best Denominational schools where a secondary education is to be obtained, if inadequate, at any rate much superior to that of the private adventure schools, these are out of the reach of the pockets of the average upper-class people, who, even if they appreciate this misfortune (which, as a rule, they do not), are unable to remedy it.

Here, then, as it seems to me, lies the difficulty; and we have now to look at the solution which the apparent tendency of things is proffering to us. "If 'A. N.,'" says Mr. Bean, "had resided in Victoria, he would have learnt that the Public schools (as they are there called) of Geelong and Melbourne are already taking something of the position, and aspiring to fulfil the functions, of the English public schools. . . . And," he goes on, "at Paramatta, Stanmore, Bathurst, Bowenfels, and elsewhere, there are already boarding-schools, not private, but belonging to Denominational corporations, which, if fostered by private assistance, will eventually grow into something resembling the Public schools of England." Mr. Bean is, of course, right. If things progress in the way in which they are now progressing, if our colonial statesmen turn all their attention, and as much of ours as we will give them, *to* the education of the People, and *from* that of the Upper-class, then, I say, more and more will the Upper-class be thrown into the hands of schools which are mere private speculations, which are really under no control but that of personal caprice (and the personal caprice, great heavens! of what a stamp of intellectual and spiritual man), which, accordingly, provide an education, even when judged by its own miserable standard,

F

superficial, incoherent, impalpable. And these other schools,
I say, the best Denominational and Corporation schools, the
Australian Public schools of the future, will become more and
more the educational monopoly of the professional and
wealthy portion of the Upper-class, just as in England they
have become that of the aristocracy and these portions of the
Middle-class. These "*great schools*," exclaims Mr. Bean justly
of the English Public schools—"*which have done so much to
form the character of the English gentleman.*" Of the English
gentleman? Yes, and alas! of the English middle-class man,
that terrible and pathetic being whom Mr. Arnold has taught
us to know as the British Philistine. "I declare," says General
Gordon, the hero-elect of this very class, "I declare I think
there is more happiness among these miserable (Soudan)
blacks, who have not a meal from day to day, than among our
middle-classes. The blacks are glad of a little handful of
maize, and live in the greatest discomfort. They have not a
strip to cover them; but you do not see them grunting and
groaning all day long as we see scores and scores in England,
with their wretched dinner-parties and attempts at gaiety where
all is hollow and miserable."

What a future for the Upper-class, the by far largest class
of Australia! What an appalling solution to an educational
difficulty is this:—*A small class made up of our squatters,
professional men, and wealthy tradesmen, forming a sort of intellectual and spiritual aristocracy; our Upper-class not only itself
intellectually and spiritually dull and debased, but debasing and
dulling all the better spirits which, in their social ascension, pass
into it from the ranks of the People.* The thought of such a
future to those of us to whom the progress onward and
upward, whether of England or of Australia, is a care, is
appalling, heartrending, unendurable! There is nothing that
we could do, by the devotion of our powers, energies, and
means, that we should not, would not, do to prevent it. And
we should be, and are, encouraged in our struggle against it by
the reflection that the real deep true spirit of the time is
against all monopoly, practical and physical, intellectual and
spiritual—that once the Upper-class, and after them the
People, is aroused to the realisation of the fact that there is a
danger here of the formation of a new aristocracy, an aristocracy which, with all its charm (let us suppose) of social
manners and of intellectual and spiritual culture (and this is

supposing a very great deal), means nothing less than the materialisation, the dulling and the debasing, of everything beneath it—when the Upper-class and the People, I say, are aroused to the realisation of this, we may be sure that they will not rest till they have prevented it.

And how, it is asked, is such a future to be prevented? how such a present to be ameliorated? By the formation, not of Denominational and Corporation schools at a charge which places them out of the reach of all save the richer among us, but by the formation of Public State schools that provide a secondary education as good, and, we will hope, better, than that of these others, and at a charge that is within the reach of the average upper-class people. " Yes, but," at once is answered, "such schools already exist in the High schools, and they have not been a success." I will not here contest, although I well might, the first assertion ; but I cannot, if I would, contest the second. I began by noticing the cause of it, this general satisfaction of "the intelligent public" with the educational pabulum provided for its off-spring. I deplore it ; I hope for the day of its removal to the gulf of oblivion. In the meantime all that can be done is to strive to assist this "consummation devoutly to be desired" earnestly and perpetually.

One word more. No one is more in sympathy (if I may be pardoned for speaking of such an unimportant entity) than *I* am, with the efforts of such men as " A. N." and Mr. Edwin Bean to reproduce, or try to reproduce, in Australia as far as may be, "that which is certainly best in the English Public schools, viz., what is called the Public school spirit." I have not the least prejudice against English Public schools, at one of the oldest and most conservative of which I was myself educated, and from which I almost entirely derived the circle of my most valued friends ; nor yet against the Denomina-tional and Corporation schools here. I have only to remark to Mr. Bean, what I am sure he will at once admit, that if the danger of State schools is the excessive interference of the State, the danger—nay, the absolute abuse—of endowed Public schools is that they become mere feeders of the uni-versities ; and in England to such an appalling extent was this the case that the State absolutely had to alter and narrow its Indian Civil Service examinations in order to bring them within reach of the Public schools, which were being quite left

out in the cold! Doubtless, then, the Australian endowed
Public schools would have their danger too, a danger which
"even no less a thinker than Herbert Spencer," as Mr. Bean
says, has not perhaps, in the application to artificial civilization
of the laws of the natural "struggle for existence and survival
of the fittest," quite comprehended.

With all apologies to you for the amount of your "valuable
space" on which I have encroached in even this far too per-
functory consideration of the matter in hand,

I am, etc.,

There is no one whose opinion on this question of
secondary education is more worthy of our attention than that
of Mr. Matthew Arnold. Our debt of gratitude to him for the
general advancement of the Idea of Culture, not only at home,
but everywhere where our language is spoken, is so great that
we have begun to accept it almost as an impersonal fact. The
work which he did long ago, and has never ceased to recapitu-
late, for the cause of middle-class secondary education, can only
be appreciated by those whose attention has been turned to it
more especially. This, I hope, will hold me excused to him
for quoting here from a letter of his to me, some expressions of
his, and the more so as they seem to show something like a
modification of the view he has so far publicly enunciated.
"I think," he says, "I see signs that the education question is
likely to present itself at no distant date in this wise : 'Shall
the majority give public money for any education except the
education necessary for every citizen ?' The education necessary for every citizen will be somewhat extended in scope, but
no account will be taken of the higher culture hitherto deemed
necessary for a leisured and governing class, and to which so
great a mass of endowment has been made to contribute. On
the Continent of Europe a great change will be produced if
this new view prevails, for the endowments have in general
been seized by the State, and the State has directly subsidised
secondary and superior instruction. In England it has not,
but the endowments which these instructions enjoyed have
been left to them. Probably they will not be taken away, but
further public aid will hardly be given. Nor do I think it will
be given in the Colonies ; and as there the endowment of
secondary and superior instruction is inconsiderable, these
instructions will be, as they are now, at a great disadvantage.

The wealthiest people will send their sons to be educated in England; private schools will, of course, exist locally, but I do not think they will have influence enough to create a class and a power out of those they train. Society will thus be, on the whole, much more homogeneous than with the old nations of Europe; but, as in the United States, this condition of things will have its own dangers and drawbacks. The best way to meet them is for individuals to keep up a love of genuine culture in themselves, and so to create an even larger force in the nation to favour it." Of the truth, or very probable truth, of the educational future here drawn out, there can, alas, be little question. M. Renan, whose work for France can well be paralleled with that of Mr. Arnold for us, takes an even gloomier view. We may count ourselves lucky, he says, if Democracy will consent, not to encourage, but to tolerate independent study. Democracy, he says, again, is the advent of universal mediocrity, of that most terrible of mediocrities, the aggressive. "Great qualities," cried Empedocles, facing the same problem as we do,

> "Great qualities are trodden down,
> and littleness united
> is become invincible."

If this, then, is to be the case in Europe, what will it be in America, and still more in Australia? Aristocracies may not be ideal, but they have their use: they establish a certain high tone of social intercourse which is certainly valuable as one element in a really fine civilization; and, when they have passed away, it still lives as a tacit influence. France to-day, for instance, is a republic, but her outward manners, despite all that has happened, bear something of the mark of the Grand Siècle. England, again, is swinging away with heavy speed from her old ideal of Puritanism, and yet, as Mr. Arnold says so well, "the seriousness, solemness, and devout energy of Puritanism are a prize once won, never to be lost; they are a possession to our race for ever." But America? but Australia? America is not leavened by Puritanism as England is, neither has she any hereditary tone of social intercourse to be compared with that of England, not to say of France. America must settle her own problem for herself, despite all the outer influence which is brought to bear on her: two hundred miles out from the Amazon mouth the water is still fresh, but it is salt at last. But consider this Australia where the Puritanism

only began to operate when its sincerity was souring into cant,
where the tone of social intercourse flourishes in the hands of
those who attain to it as the imitation of an imitation! What
can be so disastrous for Australia as the thrusting into power of
a class of this sort, to be followed by a class which is to the
first as the first is to its prototype in England? How this
future presents itself has already been considered here. Mr.
Marcus Clarke's picture of it stands like a perpetual nightmare.
What hope, then, remains to us except in that very "higher
culture hitherto deemed necessary for a leisured and governing
class," which Mr. Arnold tells us our local private schools will
not have influence enough to create as "a class and a power?"
Is the only aristocracy possible to us to be, not a broad one
like that of Athens, but a narrow one like that of Rome? We
all know the picture Juvenal has painted of the decadence of
this last, and Johnson's application of it to the London of his
time is not a memory altogether pleasant. "The lustre of a
capital," says M. Renan, with his eye on that of his own
country, "springs from a vast provincial dung-heap, where
millions of men lead an obscure life, in order to bring forth
some brilliant butterflies which come to burn themselves in the
light." And if for capital we substitute plutocracy, and for
butterflies creatures of a nature less savoury, we see something
like the sort of future with which we are threatened here.
Political life at present in Europe can scarcely be called noble,
but here in Australia it is positively so base that there is a
danger of its becoming the monopoly of men whose verbose
incompetence is only equalled by their jovial corruption. The
Plutocracy, such as it is, is being thrown in upon itself. Its
present generation, it is true, is content to work—and, indeed,
can find its only happiness in work ; but this will not be so with
the next, and still less with the third, generation. The desire
to enjoy will grow into a lust, and this lust will spread. The
end of this we know, and there will not lack writers to look
back upon the present, even as so many of us look forward to
the future, with a sort of eager envy. Well, and what is to be
done to prevent this, if it is to be prevented? To cease from
trying to obtain a secondary education for the Upper-class? to
obtain Australian Rugbies, not only for the Plutocracy, but for
the Upper-class, and for any one of the People that has the
care to climb up to them and the best education which his age
and country can afford him? to create a class and power that

shall, in their turn, create a really fine civilization?—are we to cease from all direct struggle for this, and meet the present crisis by simply trying "to keep up the love of genuine culture in ourselves, and so to create an ever larger force in the nation to favour it?" I cannot believe that this is so; I cannot even believe that, good way as it is, it is "the best way." We have all been reading lately what Mr. Arnold had to say in favour of this indirect method, this creation of a Remnant that should at last become a power, and I am sure I should be the last person to say a word against it. All I have to say is, that I have too much belief in the power of institutions (a power "the benefits of which," Mr. Arnold has just been telling us, "he had not properly appreciated" before his trip to America) to neglect anything that could bring them to the side of Culture. I appreciate the indirect method, and I believe that, in the long run, it is the method which gives permanent solidity, but I cannot blind myself to the immense importance of the direct method. If it is necessary to conduct a river into a city, the pipes must first be made, and care taken that they are not too small. The French Revolution was a violent attempt and a premature one, and yet, such as it was, it brought a greater volume of happiness into France than the abortive attempt that we made in England. *We* have still to face the problem of the happiness of the few and the debasement of the many, and I cannot see that it is an easier problem to resolve than that which is presenting itself to the French just at present. I still, then, must continue to believe that it is not wise in England, and how much more in America, and how much more in Australia, to refrain from the direct struggle for a higher education for our Upper-class. Our aim is not for the few but for the many, and not for elementary Culture for the many, but for the possibilities of a really fine Culture. We have, too, our distrust of Remnants. We dread their tendency to take to lotus-eating. They are apt to care so little for the propagation of either their species or their Culture.

> " Let us alone ! What pleasure can we have
> to war with evil? Is there any peace
> in ever climbing up the climbing wave?"

It is with difficulty, with great and perpetual difficulty, that a Goethe can keep his duty to his art and his duty to his neighbour at the perfect poise. It is so hard to keep your duty to yourself from running into your duty to your selfishness.

Light, and the love of light, and the love of bringing light to others, is after all impossible without a certain admixture of heat. Let us, then, still continue to nourish our enthusiasm for a direct purpose, which shall be the future to that great mass of average human beings who are thoughtlessly moulded by whatever they find is strong enough to mould them. Let us be jealous of individuals. "*Non Angli, sed angeli.*"

> "*Leave not a human soul
> to grow old in darkness and pain!*"

October, 1885.

CULTURE.

EVERYONE nowadays has something to say about Culture. Even the politicians have heard of it, and some morning we may read in our newspapers that one of them is of opinion that there is some meaning in the term. Naturally enough we have all of us for some time been groping after the thing itself. The Time-Spirit is like a skilful driver of sheep. He may have considerable trouble with his flock, but, thanks to his unruffled intelligence and the ceaseless exertions of his dog Genius, he brings them all in in time for the market. It is now almost a century since the Idea of Culture took definite shape in the mind of a single man, and ever since then the number of its followers has kept on increasing, until at last everyone, as I remarked, has now something to say about it. If, however, one enquires of people, not what they *think* of Culture, (For everyone from the Vatican Œcumenical Council* to the author of "In Memoriam"† is agreed as to the advantage of it), but what culture *is*, one may go far for a satisfactory answer. Women are growing dissatisfied with the sphere of their work. What is it that they need? "More breadth of culture," answers the Prince of Tennyson's Princess readily enough, "more breadth of culture!" And it will be said that it is easy to see that what the Prince means is, that women should have thrown open to them the education that has so far been the monopoly of men. But is this Culture? is this the whole truth about it?—simply the giving to the many—to women, to the Middle-class and to the People— what is the education of the few? would that man in whose mind the Idea of Culture first took definite shape have been satisfied with the sight of ubiquitous Harrows and Etons and Grammar Schools of Melbourne and Geelong? There can be no doubt but that such a sight would have pleased, but it certainly would not have satisfied him. "Schools," he would have said, "are of high importance, but what is taught in them is of importance still higher."

---

* Crescat et proficiat tam singulorum quam omnium, tam unius hominis quam totius Ecclesiae, Intelligentia Scientia Sapientia.
† "In Memoriam," cxiv.

And so we come back again to our question as to what Culture *is* with a sense that the ready answers to it are only half answers. Now everyone has heard of Goethe, and everyone has read some of his writings—" Faust,"² at any rate—and, as it is to Goethe that we owe the Idea of Culture (as indeed most things that are really good in the sphere of modern thought), it would be best to at once quote his own words on the matter, and see if we cannot find a definition, or at any rate a description, of Culture that shall satisfy us. Poetry, however, does not exactly lend itself to definitions of such things as this, or even to descriptions. In Faust himself the idea may be more or less, as they say, incarnated, but we plain practical people, who like things put as much in black and white as may be, have some difficulty in these matters, and would far rather hear of them in simple English prose which means what it says and says what it means, than in poetry (and particularly German poetry) which seems to us to do exactly the reverse. Well, then, let us turn away from this parabolic Goethe for a little, and see if we cannot find someone who shall be his expounder to us. And who else should this be, at any rate in this case, than he whom the newspapers like to call the Apostle of Culture, Mr. Matthew Arnold? Let us go to Mr. Matthew Arnold, and say: "Sir, you are constantly talking about Culture, and you have said many uncomplimentary things to us all about our want of it. Now would you be so kind as to tell us precisely what you *mean* by it? And we warn you that we are plain practical people who like things put as much in black and white as may be, and that we have a decidedly poor opinion of your efforts to make us believe that 'the Eternal not ourselves that makes for righteousness' is the same thing as our 'loving and intelligent Governor of the Universe,' and that it makes no difference to us when we eat our Christmas goose and plum-pudding whether we believe that we do so because those shepherds and those Three Kings *did* come that day to Christ in the Bethlehem manger, to the accompaniment of an angelic concert, or did not. We want, Sir, a definition of this Culture of yours, or, if you cannot give us that (But, really now, you are so clever at definitions that we shall be quite disappointed if you cannot!), then you must give us a good description of it, so that we may be able to arrive at a proper decision about it." Then an expression of bland patience would cross Mr. Arnold's countenance, as he sat in his study chair, listening with that " native modesty" of which he has told us all, to the words of our curious foreman ; and, after a short pause, he would perhaps answer : "Gentlemen, I am much honoured by this deputation and inquiry. Long ago in some remarks of mine on translating Homer. . . . But I will refer you to a more recent period. A new and revised edition of a little book of mine called 'Literature and Dogma' has just been issued in a cheap form by Messrs. Smith, Elder and Co. You will find that in the Preface to it the following words occur, which I venture to think may, on investigation, be found to answer the question with which I am now honoured. But, as you possibly may not remember it, (for I cannot expect you, any more than myself, to be always study-ing my works), I will quote it to you. '*Culture*,' I said (Culture in italics)—'*Culture*, knowing the best that has been thought and known in the world.' I can give no better definition than this. 'True Culture,' I say again, 'true Culture implies not only knowledge, but right tact and justness of judgment, forming themselves by and with judgment.' Or, yet again : 'Culture is *reading*' (Reading in italics), 'but reading with a purpose to guide it, and with system.'"--And with this, and a renewal of compliments on both sides, our jury bows itself out, and presently the sound of the closing hall-door mounts up to the silent chamber.

> " But an awful pleasure bland
> spreading o'er the Poet's face,
> when the sound climbs near his seat,
> the encircled library sees ;
> as he lets his lax right hand
> which the lightnings doth embrace
> sink upon his mighty knees."

This, then, it seems, is Culture—*knowing the best that has been thought and known in the world*—*not only knowledge, but right tact and justness of judgment, forming themselves by and with judgment*—reading, *but reading with a purpose to guide it, and with system.* And is not this something like what Goethe meant in that enigmatic sentence of his, which we have heard so often quoted by people who understood it as much as we did: "Vom Halben zu entwöhnen ; Im Ganzen, Guten, Schönen resolut zu leben." "I resolved to wean myself from halves, and to live for the Whole, the Good, the Beautiful." But even now, even now that we know what it is (And after all, we say, what much more is it than saying that we ought to try for the best article. and not rest content with anything but the best article ?), wherein are we, we plain practical people with our attachment to black and white, helped to the attainment of it ? Culture, we are told, is reading, but reading with a purpose to guide it and with system. The purpose, it is presumed, is attainment, but what is the system? We are to have knowledge, and not only knowledge but right tact and justness of judgment, forming themselves by and with judgment. All very nice, we say, but how are we to get them? You say to a man who hobbles, "Run :" he is quite as capable of saying it as you are. Either show him how to run, or hold your tongue!—unless it be that he thinks he *is* running, and even then it seems useless enough to undeceive him without you can teach him how to do what he now thinks he is. What, then, is this system of which you speak ? what is the receipt for it ? is it a system possible to *us ?*

Well, I really have not the courage to go and face Mr. Arnold again. Handlers of the lightnings like he is can be so disagreeable when they please. Where is the joy of figuring in some ludicrous or contemptible attitude in their writings for the next few hundred years or so? It is all very well to say that we shall all of us be in our graves presently, and all equally ignorant of what our descendants may think of us, but the truth is no one likes to be held up to the nations as a fool or a knave, and especially if he be both. I see nothing for it but to let the oracle alone. I for one will have nothing to do with stirring up Phoibos again. I have done so more than once already, and am too grateful for a whole hide to tempt the arrows further. We must be our own Oidipous. At most we can reverently finger the Sibylline leaves, and see if anything of "pleasant to the eye and good for food " can be extracted therefrom.

To begin with, however, does it not seem best to say at once that, after all, there is no receipt for not saying and doing foolish things except not to be foolish ? No system in the world will give wings to a worm. On the other hand, there is really no reason why the descendants of that worm should not one day navigate the sky ; and, as a matter of fact, they do. Similarly with the stupidest and the most degraded of us, I cannot see why a single moment should be lost in attempting to better them. The earth is likely to be inhabitable for the next eight millions of years or so, it seems, and I am sure that is long enough for us. We need not be in such a hurry as the Socialists would have us, nor yet creep along on all fours in the Conservative manner ; but we must not, of course, undervalue either fashion of progress, since both wheels and a drag are important parts of a carriage in uneven country. But here again, as is always the case, we are brought face to face with the question, not only of the wheels and the drag, not only of the carriage itself, and not only of even the driver of it, but of the end of the journey. "The purpose," we said a moment ago in our ready way, "is, it is presumed, attainment, but what is the system?—Never mind," we say, "about where we are going to : let us hear about the carriage we are going in ! Let us have Etons and Harrows and Melbourne and Geelong Grammar Schools everywhere, and then we shall be alright. Let us resolve to have the best article, and not rest content with anything but the best article, and that's all !"

Alas, for the impatience of mankind! In order to *try* for the best article, not to say to *have* it, must we not first know what the best article *is ?* should we not know where we are going to, before we construct our carriage and purchase our horses? And yet, in ninety-nine cases out of a hundred, are we not content to *go*, and leave more or less to chance where we are going *to?* do we not waste half our lives in over-coming difficulties with which we ought to have had nothing to do? It is so easy to talk and to act: it is so difficult to think, and mould your words and actions to your thoughts rather than your thoughts to your words and actions. It is the weary old tale of the more haste and the less speed, the weary old tale that is for ever new. And yet we will not listen to it. Sooner than trouble ourselves with the *whys* of things, we will throw ourselves with energy into the first *hows* that present themselves, and leave the rest to chance, or, as Dr. Moorhouse's good "unintelligent orthodox" people say, to God. But nothing real, nothing lasting, is achieved in this way. Nature does not work in this way : God does not work in this way. The beasts do and the vast majority of men do, and that is why, in Hamlet's words, life is such "an unweeded garden that grows to seed ; things rank and gross in nature possess it merely." No, if we are to understand, not only Culture but anything at all, we must begin at the very beginning : we must learn the *whys.* Take care of the *whys*, we might say, and the *hows* will take care of themselves. And let us not for a moment be deceived by those who tell us that our fathers got along very well without inquiring into the *whys*, into the causes of things, and so can we. This is not so. Whatever success has been achieved has been achieved by a recognition, conscious or unconscious it may be, of the causes of the thing worked upon. Instead of our fathers having had any success from their ignorance of causes, or their reliance on good fortune, they have had success in despite in these, and only so far as they banished the one and knew how to turn to account the other.

And Culture? what has this to do with Culture? Everything!—In this, as in so many other cases, we concentrate all our attention on the *how* and leave the *why* to take care of itself. "More breadth of Culture, more breadth of Culture," cry the Princes and the Priests, and everyone else, in emulous chorus. But when they are asked what they *mean* by Culture —what Culture *is*, then they have no answer ready save one (as Shelley says),

"pinnacled dim in the intense inane;"

and this sort of thing will, in the end, satisfy no man.

Well, we have heard what Culture *is—knowing the best that has been thought and known in the world.* But we have been brought up sharply at the very next step: *Culture is reading, but reading with a purpose to guide it.* What is the purpose? Attainment. Yes, but *how? how* and *why?*

But before we try to answer that, let us think a moment whether the expounder of our parabolic Goethe has given us a definition that is quite satisfactory. We have nothing to say against his definition of Culture itself. It expresses Goethe's "the Whole, the Good and the Beautiful" perfectly. But what about this second definition? what about Culture being reading, but reading with a purpose to guide it? Is this a pure parallel equivalent of the first, or has it something of a limitation in it? Can we, indeed (supposing us the happy possessors of a certain purpose and system), achieve a knowledge of the best that has been thought and known in the world —of the Whole, the Good and the Beautiful—by reading, and by reading only? is this what Goethe has to say to us? is this the lesson of Goethe's life? If it is, why is it that he lays such stress on the absolute personal experience of things? If Faust could have achieved Truth in his study, why does

Goethe show us his achievement of it by taking him away from his reading, and flinging him in the arms, first of Love and then of Life? Faust does not leave his reading and his thinking behind him : they accompany him everywhere, from Margarete's bedroom to the witch-revel on the Brocken. And what does this mean but that, to achieve a knowledge of the best that the world has thought and known, two things are necessary—reading and experience ; or, in the same words, thought and knowledge. No amount of reading will compensate for want of experience. It is useless for me to think I have attained to Truth, if I have never felt her absolute presence. Is idealization the essence of true love ? Is there a more real inspiration to be found in the faëry princesses of Shelley, than in the breathing women of Wordsworth ? Idealization is good, but it must have a firm foundation in reality, or it is barren of anything but fantasticality. So it is with thought and knowledge. No man who has not himself lived and loved can tell us the truth of love and life. Gibbon had immense reading, and a purpose and a system in it (I do not here enter upon their precise nature), and his history of the Decline and Fall of Rome is in many respects quite admirable, but he does not attain to truth in it. And why ? Because he has not experience, he has not knowledge. All his reading, all his purpose, all his system will not compensate for the want of their corollary. No, Culture, the achieving of the best that has been thought in the world, is not reading, not reading with any purpose or system that has been or will ever be devised. Culture is the combination of reading with experience, of thought with knowledge. The one thing acts as a check on the other; the one is the spirit and the other the body; the one, in Shakspere's words, the "judgment" and the other the "blood," and in their "comingling" is found the perfect man. The purpose, the system remain unchanged. We have only, as it seems to me, to develop our second definition : to say that Culture is *reading and experience, but reading and experience with a purpose to guide them, and a system.*

And so, having disposed somewhat of the *why,* we come back to the *how,* the purpose and the system. In reality the two are one. Mr. Arnold speaks once of Goethe's " profound impartiality," and elsewhere he lays the greatest stress on that which alone can help criticism " to produce fruit for the future "—*disinterestedness.* By *disinterestedness* he means the sincere endeavour, the pure and simple endeavour, to get at the truth of things, to see them as they really are. And what is this but Goethe's determination to " wean himself from halves," from partial views of things? Now nothing is easier than to say that you seek for Truth and Truth only, and nothing is more difficult to do. Who is there that does not make this profession? And yet how few, how infinitely few, are those who turn it into practice! And why is this? The answer of course is because, say what they may, the pursuit of most men is merely relative. I no more attain to Truth by saying " Go to, I will attain to it," than I should fly over the moon by a like formula. It is only the really honest and sincere, the really pure and simple endeavour to find Truth that makes me competent to even set out in search of it, and it is only by the ceaseless use of a system of resolute patience and clear-sightedness that I can hope to proceed with any success upon my way. This is indeed a hard saying; but who, except him who ought to feel it least, feels that Truth is a goal to be won by rose-crowned processions to the sound of cymbals and dances? Some people, indeed, have a conviction that a special exception has been made in their case, and that what has been hidden from the wise and prudent has been revealed to babes and sucklings; and I am sure it is a pleasant sight enough to see the way the babes and sucklings enjoy this idea, and will continue to do so as long as the milk lasts. (And, indeed, at this very hour when the milk is running rather low, what a dismal howl the poor little things are setting up, and how on earth are we ever going to wean them?) No, it is only by utter and unwearying honesty, by the obstinate determination to admit of no delusion or illusion, however attractive, however pleasant to our souls, that we can hope to attain to anything like Truth. How often, when we think we have found the jewel, must we put it down and remove ourselves, now to this side, now to that, to be sure that the cutting is indeed flawless! how much must we give up, and how much must we win, before our mind is trained to, as it were, of itself, effortlessly, spontaneously, look at things with that patient clear-sightedness which reaches to their essence! This, then, is our purpose in Culture, and this our system, and this is the fruit of it—a habit of thought which shall have *not only thought and knowledge, but right tact and justness of judgment, forming themselves by and with judgment.* And so our scheme is complete.

Now, leave this theoretical consideration of it for a moment, and see with what result it has been applied to actual things. It has been applied, it is being applied, everywhere and to almost everything. Take the domain of Science, where it has, so far, been applied in a manner which appeals most to most people—practical success, as we call it. There is no need for me to sing the praises of this practical success. It rises all round me in choruses and peans and hosannas. What I want to say about it is, that all this practical success is due solely and entirely to the fact that its creators have applied that purpose and system of ours on, it is true, a more virgin soil than most, but also with a more thoroughness than any. Look at the patience and clear-sightedness that breathes and shines in every page Darwin wrote! It was well said of him, that you could be sure no one would state the case against any-thing he had to say more fully than he did himself. What a serenity the man had, what depths of power and peace! It was my privilege to have had for father one who, to his own depths of serenity, and power, and peace, added those drawn from his friendship with this great Darwin, and from an unrivalled appreciation of his work. When I think of that method of the pursuit of the truth of things which I have myself seen in the late Professor Leith Adams, my father, I seem to myself to despair of ever thoroughly mastering the reality of anything at all. I am overwhelmed with the mystery of Butters' Spelling Book: I dare not lift up my eyes to criticise a barrel-organ, and the young lady so painfully practising scales there is a whole heaven above me. We cannot too much praise the complete singleness of heart and soul with which the Scientists have faced their problems. When I compare Lord Tennyson's consideration of the Struggle in Nature in *In Memoriam*, with Darwin's in his *Descent of Man*, the radical insincerity of the former, I confess, disgusts me, and I fear to do some one or other of its good qualities an injustice. What intellectual exercise all this despair is! The poet's mind is made up before he starts, and all this paraphernalia of doubt is really simply to show that he can enter into the opposite point of view to his own, and yet retain his original convictions! What is the sum total of it? That here is a man of the past, born into a present from which none but those of the future can evolve that future. Five are five and ten are ten, and he adds them together and makes seven! With how different a

G

temper does Darwin face his problem! He has become "as a little child " in his simple attitude towards things. " Where'er thou leadest, will I follow thee." And it was just because this was so, that what he had to say to us prevails more and more ; for, having attained to the secret of the purpose and system of patience and clear-sightedness, he had not only knowledge but right tact and justness of judgment, forming themselves by and with judgment; and so he achieved Truth for himself and for others. Nor does the good of such a man, his life and his work, end here. He has communicated to all who have anything to do with his work, his secret or something of his secret, even as Goethe did before him. Why, here we have Professor Huxley warning the coming race of Scientists against taking for granted the very things in the discovery and revelation of which he has himself toiled all his life, and the cry has been taken up with enthusiasm. "All is possible," said Professor Clifford, "to him who doubts." What an admirable temper is this. Imagine Cardinal Newman warning the young Catholics against taking the Infallibility of the Church for granted ! Or Lord Tennyson assuring us that that fine personal individuality theory of his ("I am I, thou art thou," and so on) must not be considered by young Churchmen as finally settled ! And yet it is in the possession or non-possession of this temper, I say, that lies the essential difference between the men of the past and the men of the future. Mr. Arnold laments that Cardinal Newman, "that exquisite and delicate genius," was not born a little later, so that the Time-Spirit might have touched and transformed him. The same may be said of Lord Tennyson, and will be said in another fifty years. But let us have an end to such laments. To these men, as to their contemporaries, the light came, and they chose the twilight where others chose the dawn, and, having had their hour of victory in the applause of the mass of their time, the doubters and the believers, let us recognize that, at any rate as influences on thought, they are but ghosts in the bright day-time, speechless and ineffectual.

I have, despite myself, been singing the praises of the Scientists. And why not ? Have they not shown us that they have (as Darwin says so gracefully of Mr. Wallace) "an innate genius for solving difficulties ?" But they, too, have their assailable side. I have spoken of Professor Clifford. His talent we were all bound to admire, and his sincerity ; but how wonderfully inept he was when he came to consider things outside his own immediate sphere ! We all remember what he had to say about Christianity. He had the same narrowness towards Christianity that the Christians have towards Science. In them it is excusable, perhaps. Circumstances have been all against them. They have had such little opportunity of attaining to the secret of the purpose and system of Culture. It has taken its rise outside their pale, and has been combated as a foe, and is still combated. But in a man who *had* this secret, how inexcusable the not being able to apply it outside his own immediate sphere ! and how doubly inexcusable to apply to his opponents that very method which had made them so ! Really he should have known better. And unfortunately there are so many of the young Scientists that are following in his footsteps, and not in the footsteps of Darwin. And this is a great misfortune, and should be struggled against with all our powers. But otherwise (since I cannot end here with the note of blame), how truly admirable is the temper of these men when they are only let alone in their own sphere ! Compare the teaching of Science in our colleges and universities with that of Literature ! And yet, slow as is the progress of Literature in its application of the purpose and system of Culture to things, it *is* a progress. The success of that charming series of biographies, the English Men of Letters —nay, of the little shilling Literature Primers—is a sign of it. And the same thing, too, is being done with regard to Philosophy ; but, so far, the men of Science have the lead, and they deserve it ; for, as I have said, theirs has been the most complete singleness of heart and soul with which Truth has been sought out, they have the most thoroughly applied the secret of the purpose and system of Culture.

Now, let us again leave our consideration of these things, and see wherein this question of Culture concerns us plain practical people with our attachment to black and white ; how does it, in a word, come into our daily life. I can only answer as before, everywhere !—The other day the son of a friend of mine, (say) Jones, wished to apprentice himself as a brewer, or, rather, wished to start as a brewer at once. His father sent him to a well-known brewer to be, as the father said, put through his paces. The young man returned crestfallen. What was the matter ? The father could not understand it, and I was set to find it out.—"*Tom hasn't enough Culture*," I reported.—"What do you mean?" asked the father.—"He doesn't know the best that has been thought and known in the world in the matter of brewing," I replied, "I should advise a course of practical chemistry."—"But I'm sure X . . ., the brewer's father, didn't know anything about chemistry, or his father before him."—"Probably; but, if X . . . didn't, I expect he'd have to give up brewing," I said. And it is the same in everything. More and more the perception that things move by fixed laws, which must be obeyed if we would direct ourselves with success, spreads and intensifies. The necessity of moulding our words and actions to our thoughts, rather than our thoughts to our words and actions, is becoming apparent to all men who would avoid the workhouse, actual or metaphorical. The *whys* of things press upon us. It is no use contenting ourselves with the *hows*. If we do, someone else finds out the *whys*, and we are left in the lurch. The other day an intelligent sheep-breeder told me an amusing tale. He had with much trouble and cost purchased in Tasmania a small stud of prize sheep, which he took up to his station in the North. The flower of the first generation he sent to a neighbouring show. The wool of the sheep was thick and close, unlike that of the locky sheep which are considered the best there. His sheep was laughed at by all the judges, who wondered such a sensible man should have sent such a senseless sheep! These judges were deficient in Culture: they did not know the best that has been thought and known in the world in the matter of sheep-breeding. The sheep of these men were shearing on an average less by more than two pounds of wool than the sheep of the more scientific sheep-breeders further south! It is a question, then, whether their children will be so jubilant when they are brought face to face with the competition of an enormously increased home wool-production, and a still more enormously increased wool-production from South America. You cannot now with impunity be wanting in Culture. The stream of life flows too fast for the straws that want to go exploring back-waters, or stopping to admire the scenery.

And Australia—this Australia in which we live—what a need for Culture is here! I see nothing here of the best, and much of the worst. Take this very question of sheep-breeding. Australia is in advance of England, for sheep-breeding is the staple support of the one country, and only an item in the produce of the other. But in what a backward state it is to what, as a staple support, it ought to be! By what rough and ready methods things are still done here. What a dearth of real intelligence there is! of that patience and clear-sightedness which is the secret of the purpose and system of Culture. Who seems to see that in this, as in all matters, the *why* is the important matter on which the *how* will follow, and not the reverse? There is abundance of shrewdness to hand, and finger and thumb wisdom, but who sees that the great necessity is sheer knowledge? Australia was made by men of this stamp, and they still rule it, but their rule is passing, as it was bound to pass, before the unruffled intelligence of the Time-Spirit. These were the men who gave us our absurd nomenclature of birds and flowers. If they saw a bird was black and had one dissonant cry, they called it a jay, and it sufficed. A flower is yellow and little: call it a primrose. And so on. Then their children arose in their turn, and found themselves rich, and took to building cities, and we have (what Mr. Sala calls) Marvellous Melbourne, with the Picture-gallery and Statue-gallery which we know, and the crowning glory of its Government House, perhaps the most hideous hospital in existence. Or the good Sydney people would like to decorate their Post-office with emblematic sculpture, and the result is, what has at last become, the mockery of a Continent. And at last, too, the Picture Gallery at Melbourne is coming into disrepute, and some day, perhaps, the Government House will do the same. It would be pleasant, I think, to see it turned into an asylum. No nation that calls itself civilized stands in more need of Culture, of the best that has been thought and known in the world, in each and every branch of it, than Australia does. Some faint perception of this seems positively to be beginning to dawn upon its complacency. Let us do all we can to forward this. "The Australians," said an Australian to me the other day, "are much more fond of beautiful things than the English." "Alas," I answered, "that is not saying much, but I have not yet remarked it." No, the one commendable wish that the Australians have, is that they really do want the best article in things, and for the best article they are ready to pay. The unfortunate thing is, that there seems nothing in which they are yet qualified to know the best article when they see it! "We want fine

pictures," say the Victorians, and they are befooled by
ship-loads of London tea-trays, which no one but members of
Assembly and the wives of tradespeople and squatters would
take for anything else.—And yet, how is it possible for me to
continue to pile up anathemas like this against these Australians for whom I hope so much, unless it be that I think in
this way to do the little best I can towards helping to the
realization of my hopes? But this is an old tale now, and we
will say no more of it.

In every aspect of life, then, from its highest to its lowest,
let us remember this idea of Culture, let us make for the best
article, and be secure in its possession. The other day a Melbourne lady was saying to me how pretty and charming a place
the Fitzroy Gardens were as a public park. "But the brown
plaster statues," I said, "and the concrete water-shrines."
And this Melbourne lady frankly declared her allegiance to
these things, and, when in my disagreeable unsatisfied way I
began to compare them with the marble copies from the
Antique which are to be seen in the Inner Domain and
Botanical Gardens in Sydney, she frankly told me that *after all*
it was only *a matter of opinion*, and *my* opinion was this and
hers was that! "And so," I said, "my dear lady, it is, *after
all*, only *a matter of opinion* whether the Apollo of the Bel-
videre or the Venus of Milo is more beautiful or less beautiful
than the statue of Burke and Wills in Collins Street, not to
say the brown-plaster statues in the Fitzroy Gardens?" And
then this Melbourne lady, who had read many novels and
magazines, and several volumes of sermons and even popular
"philosophy books," maintained her original assertion with the
charming assurance of her sex; and I could only think that it
was a pity she had not Culture—did not know the best, or
even the second or third best, of what has been known and
thought in the world in the matter of sculptural beauty, for then
she would not have helped to persuade her husband to vote for
the erection of any more brown-plaster statues and concrete
water-shrines in the public places of his city. But, as it is, I
am so thankful that the Sydney people have decorated one of
their public places with really fine marble copies from the
Antique (which none of these Australians, with their superior
love for beautiful things has yet, so far as I am aware, thought of
defacing), that I wonder at myself for thinking of saying it is a
pity to see beside these so many poor modern and perhaps

colonial products; for who can be wise—do I say in an hour, in a day, in a year, in a life-time? nay, rather, in a generation? Certainly not the architects and public decorators of Australia. Let us be thankful for what we have got, and diligently go on showing our thankfulness by asking for more.

But no ; the time has passed when silly people can say that silliness is, *after all*, only *a matter of opinion*—or, if it has not passed, then we ought all of us to be striving our utmost to make it be passed. Culture is possible to so many ! Its textbooks are no longer in the hands of the incompetent : we have really no excuse for thinking Mr. Martin Tupper is preferable as a poet to Lord Tennyson, or Miss Eliza Cook to Mr. Arnold ; and I will confess that I look with suspicion on the intellectual attainments of a man who sees no difference in the *opinion* of Darwin or Professor Huxley and of the popular Theologians and Mr. Lilly. Look, I say, at the text-books of Culture now, of the best which has been known and thought in the world. We have all seen Professor Huxley's little primer of Physiology. Well, that is for Science. Then there is Mr. Stopford Brooke's little primer of English Literature. That is for Literature ; and these are only examples. Really, now, we *have* no excuse for reading the wrong books and thinking the wrong thoughts any more. And we have not, either, to confine ourselves to the thought of our own language. Everywhere excellent translations of noteworthy works are to be found. We would get to know something of the literature of Greece? At the end of Mr. Jebbs' excellent little primer of Greek Literature, we shall find a list of the best translations. We have heard people talking of Professor Haeckel and his wonderful physiological work? Good translations of his best-known books are to hand. And so on throughout the whole domain of thought.

Let us sum up and conclude. We see, then, I think, what Culture is, and what is the purpose and system which should form and guide it. There is only one thing more to say about it, and that is that Culture, in this sense of the word, is the distinct product of our own times. No other country at no other time possessed it. The Jews possessed an unrivalled insight into Religion, into the sense of Righteousness. It is to a Jew that we owe most of what is best in Religion. Indeed, to the great majority of us his name is still a synonyme for

Religion. But Righteousness is not the sole necessity of life
—there is also Beauty. " Beauty," says Keats,

> " beauty is truth, truth beauty : this is all
> ye know on earth or that ye need to know."

But Keats, we remember, was a Pagan, a modern Greek, and
men like this are quite as apt to think that Beauty is " the one
thing needful " as the other stamp of man is to think that
Righteousness is " the one thing needful ;" whereas the real
fact is that both are needful. What an advantage, then, have
we over both Jews and Greeks in our appreciation of this ! At
the best, it is not possible to look upon either Paul or Plato as
exponents of anything final. It requires two wings to soar
with, and who can think that this " ugly little Jew," as M.
Renan has it, who talked nonsense about an Art which at
best seemed to him mostly diabolical, was dowered with two ?
Nor yet can we think this of that " high Athenian gentleman,"
as Carlyle retorts, with his illustrious Master who would have
been so " terribly at ease in Zion." Let us recognize it at
once : the Jews are great and the Greeks are great, but neither
of them by themselves can satisfy us. Nay, further ; to the
sense of Righteousness and Beauty must now be added that
sense which Bacon first brought with any fertility to us—the
sense of Science. " And we," says Arnold,

> " and we have been on many thousand lines,
> and we have shown, in each, spirit and power."

And it is just from the combination of the results of our
spirit and power on these many thousand lines that this
Culture of ours, this unique product of our times, springs. It
was not before this possible. How could Paul understand the
Greek Art ? how could Plato have understood the Hebrew
Righteousness ? It was not till the Renascence, till Shakspere,
that such a thing was possible, and it was not till Modernity,
till Goethe, that it was possible to find these two senses, the
sense of Beauty and of Righteousness, united to that third
great sense, the sense of Science. I do not say that our age
is necessarily a peculiarly great age : you may call it the dwarf
on the giant's shoulders, if you please ; but what I do say is,
that it is the first age which has been able to attain to anything
like a really comprehensive Culture, a knowledge of the best
that has been known and thought in the world. Possibly
we are only on the threshold of Truth : possibly it will be left
to another age to work out and complete what we have but

begun ; but this I think is certain : We *are* on the threshold, and the sooner we realize it, the sooner shall we realize that we are men in whom it is incumbent to put off childish things, the sooner shall we advance into the palace and very home.

Ah, then, let us no longer content ourselves with anything less than the best article! Let us live for the Idea of Culture, for and by it—for the best that has been thought and known in the world! Let us, too, like Goethe, resolve to wean ourselves from halves, from partial and prejudiced views of things, and to live "*im Ganzen, Guten, Schönen*"—"for the Whole, the Good, the Beautiful!"

December, 1885.

" DAWNWARDS :"

AN AUSTRALIAN DIALOGUE.

INTRODUCTION.

HORACE Gildea was the grandson of one of those self-reliant energetic men of the English upper Middle-class, who at an early period of life conceive a particular ambition, and devote themselves wholly to the successful achievement of it. Edward Gildea, the man in question, desired, or we may even say intended, to possess both wealth and position, and he was, as the expression goes, still young (between forty and fifty years of age, that is) when his intentions were fulfilled. A baronetcy was conferred on him by a grateful Conservative government : his marriage with the only daughter of Lord Mainwaring had already brought him a considerable amount of landed property ; and now, having bought more, he retired from the troublous and busy world to the " easeful dignity " of the life of a rich and respected English country magnate. Our Aristocracy is adaptive (here, indeed, lies its strength, as compared, for instance, with that of France) : it will enrol among its members of to-day an outgrowth of the Middle-class, upper and lower, professional or trading, with the same ready complacency with which it enrolled among its members of yesterday the offspring of some poor royal amour or other ; and this is not surprising, when we perceive how little difference there is, intellectually speaking, between the three classes. The aristocratic ideal in England does not, or did not, soar much higher than grouse to shoot, land to shoot them on, and savoury cooking to eat them with ; and the aristocratic ideal is, with slight modifications, the ideal of the country at large. In one generation the Gildeas were counted among, what is called, the best people. The two sons of Sir Edward were educated at public schools and Oxford and Cambridge, and passed, the one into parliament, the other into the Diplomatic-service, where neither distinguished themselves. Horace Gildea, too, an only child, was sent to a public school and Oxford, and with the same result. At Oxford, however, although he did nothing more, educationally, than take his degree, he did not spend his time in mere amusement. Thanks to the friendship of Sir James Gwatkin, the well-known æsthetic critic, Gildea learned to appreciate the delights of that wonderful modern production which we call Culture. He had sufficient knowledge of Greek and Latin to enter into the spirit of their art and poetry, and he learned French, German, and Italian in the pleasant sexual manner prescribed by Byron. He travelled more or less all over Europe, "living and loving largely," but (unlike Byron) saved from that excess whose inevitable fruit is satiety, by the talisman with which Sir James had dowered him. Gildea had, too, what the Romans called *curiositas*. The merely physical ideal of the English viveur did not satisfy him : he used to say that, if he was to be a blackguard, he should like to be a fine blackguard, and how can you be a fine blackguard if you know nothing but what can be known by any fool that can pay for it?

Several years after the death of his father, Gildea, living a life of considerable enjoyment between the pleasures of the countries and the capitals of Europe, began to perceive that, after all, his talisman was not omnipotent : it could not lay, it could only distance, that ancient spectre which he now for the first time learned to face, if not to dread, Satiety. At this point, however, Fortune, whose child he seemed, came to the rescue : he fell in love. The best definition of love is, perhaps, the care of someone else more than yourself, and (the passionate would add) than anything. Gildea, then, did indeed fall in love ; but as his care for himself or for anything was not very great, it cannot be said that he fell in love deeply. But Fortune, having given him a spell with which to once more distance the ancient spectre, now deserted him. The lady he loved did not love him in return : her friendship—and friend-ship from so sweet and passionate a nature as hers was of a somewhat intense character, partaking more of the warm sun-light than the clear moonlight—her friendship she eagerly gave to him, but her love was, past recall, given to someone else.

On the day on which he first realized this, Gildea, who had hoped otherwise, left England in his little yacht the "Petrel," alone. He had intended visiting the east with her, returning by Naples, Rome, and Paris, with many sweet years, nomadic or otherwise, in the radiant future. Now he was quite careless where he went: for the first time in his life he knew what it was to feel miserable. The loss of this woman was a loss from himself. He felt a void in his soul, in his future. "And yet," he used to tell himself, "she was not 'the twin soul that halved my own:' we should not have made perfect lovers, passionate, deep, abiding! None the less do I—or did I— long for her. She is the most beautiful soul I have yet seen, or probably shall ever see. Who would not straightway go and sell all that he had to possess her?—and willingly chance the rest!"

A violent storm caught the "Petrel" as she was about half-way down the Bay of Biscay, and hurried her past Gibraltar. When Gildea perceived this, and was asked by his skipper if they should put back, he kept silence for a moment. Then, looking up with an amused smile, said:

"No, Barry. We'll go straight on to Madeira for provisions —from thence to St. Helena, and then double the Cape and make for Australia."

Gildea had not been to Australia: it was one of the few places in the world to which he had not been. He might, he thought now, as well go there as anywhere. Several things in Australia interested him, and this was enough reason to make him, in his present state, care to go.

One bright, showery november afternoon, then, the "Petrel" passed Port Phillip Heads: was piloted up the harbour to Port Melbourne pier, and Gildea disembarked. He knew one person in Melbourne, and only one, Charles Maddock. Maddock, and his father before him, had been friends of the Gildea family. Maddock was some fifteen years older than Gildea, whom he had known well as a boy at Katharinasbury, he himself at that time being in the midst of his brilliant scholastic career at Cambridge. Almost immediately after his ordination, Maddock came out to a high ecclesiastical position in Australia. It had been the wish of his life to work in one of the Pacific Colonies, and now his wish was fulfilled. The appointment of one so young to the post he had at first held, had caused a little murmuring both at home and in the Colony, it being known that he was possessed of the highest influence ; but the murmuring had soon passed into pleasant greeting, and was now swelled to a regular chorus of applause from friends, foes, and indifferent alike. Maddock had great charm of manner : he was a more or less refined scholar, yet was not lacking in that spiritual robustness which goes so far to make up what is called a personality. It would not be too much to say that he was the most popular man in the colony. Society delighted in the gentleman : the outer world in the man, and both were right, for (here was the secret !) he sympathized with both.

Gildea on his arrival took up his abode at an hotel until he saw rooms that pleased him, and began, after his fashion, to examine the city and its inhabitants. He went everywhere and saw everything, happy to find that his *curiositas* was not after all dead in him. Pleasure, in the sense of *living*, is in Melbourne but, what Tennyson says of the pleasure of London, "gross mud-honey," and had not much attraction to one who had been through the best specimens thereof in London, Paris, New York, and Vienna. Gildea, however, if he did not go through it here, mingled with it as an amused half-spectator half-actor, seeking out its meaning as regards this dawning civilization which was interesting him just at present. He fell in with Sydney Medwin, a squatter's son and ex-Cambridge undergraduate, whom he had known by repute as an inter-university runner and would-be rake, and they spent some pleasant days together. Medwin's father wished him to take to station work, but Medwin, having tasted the "gross mud-honey" of London, Paris, and the Continent generally, was doggedly determined to do no such thing.

"Damn it all," he said once in his half-acute way to Gildea, "there's quite enough money made already in the family, and now it's time to spend it. If my governor had wanted me to look after sheep, he shouldn't have sent me to Europe."

Europe was to Medwin—to Medwin held down by his inexorable "governor" to an allowance and a place in the home establishment—a sort of far-off beautiful dream which had once to a certain extent been his and, he feared, would never be his again. His life was reckless : he was knowingly doing his best to spoil a fine constitution by his excesses, and looked forward to death within ten or fifteen years with stupid stoicism.

After a little Gildea thought that he would like to see something of colonial society, social and intellectual, and presented himself to Maddock. Maddock knew the Medwins well, and even Sydney Medwin who, in his unreflective way, had a great respect for him.

"The governor," Medwin said once to Gildea, "the governor has ruined my life! I had an ambition—I was *ambitious*: yes, I was *ambitious!* But I had to keep it dark! I can't argue about it, you know: I haven't thought for years, and now I can't. But if Christianity's good enough for Maddock, it's good enough for me. I believe in Maddock."

Accordingly, whenever Maddock was to be met at the Medwins', Sydney Medwin was to be seen listening attentively to everything the Doctor said, trying to think, trying to understand, the look of intelligence varying on his face with the look of puzzlement.

"A fuddled intelligence," said Gildea once, smiling and laughing; "now he'll be off and get drunk with one of his girls at Dicks'." (Dicks' was a private hotel where "the set," as Medwin and his friends called themselves, often met for the purposes of recreation.)

Maddock was very pleased to meet Gildea again, and during the next month they saw much of each other. Gildea mingled with the Colonial society as he had mingled with the outer world, but with less interest. The Colonial outer world is at any rate original: it does not imitate, it *is*. Colonial society, on the other hand, imitates and imitates badly. It is a case of the new wine in the old bottles. The young people wish to break away from all the old social convenances and bien-séances: they have almost a contempt for the old people; but the old people rule, and their rule is as yet too strong to be openly disobeyed. The young people, therefore, lack social self-reliance: they have no distinctive "style" of their own as in America. "Indeed," as Medwin used to say, "no one *has* any style out here, except the people at Government House.—And they," he would add, admiringly, "look down upon us all as louts." The young people, then, feel their ideas of happiness to be frail, immature: pleasure is not, as in the European capitals, provided for them; they must provide it for themselves. Pleasure, however, is their aim, and pleasure, so soon as they rule in their turn, they will have. The question is whether this pleasure is to be "mud-honey"—"mud-honey" with its grossness drained somewhat, but still "mud-honey"—or whether that wonderful modern production which we call Culture is going to intervene and complicate matters.

Gildea soon wearied of a society in such a painful state of transition. Having arrived at these conclusions on its tendencies, or what he took to be its tendencies, the painfulness of it began to afflict him. At the same time his interest in the problem of this small social hot-house did not, somewhat to his surprise, show signs of leaving him.

One evening, at a large ball, he had been dancing and talking with a singularly bright and intelligent girl, who had pleased him by herself expressing her consciousness of this state of social transition of theirs, and ascribing the true reasons for it. They sat out several dances together, he enjoying her talk as that of a clever child, she with her woman's vanity pleased to be monopolizing the most distinguished man in the room, and also glad of his mental appreciation of her. He half lay in a low chair beside her, looking at her with smiling eyes and smiling lips, amused. She was a little excited, just enough to give extra brilliance to her words and acts. She was not speaking to him alone : she was aware of the audience of guests, all of whom, she felt, were noticing her, and some catching parts of the conversation. He, who read her soul as if it were transparent, became more and more amused as she proceeded, and by an occasional movement helped her out with the impression he saw she wished to give her friends, namely, that he was more or less entranced by her. The thought of taking her to Paris and introducing her to its society, of watching her intense capacities of social pleasure expanding there in their natural atmosphere, occurred to him and pleased him. He had arrived at that spiritual state when much of our pleasure is in watching the pleasure of other people.

"Well," he said at last, "and do you not find yourself lonely here, with all these wonderful ideas of yours, Miss Shepherd ? All the other Melbourne young ladies do not, surely, participate in them?"

She was not quite sure for a moment whether he was mocking at her or not ; but, looking at his face, decided in the negative.

"Yes," she said, "I *am* lonely—rather. The other girls want to see things. They want to go to Europe—London, Paris, and all that. But they say it's such a bother, and they've no memory. They don't know *what* they want : they

only know that they don't want what they've got.—But I—,"
she added, turning to him, and catching her lower lip lightly
with her pretty visible teeth, one hand on her knee closing
slightly.

"But you?"

"*I* want to—*live!*"

A pause.

"Ah," he said, "that means that some day you will want to
die."

"I daresay! But I shall have lived *first!*—This Melbourne
s just waking up. I wish, O I wish I had not come into it till
it was awake!"

"You would like to go to Paris, then?"

"Paris!" (She stopped breathing.)—"O that," she said,
looking at him again, "is simply heaven!"

"How do you know that, Miss Shepherd?"

"Oh, I have read it! I have read all Alphonse Daudet's
novels, and a lot of Balzac's."

As Gildea strolled through the warm night streets, smoking a
cigar, he thought of her again for a moment, and laughed to
himself.

"The one Parisienne I have met out of Paris," he said to
himself, "She is of the tribe of the fine steel-pearl mangeuses
who rend life with their dear little white teeth for the pleasure
of rending. She should have been born in a concierge's lodge,
with a future in ermine—and the Morgue. And yet she is
better than the mere mangeuse: she has intelligence. She has
to thank Australia for that. For a month, or even two, she
would be supportable—but the "Petrel" would take three to
get her to Naples, perhaps, and it would be more trouble to
loose her and let her go then than now."

He had been strolling about the streets for more than an
hour. He was not quite sure where he was. He stopped for
a moment to look about him. A short well-moulded figure in
a close dress and a poke bonnet passed him and turned down a
narrow street ten or twelve yards ahead. He threw away his
cigar.

"Janet," he said to himself, "sweet child! And she recognized me and went on."

Janet, a Salvation Army "lass," going down into the Little
Bourke Street slums had indeed recognised him. The figure
of a man, in a light overcoat open in front showing that he

was in evening dress, was remarkable enough, to have attracted anyone's attention there. She had looked up for a moment: caught a glimpse of his face and, with a wild throbbing heart and quivering lips, hurried by, and on, and away. Gildea's investigations into the social condition of the place had made him many unexpected friends. Here was one who was something more than a friend, a lover, and he knew it.

"I am sick of it," he said to himself, almost bitterly, "I will go away. I want change."

At about five o'clock that morning Sir Horace Gildea was rowed aboard of the "Petrel," which passed out of the Heads a little after one, and turned to the east, making for Sydney.

I.

It was about eleven o'clock in the morning of a day late in april. The sun shone with bright warmth, a fresh breeze blowing in from the sea. Great deep masses of cloud, luminous-white or here and there shaded with that slaty black which denotes incipient rain, were moving in the blue vault of the heavens. Gildea was descending the steps of the entrance to St. Mary's Cathedral, accompanied by a young man of about his own age. At the foot of the steps they both paused.

"Well," said Gildea with a look, "You will be at my rooms in time for lunch, you say?"

The other nodded, and, in a few moments, saluting one another with a movement of the hand, they parted. The young man went with a quick firm step in the direction of St. James' Church, while Gildea sauntered across the road into the Domain. He was thinking of the young man, Francis Fitzgerald, a young Jesuit whom he had met years ago at a seaside place in the south of France, and who, as he said, for the sake of his health, had come out on a voyage to Australia.

"It is wonderful," said Gildea to himself, "how quickly and thoroughly the religious bodies are waking up to the intellectual necessities of the time. Romans—Anglicans—Lutherans, and even Calvinists are sucking lustily at the two paps of the Modern Spirit which we call Science and Culture. It is the instinct of self-preservation. If they do not suck they will starve. But ah, how many of us are cross-tempered enough to prefer to starve rather than imbibe the milk of a cross-tempered mother!" He looked up with a fine smile, suddenly

H

realizing his humour of thought. "I am quite serious," he said to himself, the smile deepening and broadening, lighting up his face with amusement, "which shows how adaptive I am. Really now, I listened to Fitzgerald's hopes and beliefs in the future of Romanism with quite as much interest as if I were a Romanist myself. I can quite conceive of myself taking very considerable pains to forward a cause in which somebody else believed. This surely was the central idea of my attachment to Olivia Bruce? I used to think I should be quite satisfied to live the life of a poet in that of my poetess? So far, this power of living your own life in the life of one you love has been a female gift. And indeed I have often thought that I should have been better as a woman. I can quite imagine myself as Lady Bellfield or d'Israeli's delightful Berengaria; whereas now, I am but an aimless wanderer on the face of an aimless planet, a pilgrim without a shrine."

He walked on half-thoughtful half-amused, till he had crossed the Domain and found himself opposite the Picture Gallery and the Botanical Gardens. He entered the gardens, and was proceeding down one of the walks when, some fifteen yards before him, he beheld a well-known figure. It was Maddock, Maddock standing at the side of the walk, observing a plant through his pince-nez with serene interest. Gildea came up to him with pleasure.

"Ah, Doctor," he said, "you here! This is a surprise!"

They shook hands : greeted one another, and exchanged health notes both of themselves and Mrs. Maddock, as they went on down the walk together, the Doctor rubbing his glasses with his silk handkerchief and keeping step.

"The truth is, my dear fellow," he said, his head up and moving from side to side as he drew into himself the enjoyment of the fine morning air and scene, "the truth is, I am here for a holiday—or rather, for half a holiday. Sydney is a favourite place of mine.—But," he added in his humorous confidential way, "you know I don't care for the *people!* They are not in earnest enough! I would sooner, I believe, have an earnest atheist than a lukewarm orthodox man. Isn't it your friend Renan who says somewhere, that the atheist has an idea of things, a quite inadequate idea, it is true, but still an idea, whereas 'the average sensual man' has none?—or something to that effect."

"Yes," said Gildea, "he says so; and he adds elsewhere that 'atheism is one sense the grossest of anthropomorphisms. The atheist sees justly that God does not act in this world after the manner of man; hence he concludes that he does not exist; he would believe if he beheld a miracle—in other words, if God acted as a finite force with a determinate object in view.'"

"That is good," said Maddock, "I did not give Renan credit for saying such a thing."

"No," said Gildea, "you have never got much further in Biblical criticism than the Germans. Strauss satisfies you as the great *Against*, and poor Westcott as the gigantic *For!*"

They both laughed.

"Come, come," said Maddock, "you must not poke fun at me!"

"It is impossible," Gildea answered, "to poke fun at an ecclesiastic who calls Heine 'a great poet and brilliant philosopher.'"

"Ah, you have been reading my last polemic, I see?—Yes, you *must* have been reading it; for no newspaper man would ever think of quoting an opinion like that."

"I have been reading it with admiration and wonder: admiration at its excellence as polemical work, and wonder that you should take the trouble to castigate a production which you yourself declare to be, as a contribution to theological knowledge, utterly useless."

"Yes, but did I not explain myself? The book is fundamentally vicious. It confirms the shallow heterodox in their heterodoxy, the shallow orthodox in their orthodoxy. It gives forth light to no one and darkness to everyone. Progress in foolishness and stupidity, that is all that it signalises; the foolishness of 'go-aheadism,' the stupidity of re-action. I have no patience with a man of presumable intelligence who could write such a book."

"But do you not think that your attack on it will only, by bringing it into public notice, increase its powers of mischief?"

"I hope not. I hope that I have sufficiently laid bare its gross ignorance of the subject of which it treats to bring it into that contempt whose fruit is oblivion."

"In England—in London or in any country or capital where there is a large intellectual life—this might be so. But am I not right, Doctor, in believing that this Victorian

Melbourne of yours is a place where pure intellectual life scarcely exists? You have the mass of intelligent money-makers who care, or who do not care, for things (I will not say religious but) sectarian. Then there are those who care for things political ; but where will you find any number of men who aim at making their life the purely intellectual life? They are all partizans here. When, therefore, you attack a Rationalist like Judge Parker, all the Rationalists rally round him, just as the orthodox rally round you ; and the result is, as the *Argus* says, a boxing match, wherein the great thing is to at all price shout down their man and shout up your own. Truth turns away in disgust from such an exhibition of blind deaf bawling partizanary. These men are not of the sort that are open to reason : you cannot lay bare to such as these the gross ignorance or perfect science of their champion ; they will only hiss or applaud as you blame or praise him. I may be wrong : my observation of your so-called intelligent public, is, you know, necessarily but small."

Maddock kept silence with rumpled brows. At last :

" I do not know," he said, " that you are not, after all, to a large degree right. We are very narrow here. A thing done in the street is done in the city, and indeed in the whole country !"

" And am I not right in thinking that the only two native subjects, which are capable of arousing public interest and curiosity here, are those which appeal to the two portions of your mass of intelligent money-makers—things pertaining to business, and things sectarian ?"

The Doctor suddenly regained his humour.

" Are," he said, the deep humorous smile playing about his mouth, " are all the fashionable young men who come out here in yachts as acute observers as you, Sir Horace ?—But I object to your word sectarian : you should say religious. I am quite ready to admit that (to put it as a Melbourne printer put it to me the other day) the only subject that will pay for book-printing here is Religion, and Religion, alas, in its polemical aspect. But I cannot look upon this, as you seem to do, as a great misfortune. I—I . . . well, I may say *candidly*, that I rather *like* a bit of polemics now and then, and the shouts of the men round the ropes do not altogether disgust me, as of course " (his eyebrows went up) " they ought to do ! No, I do not look upon that purely intellectual life of yours as by any means the ideal for us to aim at. It smacks too much of dilettantism for *me!*"

Gildea smiled.

"Dear Doctor," he said, "we all know that you prefer a climate where the sky is not always a cloudless vault of blue insipidity. The sound and feel of a buffeting wind is pleasant to you. As I said just now, you prefer Strauss to Renan, and the good secular Saint Matthew Arnold finds small favour in your eyes. Now too that you are taking to science, I expect every day to hear you tell us Cuvier was a greater man than Darwin, and that Huxley is an impudent young amphioxus that has no place beside the dignity of our dear old behemoth, Owen."

"Now I really won't let you poke fun at me," said the Doctor, "I really won't! The next thing is, that you will be saying something rude about Professor Mosley and his "Ruling Ideas in Early Ages," and scoffing at my idea of having some of his essays reproduced in our *Daily Telegraph.*"

"Oh no, Doctor, I will not do that. Even Mosley's essays are better than the sermons of the local ecclesiastics."

"You are very impudent," said Maddock, his face all beaming, "to call me a local ecclesiastic! I shall have to get you to write a pamphlet on my review of 'Religionless Religion,' so as to be able to denounce you *ex cathedra!*"

"Well, I should very much like to do so, only . . . you know my cowardice: I cannot write——"

"Even letters to your best friends, to explain that you have only gone off to sea at an hour's notice, and are not, as they anxiously expected, drowned, or murdered and secreted in some hole in the slums."

"I prostrated myself in apology to Mrs. Maddock."

"Yes, in over a week! As for Dr. Maddock, of course such a casual acquaintance as *he* could not expect. . . Ah, you are a quite too eccentric young man, Sir Horace! I wish you were well married, with a definite aim in life. Someday one of your wild freaks will end you, and then, what, what will have been the result of those great abilities with which God has gifted you?—Now," proceeded the Doctor, "this is not an extract from the *Daily Telegraph* sermon corner, but only the expression of the affectionate anxiety of one who hopes you will allow him to call himself your true friend."

Gildea kept silence for a moment. Talk of this sort only served to show him how completely his real inner view of things was unknown to his companion, and so the idea of making an answer did not occur to him : he felt how useless it would be. Then he genially thanked the Doctor for his friendship and its kind wishes, and added lightly :

"You ask what will be the result of, as you are pleased to say, those great abilities with which God has gifted me. The result (you perceive it) will be nothing ; but, Doctor, what, let me ask you, in a hundred years will be the result of those great abilities with which God has gifted *you?* In the hundred and first year we shall start equal ; and I, who have not a belief in a personal God and a personal immortality as *you* have, find the whole matter, I confess, rather absurd ! This would not probably have been so always. If I had lived in the days when action indeed contained the highest stakes of life, I should have played for them; but, as it is, the highest stakes now belong to the thinker, the writer, and I—I cannot write . . even letters! I, like all my contemporaries, am more or less under the sad dominion of the perception of, what Leopardi calls, the 'infinita vanità del tutto,' but, unlike the best of them, I have no care for the only immortality we have left, the immortality of Art or Science. I think of the hundred, or thousand, or million and first year, and find myself smiling."

Gildea was soliloquising, Maddock forgotten. He had, then, after all, drifted into making the answer, the idea of making which had, by reason of its clear uselessness, not occurred to him ; and yet he had not made it to Maddock, but to himself. Maddock, indeed, did not altogether understand it, but the feeling of it, the belief that inspired it, he felt and hastened to reply to. He laid his hand gently on Gildea's arm, bringing him to a pause, and said simply :

"*Look* ."

They had come down as far as Farm Cove—skirted it, turning off along Lady Macquarie's Walk—then mounted up onto the drive, and, having passed by the Chair, were now standing on the brow of the slope with an open view of Garden Island (Clark Island being hidden), the harbour, and the woody hills behind it. Great deep masses of cloud, luminous-white or here and there shaded with that slaty black which denotes incipient rain, were moving in the blue vault of the heavens. Light and shade lay everywhere in alternate streaks or patches. One round piece of water to the left was like a burnished blazing mirror of steel. Other parts were blue, gray, or dark, reflecting the cloud-colours above them. The anchored ships rose and fell gently, their flags fluttering. A steamer came stealing out of one of the harbour arms into the open. The only sounds of life were the far-off hammer-strokes of the builders, the occasional cry of the white fleeting sea-gulls, the striking of a ship's bells, the cricket humming at their feet.

"And," Maddock said, in his deep voice of earnestness, "in the face of such a scene as this—the free glory of nature so great and so glad, the wonderful toil and effort and happiness of mankind—you will say to yourself: ' *There is no soul in me, for there is no God to give it.*' Ah, my dear Sir Horace, you surprise and grieve me! Are you not—you, oh heavens, *you!* —at heart an atheist? are you not guilty of that grossest of anthropomorphisms yourself?"

Gildea smiled, a fine sweet smile of sadness that made even the strong steady heart of his companion turn faint for a moment and sick. There was something so absolutely inevitably hopeless, as it seemed to Maddock, in this strange soul that he saw before him, now for the first time laid bare. Here was a patient for which the physician felt he had no power of healing or even alleviation. What view of christian faith and hope and love did not this strange soul know? Maddock, for the first time in his life, felt himself in the presence of one, the breadth and depth and height of whose spiritual experience encompassed him like an ocean. The words of remonstrance died on his lips: exhortation lay lifeless in him: silence and sorrow possessed him. He turned away with a heavy sigh, a sigh which was the unconscious acknow-ledgment to himself that life and death, time and eternity, man and God, could indeed be read in two diametrically different ways. For the first time in his life he realized the truth of "the Everlasting No" in a human soul greater than his own.

They walked on together for a little in silence. Then Gildea said as simply and naturally as if nothing unusual had happened:

"Now, Doctor, tell me will you come and have lunch with me? Mrs. Maddock, you say, has shaken you off for the sake of a long morning with Lady Whitfield, and why should you not retort on her spinster's déjeuner with a bachelor's lunch? I ought to have thought of it before."

The Doctor again suddenly regained his humour.

" 'Thank you," he said, " I shall be charmed."

" Nay," said Gildea, smiling, " but I must bid you pause a moment, aimless dreamer that I am, and tell you who you will meet there. Perhaps you will want your assent back again."

"Speak on," said Maddock, " and, provided it is not some one who will object to my smoking afterwards, I . . . I don't think I shall !"

" 'The guests, then, are three in number. Firstly, James Alcock, who, they tell me, is the most secular and scientific member of all the Australian Legislative Assemblies——"

" Go on," said Maddock.

" Doctor," Gildea said, " he reads Haeckel and swears by no other prophet of Science. Pause before it is too late. They say too that he sleeps every saturday and sunday with Mill " On Liberty " under his pillow, and all Spencer's " Principles " strewed about the counterpane. He knew my father years ago in England, and his heart warms towards me as towards an incipient disciple."

" Secondly—"

" Secondly, Francis Fitzgerald, a young man learned with all the learning of the Egyptians ; a pilgrim and devotee at that simple west-England shrine which holds the Catholic pearl beyond all price, John Henry Newman ; a scholar of the Parisian seminaries ; a pupil of the inner Jesuit circle—"

" 'Thirdly—"

" Frank Hawkesbury, the young Australian poet ; a Socialist, delighting in Trades-Unions, Religious Revivals (the Salvation Army is a hobby of his), and Secular Organizations with a grand impartiality ! Nay, it is even whispered that he had dealings with Holden and the Irish and Continental Nihilists two years ago in London. Our friend Mrs. Medwin almost fainted when Sydney Medwin asked her if she would care to know him."

"I have looked through one of the young man's books of poems," Maddock said, serenely, " and rather liked them. He is in earnest. Your lunch will be amusing.—It smacks to me," he added, with a touch of grimness in his humour, "a little of those shows one sees now and then at the street-corners. They call them, I believe, happy families."

Gildea laughed.

"Yes, Doctor," he said, "but what if the animals should take to fighting? Alas, then, for the canaries and the mice, who will be worried and eaten by the dogs and the cats."

"Which are who, or who are which?"

"Let us say that Alcock is a dog, and Fitzgerald a canary."

"Then *you*, I suppose, are the mouse and *I* the cat? But what is your young Australian poet to be? You have left him out."

"Oh, he will be a rabbit. You will see that he can burrow. It is the forte of Socialists, burrowing.—Now," he proceeded, "we must go this way if we are to get to my rooms in time. And as we go, will you let me first express some tentative thoughts of mine, and then ask you a few questions about your friend Mr. Parker and yourself?"

"Ask on," said Maddock, getting into step, "and I will do my best to answer you."

II.

"It is about this little book of his," Gildea said, with slow reflectiveness, "Religionless Religion." I found it interesting."

"Indeed?" said Maddock, "As interesting as the production of your dear continental sceptics?"

"Well now," Gildea said, in a tone that implied a certain amount of candour, "to tell, what the French call, the true truth, I was struck by several things both in it and in your reply to it. I thought that it would have been difficult to have found a more typical example of the average intelligent secular view of theological Christianity than that of our good Judge."

"I agree with you, and that was one of the reasons that made me decide to attack it. It is typical."

"And, therefore, to anyone who is, though only as an amateur, an observer of things contemporary, it is interesting. Its very deficiencies will be instructive. Well, what I want you to do, Doctor, if you will be so good, is to help me with your superior knowledge of the things treated of to arrive at the spiritual condition of the treater. Perhaps you will not find the attempt too uninteresting, or . . ." He paused with a movement of courtesy.

Maddock, who had a faint suspicion that Gildea was mocking, half grumbled out humorously :

" Go on, then !   Qualify yourself as a psychologist, my dear fellow, and then we will have a plunge into social metaphysics. It is refreshing in a country where they are all partizans, and Matthew Arnold and the purely intellectual life are not appreciated. *Sic itur ad astra.*   In the name of all the lucidities, forward !"

"In the first place, then, we have to notice, have we not, that the little book is polemical, which, at any rate to the amateur observer of things contemporary, detracts somewhat from its historical value ; for, after all, is not a polemist, to a large extent a man who defends the delusions of his friends against the delusions of his enemies, and leaves Truth, like the proverbial pounds, to look after herself? But, if we always remember to take off a percentage for the polemics, we need not miss what it is that the polemist really means and feels?"

" Πως γαρ ου ?" said Maddock.

"And the more easily, as our Parker is in earnest about, what he calls, ' his most serious and difficult task.' "

" Forensic flourishes !"

" —In earnest as far as suits the disposition of a theistic polemist."

" —Microscopically, that is to say. The lawyer's, and especially the successful lawyer's, habit of thought tends towards earnestness as the sparks fly downwards."

" For the average lawyer's habit of thought is perhaps the most typical example of the average intelligent secular view of things. Is it not the final fruit of what is called common-sense, that is to say of the sense of common people? Our good Judge more than once speaks of himself and his audience as " persons of ordinary common-sense," as opposed to " meta-physicians," and especially " ecclesiastical metaphysicians." He wants clear solid statements which his mind can see, and as it were, touch and handle. He scoffs at all statements other than these, looking upon them as at bottom sophistical. It follows that, when he comes to criticise the Bible, he claims the right to criticise it, not only with the same spirit, but with the same manner, as he would criticise any other book. He will not only look at it straight, fearlessly, logically, but he will demand of its statements that they be clear and solid, that they bear the ordinary interpretation of ordinary statements. He will apply the same principles of examination to Moses and Jesus as he would do to Blackstone or Chitty. And all the secular persons of ordinary common-sense cry out : ' Hear, hear !' "

" With the Judge," said Maddock, "a metaphysician is a man who examines the Bible by the aid of principles other than those of one who is ignorant of all contemporary history save that which the Bible gives him."

" The consequence of which is, that he is capable of such a statement as, that ' without question early Christianity was far more free from paganism and from the taint of super-stition than the Christianity of our own time,' and others of a like force."

" He has no notion whatever of the philosophy of history— of, what I call, the development of divine Truth."

" And yet he is contradictory enough, while asserting the degradation of the Christian ideal, to lay much stress on the development of Divine truth in a civilization that has, till comparatively lately, been Christianic. Yes, he sees the development of divine Truth, but he does not understand the forms which that development has taken in Christianity. The Trinity—the Atonement—the Deity of Christ—are to him ' mere crude superstitions which disfigure and obscure pure and true religion.' It never seems to have occurred to him that, although these doctrines may be empty formulæ to him, they were and are passionate realities to others."

" That is very true."

" He will talk with the same ignorance of what he would call Jesuolatry as a Protestant will of what he calls Mariolatry, neither he nor the Protestant understanding any more of a deep spiritual truth than its cut-and-dried dogmatical letter." The Doctor assented, though with a movement of slight qualification.

" We agree at starting, then, that his criticism as that of an historical Bible student does not exist. The authorities he quotes are, as you point out in your Reply, ludicrous. They culminate in his poor little some ' celebrated Unitarian minister ' or other, than whom the habit of thought of the legal Biblical critic can, it is to be hoped, no further go ! He is too, we agree, careless and superficial even in his own style, but we must not lay too much stress on individual cases of this in the face of his request for ' indulgence ' for his ' doubtless many imperfections here.' "

"When a man speaks publicly of such a grave matter as religion," said Maddock, "he should *not* be careless, he should *not* be superficial! We have a right to demand of those who make explosives, that they, at any rate, do not smoke in the magazine."

"True; but, if we all got our deserts, who, you know, should escape whipping? Certainly not the producers of orthodox religious literature."—(The Doctor, after a pause, assented as before).—"Well, we will proceed further against our good Judge, and say that his appreciation of what is, as he says, 'good and ennobling' is ludicrously inadequate. What can be said of a man who seriously speaks of Jesus, 'when, in the garden of Gethsemane, he went apart and prayed, three times over, the same prayer to God, within a short period,'—of Jesus thus *'doing that which he told his disciples not to do*—*"use not vain* repetitions, *as the heathen do," for the reason that your heavenly Father knoweth what things ye have need of* before ye ask *Him.*" Habemus confitentem asinum! We can only burst out laughing : a reply to such a statement is impossible! The lawyer's habit of thought is at its apogee, and (as Heine says) '*Gegen die Dummheit kämpfen wir Götter selbst vergebens.'*— Against stupidity the very gods themselves struggle in vain." The Doctor assented smiling.

"And statements similar to this are not scarce here. Our good Judge, then, has not, it is clear, much experience of the spiritual life, of those who live in the spirit. The 'sudden conversion of Paul,' for instance, strikes him as one of the (it is supposed) 'improbabilities so forcible that no sane *thinking* man or woman can accept' the inspiration of the Scriptures which relate them. Now, any one who knows anything of human nature other than that of 'persons of ordinary common-sense,' knows that such 'sudden conversions' are not only not improbable, but passably frequent. In some cases, as in that of Staniforth, quoted by Arnold in his 'St. Paul and Protestantism,' the circumstances approach so closely to those of Paul's that we are enabled to assign to them a definite place in the science of psychology. Nor are our good Judge's 'errors,' as you say, exhausted yet. We have still to bring against him the charge of, what Celsus calls, κουφοτης, and Arnold translates 'want of intellectual seriousness.' So confused and incoherent is his knowledge of the real position that the secular biblical critic takes up, that he absolutely calls the position taken up by the orthodox biblical critic (that is to say, biblical *critics* who are orthodox; as, for instance, you yourself, my dear Doctor): he absolutely calls this position critically 'untenable,' not perceiving that it is his own only differing in degree!—This is simply appalling! The κουφοτης of the Secularists is not a whit better, after all, than that of the Christians!"

"Yes," said Maddock, disregarding the last remark, "but then you must remember that the Judge 'does not intend to resort to any process of subtle argument, nor to make any display of scholastic knowledge, nor to indulge in learned disquisitions.' He merely writes 'popular, clear, and simple' nonsense for 'the doubter who is trying to grope his way to the light, but cannot; to the Atheist who believes in nothing, neither in a Supreme Power, nor in a future life.' And your secular ingratitude to him, Sir Horace, strikes me, I must confess, as keener-toothed than the winter wind of orthodoxy!"

"Doctor," said Sir Horace, "you are poking fun at me! But I, who am, as Shelley said of himself 'rather serious'—I proceed in my examination, whose sole confirmation as truth I find in your words or gestures of approval. You will, I hope, forgive me for any repetition I may make of your own criticism, as a master should a humble disciple? It is only a proof of attention and admiration."

"Go on," said Maddock, "mocker!"

"All these faults, then, which we have remarked in our good Judge—his polemicality; his ignorance of the grammar (or, perhaps, as your Reply says, the alphabet) of historical criticism; his ludicrously inadequate conception of the good and the ennobling, of the spiritual calibre of such men as, for instance, St. Paul; his superficial acquaintance with the data of the subject of which it is treating; and, finally, his κουφοτης, his want of intellectual seriousness—all these faults, are we not agreed, are the faults of the average intelligent secular view, in its negative consideration of Christian Theology? The question that now arises is, has this view nothing but faults?—has it no excellencies? Does there remain, after the attack on it of so admirable a theological polemist as Dr. Maddock is, no residuum of real and vital truth? Let us try and see.—To begin with, did we not find that, despite a contradiction, our good Judge perceived the reality of, what you so finely call, the development of divine Truth?—

"*Yet I doubt not thro' the ages one increasing purpose runs,*
and the thoughts of men are widened with the process of the suns."

"No," said Maddock, "I cannot grant him even that! A faint glimmering of a thing cannot be called a perception. Consider this very contradiction of his! Consider, again, his unspeakably gross and ignorant treatment of the Old Testament which he brands with blood-thirstiness and impurity. He works by a rule of thumb. The higher spiritual mathematics are mere names to him. He is—I must declare—too much of a blockhead to ever rise beyond the spiritual Rule of Three."

"I agree to a large extent, dear Doctor; but you will admit, I think, that even the Rule of Three is not without its use, without its real and vital truth?"

"Not when the schoolboy cannot use it properly! I have pointed out, for example, that, in attacking the doctrine of the Divine Sonship, he only attacks a dummy doctrine of his own. Your schoolboy does not know which of the three is his third quantity! He wants, then, to be whipped and put onto the dunce's stool—to encourage the others!" The Doctor spoke for the first time with a little testiness.

"Be it so," Gildea said. "our good Judge is not to be allowed more than a faint glimmering of that fine theory of ours of the world's unseen τέλος. The 'divine far-off event' is not more than a fog-lamp to him, which he will not, then, mistake for the moon, or its light for moonshine. But that he is too much of a blockhead to even rise beyond the spiritual rule of thumb, the spiritual Rule of Three, seems to me, I confess, dear Doctor . . well, a rather strong statement. The average intelligent secular view of things is, is it not, less pedantic, less given to accepting the conventional value of things as their true value, than the average intelligent orthodox view? Are not, indeed, these tears a most convincing proof of it? Is it not just because our good Judge refuses, for instance, to accept the orthodox view of Jesus and of God that he wrote his little book, and you replied to it? Now the orthodox view of God is, if you will let me say so, excessively pedantic : it adheres to the expressions of a belief in which in its heart it does *not* believe at all. Parker's criticism on this is excellent. 'It is impossible,' he says, 'to lay down any definition of God which will even satisfy man's conception of God.' What, then, is the good, he asks, of holding up this 'magnified non-natural man' of yours, and asking me to fall down and worship it? Common-sense revolts against such an idea and common-sense, dear Doctor, is, will you not agree, for once right ?"

" You surprise me, Sir Horace," said Maddock. "Are you too going to spend your time and trouble in demolishing the survivals of verbal inspiration ?"

"Certainly *not !* I am only trying to see wherein common-sense is a safe guide as a biblical critic. We are agreed, then, —you, that is, the Judge and I—that we must unite in opposing many of 'the statements which,' as the Judge says, 'the orthodox are pleased to call evidence.' Because, for instance (to continue with the Judge's own words), 'the fallible man Paul says in a letter to Timothy that the Scriptures were inspired, it does not make them so.' We are agreed here ?"

"We are agreed here," said Maddock, with deliberation.

"Or again, to take another instance, when Matthew and Luke, for whatever purpose, strive in their genealogical tables 'to give Jesus' (I always use the Judge's words) 'a divine origin, conceived of a virgin by the Holy Ghost, and yet to connect him with David by making Joseph the natural father of Jesus.'—are we not here faced by two ideas which 'no one short of an ecclesiastical metaphysician,' or, as you say, a 'very bad critic,' would or could 'reconcile ?'—We are still agreed, of course."

"We are still agreed—to a certain extent."

" Nay, let us go further, then, and chime in with the Judge to the effect that ' on far stronger evidence (if evidence it can be called) than that which supports'—let us say, almost all— 'of the events or miracles' of the Scriptures, 'the Roman Catholic Church propound to the world their miracles,' which 'the Protestant section of Christianity reject as incredulous.'"

"Proceed," said Maddock.

"Nay, let us go further still, and notice how we no longer look on the Genesis account of the Creation as more than allegory, of the Flood as being strictly accurate ; of the tower of Babel as, again, more than allegory, and so on in many other similar cases. And how in the same way we do not look upon the statements of Christ, and after him of the author of the ' Revelations,' of the close approach of the Apocalypse, as literal but only figurative. 'The statement of Jesus,' as the Judge puts it, ' as to his coming again before the then genera-tion have passed away does not mean that he will so come : ' generation ' being merely used figuratively, but when he does come he is still to come in the clouds of heaven, and with great glory, sounds of trumpets, rushings of winds, and mourning of tribes; for' (Gildea paused)—'all this has not yet been falsified by the event.' This is, I think, undoubtedly the conclusion at which common-sense arrives, but common-sense is of course wrong."

"Common-sense is wrong," said Maddock.

"Common-sense too, as exemplified in this its typical blockhead who cannot ever rise beyond the spiritual Rule of thumb and Three; common-sense observes of the development of divine Truth, as exemplified in the Christian theology of yesterday and to-day, that its 'golden rule apparently is to adopt those interpretations' of its Scriptures 'which best satisfy the exigency of the particular position of the time being,' and thus we have no further guarantee that the God of to-day will be the God of to-morrow than that the God of yesterday is certainly not the God of to-day. 'Heaven forgive me,' exclaims 'that great poet and brilliant philosopher,' Heine, 'but I often feel as if the Mosaic God were but a reflected image of Moses himself.' And we all remember with what contempt Taine speaks of this God of Christianity, revised and amended to suit the latest edition of scientific and historical discovery—rooted up out of the earth and momentary intercourse with man—driven out of the clouds and the occasional interposition of his strong right hand—spied and telescoped from the radiant bowers of the stars, and finally lodged out of sight, and all but out of mind, in the eternal infinitudes of Time and Space! After all, then, may not our good Judge have had, not of course a perception, but a faint glimmering, of sapience, when he spoke of the position taken up by the orthodox biblical criticism as critically 'not only untenable, but absolutely suicidal?' The thought is, as we agreed before, simply appalling. Spirits of Butler, Paley, Neander, Weiss, Westcott, Lightfoot, and many another mortal or immortal immortal, rise and thunder 'No!' When this exponent of the average secular intelligence declares that contemporary Theology is an impossible compromise between Reason and Absurdity; that the Protestant is quite inconsistent who with one face rejects 'the events or miracles propounded by the Roman Catholic Church because they involve a violation or suspension of unvarying natural laws; because such things do not happen, and because *reason* refuses to give credence to

them,' and with another face accepts as truth the sojourn of
Jonah in the belly of some sea-monster (at present con-
veniently extinct, even to the bones), or the communications
of, what Gordon describes as,

'that duffer at walls,
the talkative roadster of Balaam :—'

rise, I say, and in Olympian accents demonstrate to him and
his benighted audience, that these were but links 'in the
development of divine Truth,' and that 'one lesson at a time
of this difficult kind was enough, and as history shows more
than enough, for human weakness.' "

"You are a treacherous and malicious young man," said
Maddock, laughing in spite of himself, "and have no right
to quote my words in such an irreverent and grotesque
manner !"

"It is my orthodox ingratitude," said Gildea, "—And yet,"
he added suddenly, with a complete change of tone and
manner, "in less than fifty years polemics like these will be
looked upon as childish, and, those who spent their life and
energy upon them, as we now look on the mediæval School-
men. It is a sad thought."

Maddock was a little puzzled at these swift chameleon
changes in his friend.

"And now," said Gildea, looking up with yet another change
of tone and manner, "and now we have done with the
negative side of the good Judge's criticism and can turn to
the affirmative.—But that," he added, "must, I am afraid, be
after lunch—if you will, Doctor ?"

"I will," said Maddock, "and you shall not then find me
so passive, for your treachery and malice are now quite laid
bare to me."

Gildea smiled.

"But not my loyalty and admiration ? Believe me, Doctor,
that, if it were only for this one remark of yours, I could never
fail in my interest and gratitude to you. 'Our blackfellows,'
you say, 'had no punishment for offences against their elementary ideas of purity but spearing. *And it was infinitely better that
they should spear for impurity than lose their first step towards
a higher life.*' . . But here we are," he said, "This is the
house. Fitzgerald and Hawkesbury have to leave us soon after
lunch. Mrs. Medwin and her niece, Miss Medwin, are coming
later to make tea for me, and then we are going out for a sail in

I

the yacht. Mr. Medwin is thinking of a legislative career, and so Alcock is to be cultivated. Can you come with us? You know how pleased it would make us all."

The Doctor explained that he was due at his hotel at half-past three to meet Mrs. Maddock, and both he and Gildea expressed their due regrets at his not being able to make one of the party on the yacht.

III.

Gildea led the way upstairs and ushered Maddock into the sitting-room. It was in reality two rooms joined together by a large folding-door, which was now thrown open and draped with four looped-up curtains, two of some dark-red material behind two of delicately-wrought muslin. The two rooms were of the whole depth of the house, the large bay-windows, open and with a glass-door in the middle of them open also, at one end looking out over the city, at the other over the harbour. A grass-slope, and a garden with flower-beds and rustling trees, spread all round and down to the water's edge ; while, a little way out, the "Petrel" rode at peaceful anchorage, her boat behind her. Maddock was for the moment so taken up with the beauty of the place within and without—the room with all its harmonies of form and colour, the garden and harbour scene— that he did not notice that someone was standing, half hidden by the curtains, in the next room on the hearth-rug. Then Gildea passed through and greeted this person whom he brought forward and introduced to Maddock as Mr. Hawkes-bury.

Hawkesbury was a small but well-made man with a tendency to muscular leanness. His face was striking and interesting, and betrayed a strongly-defined individuality. At one moment he might have been called handsome, and his manner frank, free, and open : at another his features took such a contracted intensified look, and his movements were so nervously acute, that the whole man seemed to have suffered distortion. It seemed as if he were suddenly seized by some keen pain, spiritual and physical, and was being racked by it. When Gildea entered, there was for a moment a trace of this latter manner in Hawkesbury : his sensitive pride found something antagonistic in, what seemed to him, the consummate luxury which surrounded him and even in the consummate culture of its owner : he was almost asking himself what right this man had to spend so much money and care in decorating a few rooms for a few months, this man whose life was so radically selfish? Hawkesbury's was, he might have said, the feeling of one who was a socialist and worker by intense conviction, finding himself opposed to one who was an aristocrat and hedonist by the mere chance of birth and fortune. But, when Gildea met and greeted him with the frank sweet unconscious cordiality of an equal whose acquaintance is pleasant, the dark look passed from Hawkesbury's face and he gave himself up to the simple pleasure of the situation. His unexpected intro- duction to Maddock, who represented to him the more or less sumptuous aristocrat of religion, for a moment, it is true, threatened to bring back the evil spirit to him ; but Maddock, with his fine social tact, almost divining the state of affairs, was equally frank, sweet, unconscious and cordial in his manner, and Hawkesbury was at his ease.

The three men stood talking together, Maddock in the middle, in the bay-window that looked out over the harbour.

"Why, Sir Horace," said Maddock, "you will never be able to get away from this enchanting place again ! Are you sure you do not intend to make it into a home ? You did not honour your Melbourne rooms with such care—such choice of furniture, and . ." (He raised his arm and outspread hand, smiling humorously).

"'Man delights not me,'" answered Gildea, "'No, nor woman neither, though by your smiling you seem to say so.'" The smile broke out on Hawkesbury's face too. It was soothing and very pleasant to find these two talking in his presence of such an intimate matter as that alluded to here : he was not accustomed, in the company of, what in Australia and even England goes by the name of, ladies and gentlemen to this complete absence of social and individual constraint.

Then Edgar, Gildea's valet, ushered in someone else, Mr. Fitzgerald, and there was a movement and introductions between Maddock, Hawkesbury, and the new-comer, the three being left alone for a moment while Gildea was giving some directions to Edgar about domestic arrangements.

Maddock and Fitzgerald fell almost immediately into a con- versation, Hawkesbury playing the part of silent member. The Doctor was interested in finding out what the impressions of a cultured Roman Catholic were of Australia and more

particularly of Victoria and New South Wales. He asked a
few questions, the answer to which, he thought, would show
him whether Fitzgerald had observed things with care and
sympathy, and was answered with a gentle readiness that
pleased and satisfied him. The two men felt themselves to a
certain extent on common ground, and, Fitzgerald touching
incidentally on the education question, they began to parallel-
ise each other's views with cordiality.

"We quite recognise," said Fitzgerald, "all the difficulties
of the case—the danger of the unfair influence of catholic
teaching over protestant children, or vice versa, just as each
happens to be stronger in the particular place and school.
But we would accept this danger—accept it, even supposing we
were the losers by it—rather than have the present state of
things continue. As our Archbishop said only the other day at
Leichardt : 'Besides the faculties of intellect and of reason,
there are certain passions of the soul,' and to develop the
former and wholly neglect the latter is to send a boy out into
the world with *only one eye*. You have prepared him for the
temporary business of life, and unfitted him for the glorious
service of eternity : you have given his ship fine sails, and forgotten to add a rudder ! He may be an acute man of
business, but he will be a bad citizen ; for, in taking away from
him his sense of religion, you will take away from him his
sense of morality, of honesty, of integrity ! We can, at the
present stage, see for Australia no future save that of corruption
—a corrupt political life, a corrupt national life, the unlimited
worship of Mammon !"

"I agree with you to a large extent," said Maddock, "and
we all know that, practically speaking, the talk about 'religious
education at home' is mere verbiage. If the education of a
child is secular, his spiritual lungs, so to speak, end in being
able to inhale no other air and thrive on it."

"And," Fitzgerald said, "the education *is* secular ! Every
effort is being made to drive the voluntary schools out of the
field. Their state aid here in New South Wales is withdrawn :
in England it is reduced to a pittance and hedged about with
annoyance. And this, although the educational reports, drawn
up by a secular commission, show that, at any rate the
catholic schools educate on the average both better and more
cheaply than the state-schools do ! We only ask for fair play,
and now it has come to this pass that we cannot get it ! All

over England the protestant voluntary schools are failing and disappearing. But we, we Catholics, who cannot, as Protestants do, console ourselves with the reflection that the atmosphere of the state-schools, if secular, will be tempered by that of our own beliefs—we *will* not fail and disappear! We are the poorest of all religious bodies in England; but I will venture to say, that not a single case can be found of a catholic school which has surrendered itself up, as these others did, into the hands of the Secularists. Our educating priests and laymen have to suffer much privation : I know, shall I say hundreds, of them who deny themselves all but the bare necessities of life ; but—*we stand our ground!* . . . You see," he added smiling gently, "we Catholics cannot labour under any delusion here. We recognize that this is a stupendous crisis in the world's history. We will have no compromise and secular tempering of the wind to the shorn Christian. We will stand to our guns, and, if we must perish, perish there !"

Maddock was impressed, and so even was Hawkesbury. This man's enthusiasm was so quiet, so clear, and yet so radiant. Gildea returned and joined them.

"We were speaking of the popular education," said Fitzgerald, turning to him, "and I would persuade Dr. Maddock that his cause and ours are here identic."

"I need no persuading," said Maddock, "I have for some time been persuading *myself!*"

"And yet," Fitzgerald put in gently, "the alliance between us and you seems farther off than between us and the Dissenters."

"And that, I think," Gildea said, "is because you have more in common. You are afraid of one another. In the one case, you know that the frontier of your alliance will be observed, in the other there is a chance that it may not. At present the most dangerous opponents of Catholicism in England are, what they call, the High Churchmen. The Church of England is a compromise between Catholicism and Protestantism ; hence its adaptiveness, hence its strength ! It more nearly, in my opinion, approaches ideal Christianity than any other sect in existence. It unites the Faith, the Poetry, of Catholicism, with the Freedom, the Prose, of Protestantism."

"We thank you," said Maddock.

"Logically speaking, however," added Gildea, " it is an absurdity. '

They all began to laugh.

"Ah," said Maddock, "I was right when, even while thanking you, Sir Horace, I thought to myself: *Timeo Danaos, et dona ferentes.*"

"The Christianity of the Future," Gildea proceeded gravely, "lies, I believe, in two transformations—in Catholicism learning that its kingdom is not of this world, that it no longer requires a Pope, a Rome, as a Palladium whereby it may fight; in a word, in learning the lesson of Protestantism, of Freedom : and in Protestantism doing the converse, and absorbing into itself the catholic Faith, the catholic Poetry!"

"And what are the Secularists going to do in your Future?" asked Hawkesbury, "are Messrs. Arnold and Huxley to be put up on a shelf in your spiritual Museum, in two large spirit bottles, labelled respectively ' Culture' and ' Science?'"

"Culture," answered Gildea, "is, after all, but Secular Catholicism, just as Science is but Secular Protestantism. They too will each learn their lesson of the other."

"Humph!" said Maddock, who again had a faint suspicion that Gildea was mocking, "and so, after all, Sir Horace is an optimist."

"We do not lay stress," Fitzgerald said gently, " on the temporal power of the Holy Father. As Sir Horace implied, this temporal power was once the one shining light in a chaotic world, and it was well that it should be set on a hill. But now the light is diffusing itself. It is our wish that, as the Vatican Œcumenical Council declared : ' Intelligence, Knowledge, and Wisdom may grow and perfect themselves—as much with the mass as with individuals, with one man as with the whole church!' We are no foes to Freedom. What we *are* foes to, is Anarchy! At the Reformation you gave the right of deciding on the deepest religious questions to every ignorant man that chose to discuss them, and the seamless robe of Christianity was rent into a hundred pieces ! Look at all these miserable little protestant sects and sub-sects, Plymouth Brethren, Primitive Methodists, Ana-baptists, and I know not what noisy, ignorant fanatics. At the Revolution, you did the same for social questions, and what is the result ? The Dynamiters of Russia, of Germany, of Ireland, initiated by what you, Dr. Maddock, so well call ' such gentleness as was revealed in the diabolical deeds of the Commune,'—to say nothing of those of the Reign of Terror."

Maddock half-deprecated, half-approved by a gesture and an inarticulate sound.

"Yes, but," said Hawkesbury with the thrilled voice of suppressed passion, "has not history justified the Reformation? and how can you say that it will not justify the Revolution? These, as it seems to me, are the two fiery portals which lead to Religious and Social Liberty. But you are right to depreciate them : they knew nothing of the poetry of Culture and Catholicism, or of the prose of Protestantism and Science. They were volcanic eruptions of the People. Heine says well, when he talks of 'the divine brutality' of Luther, and we do not shrink from the same phrase for Hugo or Whitman. Sir Horace has painted us a Future which is indeed heavenly. It is thronged with sweet-singing angels, and there is not a shadow in its perfect light. But what has become of the *men*, and what, O what, has become of the *devils?* They have no place in this Future. You do not care for the People, I say, except as you care for your dog which, if he is quiet and docile, shall have a kennel and the bones and scraps from your table ; or, if he is surly, shall be chained up ; or, if he goes mad, shall be shot ! Ah believe me, gentlemen, the People *has* a place in the Future, for the People, and none other, *is* the Future ! '*All for the modern,*' cries Whitman, '*all for the average man of to-day.*' But you—you only care for the Upper and the Middle-class. Your scheme of civilization does not reach to the People. The Upper-class is exhausted : it needs invigorating. '*Cultivate the Middle-class,*' is the cry, ' *Give us Higher Education for the Middle-class !*' This is the whole social teaching of the best representative man you have, Matthew Arnold. Now we, we Socialists as you call us, *love* the People, and (you will pardon me) *hate* the Middle-class ;— the dispossessed, the sufferers, *not* the possessors, the usurpers ! The People is the Prodigal Son. What sympathy have we, then, with a man like Arnold who has devoted himself to the edification of the Elder Brother? Arnold says once that he has evolved that perfect style of his which we know so well—that style which encloses a minimum of ideas in a maximum of catch-words—or, as he likes to call it, 'plain popular exposition '—for the especial benefit of the British Philistine, the divine Middle-class, who otherwise could not be got to read him ! He would have done better, perhaps, if he had not turned to the setting, but to the rising sun. The People are the masters of the Future, and the People's great men will be the great men of the Future."

There was a pause. Then :

" There is much truth in what Mr. Hawkesbury says," says Gildea, " Just at present we think too much of the ultimate Culture of the Middle-class and too little of that of the People. But the fact is, that the question of the Middle-class is pressing : they are, as you say, Hawkesbury, the possessors ; they are the Present ! And this, I think, is why men like Arnold, who believe that, in the organization of the Present, lies the only hope of the success of the Future, are so anxious about it. It is a case, as he believes, of ' Culture or Anarchy ' —Culture now or Anarchy then. And Carlyle, a disciple of whom Mr. Hawkesbury has, in the admirable Preface to his second book of Poems, declared himself to be ; Carlyle too, who laid much stress on what he calls 'the radical element ' in himself, yet mocks at ' Mill and Co.' as he says, in whom he declares the opposite element was ' so miserably lacking.' Carlyle had no respect for ' Rousseau fanaticisms,' even in a man like Mazzini : he saw that, if the Middle-class were pur- blind and slow, the Socialists were only purblind and quick. Supposing that we grant that the Dynamiters of Russia are justified in meeting an absolutely dense despotism with violence, what excuse but impatience can we find for the Dynamiters of Ireland ? The first have no means of free agitation, the second have every means. Ireland has been wronged : no one denies it ; and never, in the whole course of her history, has England shown such alacrity as she is doing now to right the wrong ; never, not even for herself. But the Irish Socialists are impatient : their cry is for everything to-day, this very hour ! To grant it them would be the greatest unkindness possible. Well, they too have taken to dynamite as a hypochondriac takes to opium. The Russian Nihilists are noble people, none nobler, but they taught fools and knaves an appalling lesson when they inaugurated the reign of terror in Petersburg. At the present moment, as Heine clearly foresaw, the Civilization, not of Europe, but of the whole world is in danger."

" You speak well, Sir Horace," said Maddock, " and express my opinions better than I could myself, but— *Timeo.*"

He, Gildea, and Fitzgerald smiled. Hawkesbury was grave. There was a pause. Then :

"I think," he said, "that you do the People wrong. These extreme Socialists, the Nihilists as they are called, are not from the People, but from the Middle-class. They are, as a rule, men who have received the best education of the time, and who yet find themselves unrecognized and unrewarded. Most of them are journalists. It would astonish you, I think, to see the amount of really first-rate talent that is being flogged to death in the shafts of the modern Press. These men cannot work in shops and banks : the narrow material life has been made impossible to them. The only opening for the life they would—nay, that they *must* live, or perish, is that of Literature. Literature caters for the Middle-class, the ruling class. These men, then, are the slaves of the great caterers, the news-paper editors. One of the most thorough Socialists I ever knew, Holden, in fact, was on the regular staff of the English *Spectator*, the organ of the enlightened portion of the Middle-class ; and there, as he said to me, he went as near Socialism as he could for threepence ! (Threepence is the price of the paper.) This same man wrote, too, political articles for a distinguished radical politician, and I have seen the proof-sheets of these hacked and mauled by the patron to suit the palates of the Radicals. It was this man who once seriously contemplated dropping a bomb in the House of Lords, to show that herd of hereditary liars, as he put it, that there was such a thing as justice in the world ! He loved the People : he hated the Middle-class, but the People cared nothing for him. It is, then, I think, a mistake to lay the paternity of Nihilism to the charge of any but the over-fed tyrannous Middle-class."

"What you say," Maddock said slowly and courteously, "is very interesting and instructive, Mr. Hawkesbury, and I perceive that the ground which you, and I think I may say Mr Fitzgerald," (Fitzgerald smiled and bowed), "and myself have in common is large enough to admit of our working—at any rate not in opposition to one another. Is not our mutual object the enlightenment of the unintel-ligent mass of the People and of the Middle-class ? I am, I am sure, grateful to you, sir, for the manner in which you have brought this home to me. I always felt that underneath all our differences—I mean, the differences of our beliefs, religious or social—we had a common ground, the advance-ment of a really good and true Civilization, and now, I think,

I know this. He renders us a great service who makes our feelings self-conscious, who turns them into the articulate thought of words."

There was a slight pause.

"And now," said Gildea, in his half-amused way, " we will, if you please, go down to lunch. Mr. Alcock particularly asked me not to wait for him, and we have waited, it seems unconsciously, for over half-an-hour."

They went down together into the dining-room, chatting lightly and pleasantly.

IV.

The dining-room was the corresponding room on the ground story to the sitting-room up above. It was quite as well furnished, but in a different style. A fine rather than an exquisite form of beauty had been sought after. It was a saying of Gildea's that a dining-room ought to give you an impression somewhat similar to that of a beach-brake in spring : the architecture and furniture should have clear outlines, the colours should be clear, the lights should be clear. All massiveness and duskiness was to be avoided. A meal ought to be a repast, not a feast : we should rise pleasantly satisfied, not dully satiated. In a sitting-room, on the other hand, the sworn abode of the sweet and delicate talk and music of women, just as the dining-room was that of the serene discussions of men, there should be something of the lush luxuriance in shape and colour of the midsummer woods, knights and ladies and all the figures of romance and fairy-tale passing together. But such an arrangement of rooms as this, he would say with his bright half-mocking smile, was at present like a damsel of the Middle Ages suddenly awakened in the dull derisive streets of London or Manchester. This will only come to pass in that wonderful Future, when we have all learned that Beauty and Truth are synonyms, and Keats has statues and altars like Sophokles of old.

Considerable time, wealth and trouble had been spent on this house. Sydney and Melbourne had been ransacked for beautiful things worthy of Gildea's ideas of "the nest," as he called it to himself, that he desired ; for this was indeed one, and not the least remarkable, of his freaks. It had been aroused in this fashion. One afternoon, sauntering across a

road in the Domain, he had almost been run over by someone
riding a splendid bay horse. Looking up, with a fine touch of
anger, he had perceived that it was a lady, who was looking
down at him with a look, he suddenly felt, so precisely his own
that, the ludicrous aspect of the thing coming upon him, he
smiled. She too, at once following his change of feeling,
smiled, and then in a moment, with a slight courteous movement of hand and body, had passed. It had all taken place in
a few seconds. Her face and form made up between them, he
thought, the most beautiful woman he had ever seen, and he
had not seen few so-called whether in Europe or elsewhere.
Beauty in women was, according to Gildea, a thing which was
not *in reality* to be seen in the present world, implying, as it
did, perfection of form and perfection of spirit, καλον κάγαθον.
The Athens of Perikles had produced female beauty; in the
face and form of the Venus of Milo the highest physical and
spiritual perfection of the time is apparent. Florence too, in
such a woman as Vittoria Colonna, had produced female
beauty, and the Renascence had incarnated it in a Marie
Stuart; but, so far, our Modernity was not ripe for it. Lovely
female faces it, as all times, had in abundance, but these faces
knew nothing of spiritual perfection : they knew nothing of
life, they were not beautiful. And the female faces that *did*
know of life, the faces of women like George Sand, Char-
lotte Bronte, George Eliot, were quite wanting in physical
perfection. They imply mental passion, the struggle of pain :
they have not reached to the serene pleasure of spiritual
sovereignty. No, Beauty, καλον κάγαθον, is to be a produce
of the Future when Modernity has passed through the pangs
of its travail and, in the bright light of health and youthful-
ness, "grows in wisdom and stature" to the perfect self.—But
this face that he had seen for a moment, was, he thought, really
beautiful.

A few yards from him a man was standing looking back at
the rider passing along under the trees. Gildea came to him,
and asked him courteously if he happened to know who the
lady was?

"No," said the man, "I don't know who she is, but I often
see her."

And on this incident Gildea had founded a freak which had
for some time amused him. He intended to see this woman
again, and, if he was correct in his supposition (which he used

amusedly to doubt to himself) that she was some phenomenal anticipation of the Future, to possess her. He set about choosing and furnishing a house, therefore, which should, as far as possible, be worthy of such an individual, and much amusement it occasionally afforded him. A private enquiry-office was meantime seeking her out ; and, about a month ago, Gildea to his surprise had been informed that she was, beyond doubt, a Miss Medwin, niece of the well-known squatter, english, eccentric even to the extent of riding about and shooting in man's clothes on one of Mr. Medwin's stations in New South Wales, and, moreover, strongly suspected of having had, and of still having, an intrigue with a Mr. Frank Hawkes-bury, a writer and man of uncertain means, in Melbourne. Gildea laughed much on receiving this unasked-for report, (He had just by accident made the acquaintance of Hawkes-bury), and his interest in his freak somewhat revived ; but his all but conviction that he was incorrect in his view of Miss Medwin (if it were indeed she), prevented him from having any great interest in the matter or any great anticipations of suc-cess. As usual, however, he was satisfied to find that he had any interest or anticipations at all. He learned from Mrs. Medwin that she was in a short time coming to Sydney for a week or so on her road up to one of Mr. Medwin's New South Wales stations to which she had not been for years, and would be pleased to see him. A few days ago, then, she and Miss Medwin had arrived, and were waiting for Mr. Medwin who was detained by business in Melbourne. Hence Gildea's invitation to Mrs. Medwin and her niece, to come and make tea for him and go for a sail in the " Petrel."

The party arranged itself round the table, Maddock at one end, Gildea at the other, an empty place on Gildea's right hand for Alcock, Hawkesbury on his left with Fitzgerald next to him. Maddock, as before, could not help observing with admiration the beautiful room in which they were sitting. Hawkesbury, however, following out a train of thought sug-gested by his own last words, sat serious, looking at the table-cloth.

The lunch began. Gildea and Fitzgerald could both, when they pleased, excel in that graceful sweetness of manner which is supposed to be the peculiar gift of women. They pleased now. The talk flowed lightly and pleasantly, and soon re-turned to, what seemed to be to them all, the most interesting topic—the People. Fitzgerald spoke of the far greater ease and leisure of the People here than in England, and that led on to a consideration of the question of Labour here.

"Carlyle declared long ago," said Hawkesbury suddenly, "that the great question of the time was no other than the organization of Labour. Well, Labour is at last organizing. The consequence is that, as Mr. Fitzgerald remarked, there is greater ease and leisure among the People, not only here in Australia where Labour is comparatively scarce, but even in England where it is plentiful.—The question here, however," he added, "shows signs of complication. The employers are to form—nay, have already formed—a union: 'The Victorian Employers' Union.' The only wonder is that it is in Victoria and not in England that this idea has first been adopted. In Trades-Unionism in England, let me say it at once, there have been many abuses; but, let me hasten to add, not nearly so many abuses as there were under the old despotism of Capital. Trades-Unionism, which so few people seem to understand, originally meant the combination of many oppressed small units against a great oppressing unit. *Now* it means more: it means the determined effort of the People after happiness."

"That is very true, I think," said Gildea, "The People, ever since the deception practised upon them by the compromise Reform Bill of '32, have been slowly learning to organize themselves and to rely on themselves alone. Such a fact soon makes itself apparent. There is not a single considerable political measure since '32 which has not a socialistic tendency."

Hawkesbury acknowledged Gildea's remark, and proceeded:

"The People, and by the People I mean of course the masses, is everywhere realizing that there is something better worth living for than frantic competition and the scramble for wealth. Trades-Unionism, then, is the sworn foe of all this. I am not speaking either for or against Trades-Unionism: I am simply stating what it *wants*, what it *is!* The Trades-hall delegates, in the late conference anent the Bootmakers' strike in Melbourne, refused to let a bootmaker work for more than eight hours a day, although, by so doing, he might better him-self, and by not so doing might keep himself for ever a mere journeyman. 'Further argument with men of such a way of thinking,' says Mr. Bruce Smith, the chief mover of the

' Victorian Employers' Union,' ' further argument seemed useless.' And it was indeed as it seemed ; for these men were of
opinion that if, in the frantic competition and scramble for wealth,
one or two journeymen *did* rise and become rich, hundreds and
thousands would have to lead lives which would not stand
too favourable a comparison with those of dogs. ' Therefore,'
the delegates would say, ' we will check this frantic competition
and scramble for wealth, and we will even be so wicked as to
sacrifice the one or two possible journeymen who might rise
and become rich, for the sake of the actual hundreds and
thousands whose lives otherwise would not stand too favourable a comparison with those of dogs.' Well, and what will be
the end of this new phase of the great battle of Capital *versus*
Labour on which we seem to be now entering here ? Let me
not be thought a terrorist, if I remark, what is indeed patent
to all, that, in a country with a franchise like ours, Labour, if
driven into a corner and confronted by Capital triumphantly
brandishing its sword of ' Frantic-competition-and-the-scramble-
for-wealth—Labour, I say, might make things excessively
uncomfortable for the community in general and Capital in
particular. I am not hinting at mobs and sticks and stones. I
am merely stating a fact that is patent to all. Our good
friends the Landed-proprietors, videlicet the squatters, have
experienced in Victoria and elsewhere—are indeed now ex-
periencing even in Queensland *—the undoubted benefits of
a little judicious legislation. Might not someone suggest to
the ' Victorian Employers' Union ' and Mr. Bruce Smith, who
seem to have such quaint notions of what Trades-Unionism
really wants and is, that the same fate may possibly be in store
for our other good friends, the Capitalists ?"

"It is a pity," said Gildea smiling, "that we have not
a Capitalist here to answer you. But, I think, I know
what one of them, Mr. Alcock, would say. He would
say that the great law of Nature is this very frantic struggle
which you deprecate, and that, if you attempt to put
a check on it, you will only end by first arresting and
then destroying all progress. He would oppose the interference of organized Labour quite as much as of organized
public opinion, that is to say the State. He would of course
recognize all the evils of the frantic struggle, but he would say
that it yet contained the great ascending and progressive power

*In the Land Act that came into force in March, 1885.

of Nature, it was yet capable of Evolution; whereas the artificial state of popular leisure and ease contains the great
de-scending and retrogressive power of Nature, Dissolution.—
But here," he said, "at the very nick of time, he comes himself."

Edgar, who had just left them, returned ushering in Alcock,
who came forward with somewhat off-hand apologies to shake
hands with Gildea. He was then introduced to Maddock and
shook hands with him, compromising the matter, as he thought,
with the others by a bow and an expression of his pleasure at
making their acquaintance. He sat down in his place and,
having told Edgar what he chose to eat, was ready for a few
moments' talk before setting somewhat vigorously to work on
the victuals. Gildea explained to him the conversational con-
text, and what he himself had ventured to say in the person of
the typical scientific capitalist.

"Well," Alcock said, with a half-pleased half-amused look
on his face, when Gildea had finished, "I will observe that, on
the whole, you didn't put my sentiments so badly, Sir Horace.
—I am opposed to all state interference," he declared, turning
to Maddock, "It doesn't pay in the long run; it enervates
people! Look at this New South Wales here. They can't put
a bridge across a creek now, without petitioning government
for assistance! In England a half-dozen men or so would have
got together and settled the matter themselves. And they
want more state interference in Victoria! Why, it'll drain out
all their independence, and energy: and, in twenty years, they'll
be as lazy and lackadaisical as they are here in New South Wales!
Competition's the law of Nature." By this time Alcock's mouth
was full, and he was beginning to enjoy the delicate food and
wines, for he was hungry and thirsty. There was a pause.

"True," said Fitzgerald, gently breaking it, "but does not
Mr. Alcock too think, that it is just where the law of Nature
ends that the law of Humanity begins? Surely this is the
essential position of Christianity, that it says to the brutality of
Nature: 'Thus far shalt thou go, and no further.'"

"You can't," answered Alcock with his mouth full, too intent
on the victuals to be more explicit, "You can't interfere—
impunity—great law—nature—struggle—existence—survival
—fittest."

"Here, then," said Fitzgerald who ate little and drank less,
turning to Hawkesbury, "*we* are at one, I think, as opposed
to the pure Scientists?"

" I do not believe," Hawkesbury said, "and I do not think any Socialist believes, in carrying the initiative of the individual to the extent that Herbert Spencer would like. But we are not in favour of state interference. We want to nationalize things, the land, the unearned increment, the great public enterprises, but we include in this term the State also. The State at present means the tool of the Middle-class, worked by Capital and the Land Interest. This arrangement partakes too much of the nature of a political joint-stock company to please Socialists."

" And you think," asked Gildea, his hand on his wine glass, looking at Hawkesbury, "you think that when the People wins, as it of course ultimately will win, the control of things, that it will not work the State in its own interest, just as the Aristocracy did and as the Middle-class does ? "

" You know," Hawkesbury said, " I *believe* in the People ! The People is the only unselfish part of society. Their one desire is for justice and mercy ; and, when they could not get it themselves, they have always died readily for those who, they believed, wished to give it them. Herein lies the secret of all great popular devotions—from that of Christ to that of Napoleon."

" I," said Alcock, "do *not* believe in the People, as you call them, and their unselfishness has not yet come under my notice. The People, like everyone else, are led by what they believe to be their interests, their immediate interests, and our great effort should be, by giving them a good sound practical education, to get them to see that their true interest lies in e-volution and not in re-volution. Let us have a fair chance for everybody, and let the best men win."

" Yes," said Hawkesbury, with suppressed eagerness, "but the trouble is that, in this so-called free competition of yours, the best *don't* win ! In Nature the best win, I agree ; but Civilization has complicating clauses that modify and all but change, what you rightly call, her great law—the struggle for existence and survival of the fittest."

" I do not see that," said Alcock, returning to his victuals which he had left for a few moments.

" I will give you an instance," said Hawkesbury, " A, B, and C are three men who start as beggars in the market of free competition. A has the best wits, and A accordingly wins, and makes a fortune. Good: we applaud ! Then A, B, and

C all die, leaving sons D, E, and F, the best-witted of whom
does not happen to be D, A's son, but E, the son of B. Does
E therefore win and make a fortune, and D sink down to his
proper level with F? Not a bit of it! D has not only his
own second-rate powers to help him: he has also the wealth
which he inherits from his father. E, then, has no chance
against him : the second-rate man with wealth overwhelms the
first-rate man with beggary. What are the consequences,
generally speaking? Why, that, instead of the best surviving,
the second or third or fourth or fifth-best survive, and the
market is drugged with successful mediocrity. Here, I think,
is the delusion under which Herbert Spencer's social philosophy labours: he does not see that Civilization, as we know
it at present, is not a natural but an artificial state, and that
therefore the laws which hold good in Nature by no means
necessarily hold good in Civilization. Look at the bees or ants,
whose Civilization is a natural and not, as ours is, an artificial
one : do *they* encourage free competition with its inevitable
concomitants of wealth and power accumulated in the hands of
a few to the prejudice of the community? Not so. To each
is assigned an equal, if varying, share in the economy of the
community. With them work has its duty, and, as for idleness, it is not possible. But what duty has the successful
business man, except to his own success? what duty has the
wealthy aristocrat, except to his own pleasure?" There was a
slight pause.

"It won't *work*," said Alcock, his eyes a little opened,
sitting considering this young man with sudden interest.
(Alcock had so far thought that, in the present company,
nothing would be acceptable save, what he called, a popular
exposition of his own views)—"Believe me," he added with
gravity to Hawkesbury, "I have gone through all this at length,
repeatedly, and with care, and I am convinced that, with many
drawbacks, free competition within and without is the only
thing which will give us a civilization of progress. The real
tendency of everything else, I say, is towards stagnation or
retrogression. Free competition universal, the great problem
of which is to be the dominant race will proceed to settle itself
quickly and thoroughly. Until that problem is settled, we
cannot hope for a Civilization worthy of the name. All the
inferior races must be stamped out, all the stagnatory or
retrogressive ideas eliminated, and the best men with the best

K

knowledge left masters of the situation. It is impossible to foresee what such men may achieve. We may yet, perhaps, open communications with the planets and even modify the courses of the stars."

"Well," said Fitzgerald smiling, "we have had the Vision of the Future from the Christian, the Cultured, the Socialistic point of view, and now we see that Science too has her dreams. I have no objection myself to any of these Visions which, as I take it, all contain a not inconsiderable amount of truth. I would only observe that I believe them to be all impossible solely and individually. The Socialistic Future that would banish Christ, the Scientific that would also banish God, can no more exist as, in Mr. Alcock's phase, masters of the situation, than the Future of Christianity that would ignore the glory of our discoveries in Natural Law, or the Future of Culture that would deny to the People our highest joy."

"No," said Alcock drily, "we don't want Superstition mixed up with Religion, *that* is clear enough."

"Nor yet," added Fitzgerald sweetly, "do we want Superstition mixed up *without* Religion." (Alcock, with the look of a man who does not understand a thing and does not much care to, took a drink at his champagne, which, it was evident from the new expression on his face, was to his taste. Fitzgerald proceeded suavely to the table at large and more particularly to Maddock.) "For, as perhaps Mr. Alcock," (with a slight bend of the head to Alcock), "will permit me to say, the purely scientific view of things, which sees, in the unrestrained application to civilized life of the brutality of Nature, the undoubted parent of a Civilization worthy of the name, may be after all, and I believe is, a great superstition. Is not a superstition a belief in a thing not worthy of that belief? And is it not, then, a superstition, in calculating the progress of Humanity, to leave out of all account, as the pure Scientists seem to me to do, the most distinctive thing in Humanity—Religion."

"*I* should say," observed Alcock, "that *Reason* is the most distinctive thing in Humanity."

"Indeed?" asked Fitzgerald, "You surprise me! Is it not generally admitted now that the rudiments of Reason, and considerably more than the rudiments, are to be found in the animals? But I am not aware that anyone, not even Ernst Haeckel, has discovered in them the rudiments of Religion.

Can we not, then, agree with Max Müller that it is 'certain that what makes man man, is that he alone can turn his face to heaven ; certain that he alone yearns for something that neither sense nor reason can supply?'"

Alcock had the look of a man who feels the prompting of flippancy and, restraining it, is amused at what his flippancy would have said. Fitzgerald, perceiving this, answered it :

"Müller," he proceeded, "in criticising Kant, who is of course the Father of all the worshippers of Reason, again says finely that 'he closed the ancient gates through which man had gazed into Infinity ; but, in spite of himself, he was driven, in his "Criticism of Practical Reason," to open a side-door through which to admit the sense of duty, and with it the sense of the Divine.—This is the vulnerable point in Kant's philosophy,' he goes on, 'and if philosophy has to explain what is, not what ought to be, there will be and can be no rest till we admit, which cannot be denied, that there is in man a third faculty, which I call simply the faculty of apprehending the Infinite, not only in religion but in all things, a power independent of sense and reason, a power in a certain sense contradicted by sense and reason, but yet a very real power, which has held its own from the beginning of the world, neither sense nor reason being able to overcome it, while it alone is able to overcome both reason and sense.'"

"That it has held its own from the beginning of the world," said Alcock, "is no proof that it will do so to the end."

Fitzgerald smiled.

"What you say," he answered, "makes clear to me, then, that you do not accept this 'faculty of apprehending the Infinite,' and philosophically make the best of it, but you wish to call it mere childishness or, as you say, superstition and— 'eliminate' it! And yet you talk of Religion! What, may I ask, does a pure Scientist, as you seem to be, Mr. Alcock, *mean* by Religion?"

"Well," said Alcock frankly, "I confess that, to me, it means little more than credulity. I am not, of course, hostile to Religion; on the contrary, I support it. It helps to keep society together."

"It will do," said Hawkesbury, "for the People ! Pending the arrival of that education, which is to teach them the high satisfaction of social evolution, the masses may amuse themselves with such used-out mummeries as the Devil, Christ, and

God. The People is grateful. It has, it knows, as much to expect from Science as from Culture."

Fitzgerald was quite amused.

" Mr. Alcock," he said, "since you pure Scientists are generally reckoned as the foes of us Christians, we can ask you to do us no kinder service than to nail these colours of yours to the mast in the sight of all men. I do not alone mean your belief that Religion is all but a synonyme for credulity ; but this general conception of things of yours which includes no further consideration for Religion than elimination. We can have no doubt of the results. The world will doubtless find in *our* conception of things a certain amount of, what Mr. Hawkesbury has called, used-out mummery (for man's free-will has ever turned use into abuse), but it will find also things which savour of the kindly earth and the genial sun ; whereas, if you will let me say so, in *yours* all that it will find will be the steel-cold atmosphere of some heatless planet, filled with the dreary whirr of abstract machinery. Superstition *with* Religion, they will say, is better than Superstition *without*. And then, after they have given you a trial—and a trial they will give you, and such a great and long trial that we shall be eliminated almost as much as even you, Mr. Alcock, could wish us to be—then they will come back to us, and, having been driven by sore anguish of soul to re-discover, as their Father did, the sense of duty and of the Divine, they will find that this first step leads inevitably to another, and that to yet another. And, in the end, all high souls, and after them of, course all other souls (for the wisdom of to-day is the common sense of to-morrow), will see that their best and truest Father was a man who, passing through all this before them, has these years stood with clear and radiant faith, his longing hands held out to all that would take their strong help and guidance to that place of joy and of peace !"

Alcock, supposing this man to be Jesus and having made it a rule never in mixed company to speak of that to him, under such circumstances, embarrassing personage, kept silence, looking at the table-cloth. Hawkesbury too did not understand the allusion, which even Maddock, unless he had been warned by Gildea of Fitzgerald's connection with Cardinal Newman, might have missed. As it was, Gildea, perceiving and amused at Alcock's misunderstanding, was ready to at once dissipate it.

"Newman," he said, "is indeed the great modern example of a man of high intellect and all spiritual powers giving, not only, as Heine did, 'his tribute of admiration,' but everything he had, 'to the splendid consistency of the Roman Catholic doctrine.' I remember once hearing a rather able High-churchman say that he could not see, any more after than before reading the celebrated *Apologia*, why Newman had joined the Church of Rome : which is to say, that he could not see that, to a certain type of mind, the only two logical positions for a man of thought to-day are those of Scientific Atheism or of Catholic Faith."

"He leaves no place, then," said Hawkesbury, "for the Theists or the Pantheists ?"

"The Theists," answered Gildea, "leave no place for them-selves—except in the spiritual out-houses and the Unitarian chapels. There is not, I think, in modern times, one man of first, or second, or even third-class intellectual power that has believed in a personal God and not believed in a divine Christ. All men of thought are really now divided into two classes, Christians and Atheists : the first believing in a personal Christ and a personal God, the second in Law. All other differences are, as it seems to me, at heart mere divergences of symbolism. We are accustomed, for instance, to call those who hold that matter produces spirit Materialists, and those who hold that spirit produces matter Idealists, and those who hold that matter and spirit are identic and divine, Pantheists ; but really they are all Atheists. There is no Atheism, no disbelief in a personal God, more intense than that of our Idealists, Renan, Arnold, Emerson, who never cease, however, to talk of God and bid us find in Him our only comfort and guide : they are the true children of Goethe whose conception of God was Humanity in Nature, and of Religion Humanity in Art."

"So we Catholics feel," said Fitzgerald, "and this is, as I have implied, the great truth which we owe to the life and work of Newman. He has saved us from any temptation to compromise with Atheism. We are to stand to our guns, and, if we must perish, perish there !"

"The only thing is," Gildea answered ruefully, "that no great spiritual movement, religious or otherwise, was ever yet produced, retained, or destroyed by the action of logic, and they have all partaken largely of the nature of compromise. Voltaire and the philosophes sent such a douche of logic onto

Christianity in France that they literally beat it out of the country, but it came back again. And why? Because it contained the satisfaction of the demands of one side of Humanity which Logic had not, and could not have. Well, they compromised the matter, and the result is, (Dare I declare it, Fitzgerald?), none other than men like the fine and intellectual ecclesiastics who presided over the education of that lay priest, as he calls himself, Ernest Renan. History repeats itself. What Logic tried to do yesterday, Science is trying to do to-day. And, as you," (he turned his eyes to Fitzgerald), "foresee, Christianity, and Religion generally will suffer a defeat and even decapitation, only to return with processions, ringing of bells and the glad shouts of the populace. Then the Parliament will shut up all the sunday theatres, and the skeletons of Professor Huxley and Herbert Spencer will be removed from the Pantheon at Westminster and lodged in Madame Tussaud's, and the land have rest—for the space of forty years!"

"Well," said Alcock, "you young gentlemen are getting too far head for steady-going seniors like Dr. Maddock and myself. We will ask for matches, and smoke a cigar, while you tell us all about our great-great-grandchildren."

Cigars, cigarettes, and lights were brought and, with some pleasant small talk, the party loosened and eased its position at table and physical and mental state generally.

"Talking of compromise," said Hawkesbury, taking his cigarette from his lips and leaning the elbow of the hand that held it on the table, "between Religion and Logic, or Reason, is not, what is called, Positivism an attempt to organise such a compromise?"

Gildea began to laugh.

"Ah," he said, "is not Arnold's 'grotesque old french pedant,' a late foolish Monsieur Comte, as Carlyle would say, to leave me alone even beyond 'the long wash of Australian seas?' Am I to be persecuted even here by his tiresome adaptations and school-boy notions, all bundled up in superlatively bad French?—You do not know," he added, "what I chance to have suffered at the hands of my positivist friends at home, or I am sure you would not ask me to discuss them here where I am come for a holiday. They and Mr. Mallock are the most tiresome people in existence. You have heard of Mr. Mallock out here? and of his tilts with the junior Positivists?"

Hawkesbury acquiesced.

"We have heard of everything out here," he said smiling.

"Mr. Mallock," said Gildea, "was a young man who wrote a charming book called 'The New Republic,' one of the most charming books that had been written for several years, and then took to polemics, and has been logically agonizing there ever since. For this too we all ought to owe this religio-intellectual pedantry called Positivism a grudge. And, when we remember what Positivism did for George Eliot,—reduced a good quarter of herself and her characters into edificatory machines—I think that all of us, to whom Nature and Art are precious, should look upon Positivism as the contemporary accursèd thing." Gildea spoke with a certain exaggerativeness of tone and manner that to Maddock, observing and listening to everything with humour, was somewhat puzzling. Maddock with average profundity suspected that here was a case of some personal memory of a more or less disagreeable character; but average profundity, when it has to deal with that which is out of the range of the average, nearly always makes mistakes. Gildea was subject to sudden losses of interest in what he was saying or doing, spiritual twinges of that terrible wound from which he suffered : to those to whom "the endless emptiness of all things" is a reality, moments of acute weariness and disgust are ever lying in wait, and then the harness of life and living is often resumed with impatience or even pettishness. It had been so just now with Gildea. He had looked forward to his meeting with Miss Medwin, and heard those beautiful lips open and sounds come forth that showed that, however fine the harp, its strings were unattuned. The sense of his intense and perpetual loneliness had rushed upon him, and he had gone back again into his surroundings with an irritation that in a few moments amused him at himself.

The talk passed onwards, Maddock for the first time taking his share in it. And yet again it came round to the People. It was clear that the strongest impression that had been given to the party was that of Hawkesbury's Socialism.

"If I had been speaking of it some five or six years ago," said Fitzgerald, "I should have certainly said that I thought the Secularists had made most impression on the People of late years. But, in the face of the American Revivalist meetings and the Salvation Army, I have had to modify my views."

"'These movements or rather this movement," said Gildea, "strikes me as reactionary. British Middle-class Liberalism and Secularism have been at work, with much cry, and the egregious littleness of the wool has disgusted the People who have rushed off into the opposite extreme. The workmen, the skilled workmen, are I think secular. I remember hearing a lecturer on art who had been on a tour in America say, that the American workmen all asked him if he knew Darwin or Huxley or Tyndall, and expressed little or no care about anyone else, which seemed to surprise him."

"Cardinal Manning," Fitzgerald remarked, "said well, then, that 'the spiritual desolation of London alone would make the Salvation Army possible'—'this zealous but defiant movement.' Are we right in our supposition, do you think, Mr. Hawkesbury?"

Hawkesbury assented.

"There are three movements," he said, "at present going on among the People—the Socialistic, the Religious, and the Secular. They are all strong. In Ireland I have seen the two first clash, and the first was almost invariably victorious. If the priests will not go with the People in their socialistic views, (For of course the Irish Question is really a socialistic one, although it is not spoken of as such), then the priests are given up. Usually, however, the priests, being themselves of the People, are in full sympathy with them. The Socialists are by no means necessarily Atheists, but they are not Christians. 'The sooner,' I heard one of them say once, when pressed on the point, 'the sooner Christ is made a thing of the past and Jesus a thing of the present, the better it will be for all of us.' That expresses them excellently. The same idea lies at bottom in the popular Religious movement.—We Socialists," he added with a touch of bright humour, "like the Booths better than we like the Bradlaughs, but we recognise that both are in earnest and working for the People."

"And what, religiously speaking," asked Fitzgerald, "do you believe is to be the future state of the People, and of us all?"

Hawkesbury had another touch of bright humour.

"Socialism," he said, "nothing but Socialism! We are all Socialists, whether we know it or not. Just, then, as in the first and second centuries the platonistic Time-spirit radically influenced before it was absorbed into the christianic: so in the eighteenth and nineteenth centuries has the christianic

Time-spirit radically influenced, before it shall be finally absorbed in, the socialistic. Socialism has, after all, its universal modern expounder in Goethe. Goethe was the first to look upon Civilization as a great organic whole, every part of which has fixed pleasures and duties. He was the first, we believe, to conceive a natural as opposed to an artificial Civilization. Carlyle, too, felt something of the sort, although he could not express it, any more than he could not express what he took God to be. But we know Carlyle loved us, and therefore we love Carlyle. As for your Idealists, Sir Horace,—Renan, Emerson, and Arnold—we have no care for them, nor they for us. I remember once hearing Holden call Arnold 'the man who slew so many Philistines with the jawbone of an ass.' Well, the remark is expressive of his attitude towards Culture." Gildea and Fitzgerald were laughing, Maddock smiling.

"The end of it all," said Maddock, "seems to be, then, Mr. Hawkesbury, that 'the People,' as we say, is the great unknown quantity of the social equation. We all more or less feel its power, and we all more or less wish that power to be arrayed on our side, but no one quite knows what it is and everyone is a little afraid of it."

"You say truly," said Hawkesbury, "The People is the great unknown power, and it puzzles us. Pharaoh has dreamed a dream, and there is none of all the magicians of Egypt and all the wise men thereof that can interpret it unto him. What to make of the People's noisy Tichborne or Salvation Army devotions but political and religious infatuations? Be it so! But I will say this, that the People has a shrewd humorous instinct for both politics and religion that is a whole heaven above the purblind prudence of the Middle-class." He sighed, the sigh of a man who has somewhat outspoken himself. "'—And all these things,' he added as if to conclude the matter, 'are only known to the Deity.'"

Gildea smiled.

"Well," he said, "Are there not those among us who look forward to what is to come with the brightest faith or with the darkest despair? And there are those who dream and those who doubt,—and those too who possess their souls with patience, nourishing a modest hope. For

"what was before we know not,
and we know not what shall succeed.

" Haply the river of Time—
   as it grows, as the towns on its marge
   fling their wavering lights
   on a wider, statelier stream—
   may acquire, if not the calm
   of its early mountainous shore,
   yet a solemn peace of its own."

Little more was said after this of the chief subjects of their talk, and presently both Fitzgerald and Hawkesbury took their leave, Maddock and Fitzgerald, and Alcock and Hawkesbury, expressing mutual hopes of seeing one another again.

V.

Maddock went out into the balcony and stood there, leaning on the rails, reflectively smoking his cigar and looking out at the scene stretched before him like a panorama.   Alcock held quiet converse with Gildea for a few moments, apologetically asking permission to go and write a letter, the importance of which he would have explained at length, had not Gildea interposed.

" By all means," said he ; and, with a word of excuse to and gesture of acknowledgment from Maddock, took Alcock off into a room opposite, a study, where he ensconced him at the desk and, having pointed out the position of all the epistolatory necessities and told him to ring the bell for Edgar who would see that the letter was posted at once, withdrew and rejoined Maddock on the balcony.

" You will excuse Alcock," Gildea said, lighting a cigarette, " He has a letter of importance to write, which he does not care to leave till we come back."

Maddock at once acquiesced.   There was a pause, both smoking with leisure.

At last :

" Well," said Gildea, taking his cigarette from his lips, " and how did you like the happy family?   You were a very quiet member of it."

" Yes," said Maddock, " I refrained from mewing and sat still, purring and pleasantly watching the others.   It struck me, shortly after Alcock came in, that we were a very representative happy family."

" We only wanted a genial Theist to make the pile complete. Your good Judge is a Theist.   Now if we could only . . ."

"Ay, ay," said Maddock with something like a chuckle, "Judge Parker is a Theist! As your friend the *Argus* said, he was 'the learned gentleman who discovered Unitarianism in the early months of 1885.'—Come now," he proceeded with a sudden concentration of interest, "what are you going to say of the affirmative side of this man's criticism, after your remark that there was not, in modern times, one man of real intellectual power that has believed in a personal God and not believed in a divine Christ? Are you going to turn upon me again with your precious purely intellectual view of things. and say : 'The question that now arises is, has not Theism, after all,' et cetera, et cetera, et cetera?"

"Certainly I am," said Gildea laughing, "but all hope of utilizing the purely intellectual view seems lost after my unwary committal of myself.—No," he added more seriously, "I have of course little more left to do than to try and get you to join me in abuse of the good Judge for his superstition, that is to say his Theism, and that other egregious vice of his—his ludicrously inadequate conception of what is 'good and ennobling.' To take the last first, I will say, as I once heard Hawkesbury say on a like occasion, that I would far sooner believe in the Orthodox Christ than in the Unitarian Jesus. Indeed I might broaden my saying, and declare to the whole Rationalistic conception of Christ and Christianity generally, what Carlyle declared to Voltaire : 'Cease, my much respected Herr Von Voltaire, shut thy sweet voice ; for the task appointed thee seems finished. Sufficiently hast thou demonstrated this proposition, considerable or otherwise : That the Mythus of the Christian Religion looks not in the eighteenth century as it did in the eighth. . . . Take our thanks, then, and—thyself away.'"

"Judge Parker's view of Our Lord," said Maddock frowning, "is,—not to say blasphemous,—simply *fatuous!* I do not know whether indignation at impudence or contempt at stupidity the most possesses a man, when he is told, by such an one as this, that 'the Christian Theist, who regards Jesus as man, considers, and rightly from his point of view, that it *is* within his power to attain to the life of, and to follow the example of, Christ.' Imagine Judge Parker attaining to the life of anyone but a blatantly successful lawyer in the truculent spiritual quagmires of a colonial capital !"

"Our good Judge's discovery and investigation of the character of Jesus," said Gildea, almost ready to laugh outright at

Maddock's concluding dythramb, "are certainly not unlike those of a man who should charter a penny steam-boat for a trip up the Nile, and proceed, on his return to England, to give a lengthy description of certain large triangular-shaped buildings which, he should say, bore considerable resemblance to the common-sense conception of pyramids! And it *is* possible perhaps to denominate such a description as fatuous. His conception of Jesus *is*, we are agreed--inadequate : 'an exemplar . . . who merits all praise, all esteem, and love, and admiration for that, *being human*, he led so pure, so blameless, so noble and unselfish a life.' This, what this with our good Judge *means*, is an inadequate conception of Jesus. He perceives nothing of the real essence of Jesus. Anything that Arnold, whom he quotes so often, may have said of 'the mildness and sweet reasonableness' of Jesus, or that Renan may have said of the wonderful powers of personal attraction that are in Jesus—all this has fallen like water on the judicial back of our duck here! It is for none of these that our good Judge, our typical man of common-sense, goes to his New Testament. 'Mildness and sweet reasonableness,' the yearning of a consuming personal love, are not clear solid spiritual qualities which his mind can see and touch and handle. They have no place in the copy-books of the soul, nor yet in the sum-books thereof, and you shall search its 'Little Arthur's History' from beginning to end and find no mention of them. Their only place is in the thoughts, words, and actions of the men and women who have moved thousands and millions of their fellows, in the radiant days of high civilizations, in the agonies of the travail or the destruction of peoples and races. 'It is apparent,' says he, 'that we can collect from the Christian Bible, a purer, more beautiful, and more advanced ethical code, than is to be obtained from any other book or books.' O good Judge, O belovèd Judge, if all that is to be got out of the Christian Bible is an 'ethical code,' then the sooner Martin Tupper and Mr. Harrison are deified, the sooner will the human soul have reached its apogee ! "

"That is well," said Maddock, "but, at the same time, there are few things that disgust me more than the man of the opposite sort—he who, like so many of these Socialists of yours, will sing the love of Christ with passion, and then go out and commit a hundred of the grossest sins. Christ is morality."

" Ah no," said Gildea, " he is something better ; he is religion ! It is immoral to commit adultery : it is moral to punish
it : (' Infinitely better that they should atone for it, than lose a
step towards a higher life ') : it is religious, not to condemn it,
but to bid go and sin no more. It is immoral to take
your share in your father's substance and waste it in violent
living : it is moral to punish this prodigal, to whom repentance
has only come with a belly that was fain to fill itself with the
husks of the swine : it is religious to kill the fatted calf for such
a penitent, and rejoice and make glad. Jesus' sole criticism
on practical morality, on the realization of an ethical code in
everyday life, is, that ' it was not so from the beginning.'

" Just so ; but this is precisely the difference of the ethical
code of the Old and of the New Dispensation."

" Will you let me say, that it has nothing to do with any
ethical code at all ? For, surely, the essence of ethical codes is
justice, and the essence of the religious code, of the code of
Jesus, is love. The Amazon may be a big river, but you shall
compass all time in trying to put into it the unspeakable ocean.
—No, it is just here that, as Fitzgerald would say, all these
good people are superstitious. They believe that the spiritual
progress of humanity is synonymous with the progress of one
portion of the spirit of humanity, namely the ethical portion ;
and this, being a belief in a thing not worthy of that belief,
may justly, as it seems to me, be denominated a superstition.
It is superstition without religion."

" And what, then," asked Maddock, " do you call the belief
of men like your friend Hawkesbury ? "

" Those who are immoral ? men and women who, as most
of these Socialists, work in the spirit of Jesus and act (as a
polemist would say) in the manner of Bradlaugh ?—what is
their belief ? "

" Yes," said Maddock.

" Why, clearly," answered Gildea smiling, " religion *with*
superstition ! The men of enthusiasm like Hawkesbury, and
the men of morality like Judge Parker, are surely both of them
right, and surely both of them wrong : right in their appreciation of the truth of one portion of the spiritual life, wrong in
their ignorance of another portion. They both possess truth,
and they both possess superstition."

" And what of a man like our friend Alcock here, who is
ignorant of religion and more or less lax as regards morality ? "

"He too," answered Gildea, "as Fitzgerald clearly demonstrated, is a victim of superstition. But he is not, for all that, without his belief, without his appreciation of truth. He believes in that portion of the spiritual life which we call intellect. Men like him have their enthusiasm, for which they are ready to suffer and do suffer all things ; and that enthusiasm is the enthusiasm for that portion of truth which we call Science."

"And your Fitzgerald—is he too both right and wrong?"

"Of course he is ; for has he not both belief and negation? All belief is truth, not *the whole* truth, but *a part* of the truth. There is but one thing that is the whole truth."

"God?"

"No, not God, for God does not include Nature, from which He is the outcome—not God, not Nature, but that which contains them both, Everything, the All!"

"Pooh," said Maddock, "flat Pantheism!"

"*And suppose,*" cried Gildea, "*it were* Pot-*theism, if the thing is true!*" (He laughed outright.) "—That answer of Carlyle's," he said, "is immortal."

"Oh, it was Carlyle said it?" said Maddock, "I had forgotten.—And so," he proceeded, "the secret is out, and Sir Horace Gildea 'stands confessed a Pantheist in all his charms!'"

"Two of the happy family still remain unaccounted for," Gildea said, "although they too have not probably attained to perfect truth."

"Oh, that is you and I. As for me, I can describe myself without your aid. I believe in morality and religion, with a touch of superstition in both."

"Worse," said Gildea, "worse!"

"What, then?"

"You believe in theology which is as bad a superstition as, what Judge Parker calls, 'the calm blissful sea of pure *theistic* belief.' (You notice how emphatic he is about his superstition and casual about his truth?)"

"Stop a moment now, my bright Apollo, and explain to me, what you have not yet attempted to, what the superstition of Theism is?"

"*What is Theism?*—'It is a faith,' answers our good Judge, 'which is *the* faith of all others' (that is to say the faith of Judge Parker and all the 'celebrated unitarian ministers'), 'to be clung to, cherished and maintained as long as man exists

—belief, trust in, and love for the All-loving, All-righteous, All-wise Universal Spirit of God.' Now observe that this faith, this unique faith of faiths, is 'refreshing, and invigorating in its simplicity'—(as, we might add, is also its formulator, if we did not shun flippancy as we would the pest)—'warm and glowing in its absolute unclouded devotion to, love for, and perfect trust in God alone—*proclaimed by* NATURE !' O wise Judge, O upright Judge, O Judge much more elder than thy looks, where, when, and how, in the name of all observers of Nature from Darwin through Haeckel to Tennyson, did you discover therein either this love or righteousness of which you make such mention ? 'The struggle for existence and survival of the fittest,' the parent of theistic righteousness and love ! '*Proclaimed by* NATURE !'—and Nature in italics ! O immemorial phrase that eats up all the others even as Aaron's rod swallowed up all the rods of the magicians !—Who, after this, would care to trouble himself with all the other potent items of this faith of faiths ? The idea of God, God 'the All-loving, All-righteous, All-wise Universal Spirit ' 'originated in instinct,' and is not the slow and painful growth of time ? Think of the love of Jehovah ! the righteousness of Baal ! the wisdom of Moloch !—The beauty and sympathy and warmth of the theistic form of belief," he added, "are recognizable as a half-hearted mixture of the clap-trap of Religion and Science—Superstition, which knows that it is naked, and sews fig-leaves together, and make itself an apron !"

Maddock, however, could have no confidence in the expressed views of this man, from whose face the light of amusement, amusement at others and himself, seemed never to be absent long. There had, indeed, been moments when it required all Maddock's intuition to prevent his perception rising in absolute revolt against what seemed Gildea's flagrant insincerity : then his perception had said to him that this was but a youth, endowed with brilliant abilities, the mere exercise of which was a pleasure and satisfaction to him, caring too little for any one thing to owe it loyalty. Whereto his intuition had replied that this was not a youth but a man, and a man whose secret could not thus be read. And the feeling that Maddock had, once before that day, felt towards Gildea returned now with an intensity and strangeness that seemed to Maddock, when he afterwards considered it, as little short of wonderful. Maddock's profundity was often beyond the average, and herein indeed lay his secret, herein nestled "the heart of his mystery."

"And yet," said Gildea, "here, as in the other case, the common-sense view of belief has, of course, its excellence. 'To take nothing else,' says the Judge, 'the very idea of "space" and "distance" that astronomy has given us fills the mind with wonder and with awe, clothing nature with a sublimity, a majesty, and a beauty which, otherwise, we had never known.' For observe that *Space* and *Time*, these two inexhaustible ideas, are not, to our average intelligent secular view of things, the mere words that they are to the orthodox : they are realities thus far, that they help us to perceive that 'there exists throughout space,—throughout the vast limitless universe,—motion, order, beauty ; that there is behind all motion, all order, all beauty, a force that produces the motion, the order, and the beauty.' And further. They are realities thus far, that they help us to be (whatever Dr. Maddock, in a polemico-theological spirit, may declare) earnest in our life and earnest in our wish to bring home to others the truth of that life, a 'most serious and difficult task !' They help us to all this, and an unrecognized intuitional belief in the essence which, in other forms and other men whom we fail to appreciate, not to say understand, we condemn—our intuitional belief, I say, in the Faith, Hope, and Love, which are the great movers of the progress of Humanity both upward and onward, will not let the forms that portions of this belief may take in us make the whole grow cold, lifeless, petrified, but the beauty and melody of our acts will often be found to contradict the deformity and discord of our words."

"I confess, Sir Horace," said Maddock, "that you are a puzzle to me. I really should not be surprised to see you some day walking side by side with the Judge, the best friends in the world !"

"And perhaps," said Gildea, "the Judge would not subsequently be surprised to see me doing the same with yourself! For that indeed is the only use of such poor creatures as I : we see the good in opponents and serve as links in the spiritual bridge of Humanity."

"I should very much like," said Maddock, "to hear how you would abuse me to him. I think I see the urbane expression with which you would delight him by shewing how, in this ecclesiastical, metaphysical, theological polemist here, habemus confitentem asinum ; and then turn upon him and say : 'The question that now arises, my dear Judge, is, has this man nothing but faults—has he no excellencies? does there remain, after the attack on him of so eminent a biblical critic as Judge Parker is, no residuum of real and vital truth? Let us see.'"

"Doctor, Doctor," said Gildea, "to make me laugh so, is cruel!"

"You do not consider me," said Maddock, "in the least."

They both laughed heartily.

"And now," said Maddock, "in order to complete the matter, tell me, what is *your* superstition? Here are Alcock and Parker with their respective superstitions of Atheism and Theism, of purely scientific and purely ethical progress. Here is Hawkesbury with his superstition about the unselfishness of the People and the practical neglect of Morality. Here is Fitzgerald with his superstitious belief in a Church whose splendid logical consistency will prove its ruin. Here am I, a member of a sect that more nearly approaches ideal Christianity than any other sect in existence, and is a logical absurdity—blessed with the superstition of theology and, worse, of polemical theology, with . . . But I cannot express all my superstitions : they seem more in number than the hairs of my head!"

"Let us say broadly, then, that Alcock and the Judge are those who have superstition *without*, and Fitzgerald, you, and to a certain degree Hawkesbury, those who have superstition *with*, Religion."

"And that you?"

"And that *I* am he who unites in my proper person the superstitions of all with the actualities of none."

There was a pause. Then :

"Sir Horace," said Maddock, "I take you seriously. And I will confess that I would sooner, far sooner, be any one of us than you.—Verily and indeed," he added, solemnly, "I cannot see why you should care to live."

"Nor yet," said Gildea, "why I should care to die?"

Maddock was possessed by sadness. The absolute, inevitable hopelessness of this man made him again turn faint and sick at heart.

"Nor yet," he said, "why you should care to die."

There was a long pause. Never again could Maddock be illuded into momentary misunderstanding of this man : he had now not only seen this strange soul laid bare before him and felt the influence of that sight, but had felt as if he had, as it were, almost received it into his own, almost made it a part of himself.

At last :

"I asked you to believe," he said with a touch of wistfulness in face and tone, "that I was your true friend. You will perhaps, forgive me if I . . if I offer you the one token of it that seems left to me to offer. Some day—I cannot tell, but so I trust—you may care to think that, each night you close your eyes in sleep, there is one whose prayers for you are rising, as he believes, to the God and Father of us all, to bless and keep you, to lift up the light of his countenance upon you, and to give you peace."

The two men stood facing each other for a few moments in silence : then their hands met in a close, long clasp, and parted ; and they turned, standing almost touching each other, looking out over the lovely scene of earth and water and sky.

At last :

"Those clouds," said Gildea softly, "they have a peerless radiancy. One seems to understand how the men of the past days saw a spirit therein, and held converse with it with wonder and delight and awe. Those were days of a music and beauty and sweetness such as we shall never know again."

"*If not*, said Maddock as softly,

> *if not the calm*
> *of its early mountainous shore,*
> *yet a solemn peace of its own."*

A footstep was heard behind them. It was Edgar, come to say that Mrs. and Miss Medwin had arrived and were up in the drawing-room with Mr. Alcock.

Gildea stepped out onto the lawn.

"Let us go up by the balcony," he said to Maddock.

VI.

Mrs. Medwin was the only native-born australian lady who was "good style." So at least a Governor's wife, about the "goodness" of whose "style" there could be no question, had declared. It was not, this Governor's wife had explained, that there were no ladies in Australia, (There were not however many, par parenthèse, and such style as they had was at best but second-rate american), but they none of them had that

manner of dressing, moving, and speaking which charac-
terizes what (to use this rather objectional term again, for
want of a better) we call "good style." This Governor's wife,
with her usual delicate feminine instinct, had felt on the occasion of this now socially celebrated description of Mrs.
Medwin, that she had not quite satisfied herself, that the
description did not contain the truth, all the truth, and
nothing but the truth, of the matter; and she was right, it
did not. Mrs. Medwin undoubtedly possessed that serene
refinement of movement and speech which go so far to making
up that all but defunct individuality, a "lady," but she was
wanting in the final gift of a "lady," social charm. The flower
was scentless, or rather the scent it had was of another description. Her life had not, indeed, been favourable to the
development of this final gift. She had been married early, a
ready enough victim to the convenience of her family, to a
man with whom she had little in common and much in opposition. He was liked by none and feared by all those who had
any personal dealings with him: his savage outbursts of passion recalled to memory the dark stories that were told of his
father who had, as the Australians euphemistically put it, come
out at the government expense. But she, having calmly decided
to accept Medwin and life with him, set herself by the sheer
intrepidity of her sweet high beauty, to dominate them. She
succeeded. And she won, not only the control, but the deep,
admiring love, of the man. Then came the catastrophe which
those who knew him had prophesied and recanted. In one of
his savage outbursts of passion, he struck her. The blow was a
cruel one and its results life-long. Much as she then suffered
in body and soul, she could have no other feeling for him than
that of pity. For days he would take no food, but sat in a chair
outside her door, like a dog that waits in silence on an idolized
master; and, when he was first permitted to enter, flung himself onto his knees by the bedside, sobbing and moaning and
covering her hand with kisses. And she, who had had little or
no care for him before, save as the principal incident in her
life, now to her own surprise found that from out this appalling misery was born affection for him and even love. Her
life from then onwards had been spent in a struggle far more
terrible than that which she had waged with him. At first the
idea of wasting away inch by inch on a diseased sick-bed
almost overwhelmed her: she longed, she prayed for death.

But death did not come : and then her spiritual pride began to reassert itself, and, like the captain of a battered ship, she once more thought how she could rule these waters that had ruled her. For long it seemed as if the effort would be too much for her : she said to herself one sleepless horrible night that she was being consumed alive. Her very latest gift seemed but as an added thorn to her; for now that she had affection and even love, she had also jealousy. The spell of her sweet, fearless health and strength and beauty was passed from him save as a memory : his love, deepened it might be by his abiding remorse, was (as she thought) deprived of that admiration which had been her first and strongest hold on him. Nothing more pitiful, than to see the womanliness in her assert itself against her pride and speak in jealousy ! With wonderful intuition, however, she divined and with wonderful determination carried out, what was the only plan of still keeping for herself his admiration. She, who since she had married him had not given his business affairs a thought, now gave herself up to the mastery of them. She had herself taught all arithmetic thoroughly, and, in little less than three years after her misfortune, knew more of all his business affairs than he did himself. And more. She stirred up in him the ambition to become the leader of that great amorphous section of colonial society of which he was a member, the land-owners, the "squatters." She had a certain liking for society, and when she was in England went into it as much as her extremely delicate health would permit her : in Australia, however, where, as she said, there was no society, or only of a sort which she did not like, she yet entertained a good deal, as she wished her husband to be popular in view of his entering parliament and attempting to organize his party. But her entertainment was more after the fashion of a listless social empress than an interested hostess : she did not care enough about these people to make, what would have been to her, a painful physical effort to attract them. She had indeed something of the feeling of one of the old aristocrats forced by the pressure of the time to open their houses to the Middle-class ; she acknowledged the salute of her guests, and provided them with fine rooms, music, amusement, foods and drinks, and what more could they want ? Her coldness was generally ascribed to her notorious ill-health, but the young people felt instinctively that she condemned them, and were not drawn to her. Between her and Gildea, however, there was an understanding that was not without either charm or brightness to both. He understood her, and she half-felt this and, never having been really understood before, was in a way pleased at it and drawn to him. She amused him and at times, thanks to the pity with which her sweet courage inspired him, affected him. He was not too without respect for her intuitional capacities. He said once to Sydney Medwin, who was complaining that his mother was fifty years behind the time, (Mrs. Medwin supported her husband in his views for their elder son), that, on the contrary, she was fifty years before ; for she was the only person he had met or heard of in the Colony who clearly saw that the Land Question was upon them. Mrs. Medwin indeed, as has been noticed, saw that the attempt of the Australian land-owners to repeat the performance of those of England and form a dominant aristocracy, would be met with keen opposition, and that the only hope of success lay in creating out of an amorphous class a party, and organizing it. The feeling of possession and caste had grown a strong one in her, in her more or less absorbed in the life of her husband. Hers, then, with all its powers of passionate attachment to an individual, was one of those not frequent female souls that see beyond a man into the cause which he represents. Her elder son she looked upon as a failure, as useless, as worth no more than making behave himself. Her younger son, Stephen, she was training with some care, and to him the far greater bulk of his father's wealth and property was at present destined. Miss Medwin, whom Mrs. Medwin called her niece, and who called Mr. and Mrs. Medwin respectively uncle and aunt, but who was in reality no such relation, being the daughter of Mr. Medwin's father's brother's son ; of Miss Medwin it will perhaps be enough to state, that the report which Gildea had unexpectedly received of her from the Private Enquiry Office was correct, and that she was the possessor of a moderate fortune who had come out to Australia, half for a change from her english life of which she was weary, half in search of an old schoolfellow to whom she was much attached.

Gildea and Maddock stepped out together along the lawn and mounted the steps that led up to the sitting-room balcony. The sunlight, intercepted by an angle of the house, covered half of this portion of it, almost so exactly half that the glass door, open in the middle of the bay window, was partly in the sun and partly in the shade. As they reached the balcony, Gildea, with the gesture of a courteous host, indicated to Maddock to enter first, but he, with the no less courteous gesture of a guest, refused and returned the indication. Gildea stepped into the open doorway and, as he stood there for a moment with the sunlight and shade playing upon him, met the gaze of Miss Medwin, seated upright, looking almost proudly before her. Behind her was the dark red of the curtain with its subdued white of delicately wrought muslin. Two rays of sunlight lay along the rich variegated colours of the carpet, diffusing a little light about her. She was very beautiful. They had recognized one another at once. And more. They both were undergoing that feeling of half-forgotten recollection that affects us with such unprepared and mystic strangeness. Had they, then, seen one another before that day when she had almost ridden over him under the Domain trees? had they met in some way similar to their meeting now? At such moments the past, the present, and the future, all half unknown, seem to join hands, and kiss, and part with eyes dimmed with a regretless regret.

It had passed in a few moments. Gildea, with something that might be called a sudden freak of tact, stepped into the room, turning a quite self-possessed face to Mrs. Medwin. She was sitting on a sofa dispensing serene little nothings to Alcock, whose face and manner beamed with social polish. Gildea came straight to her and made his greetings with winning grace : then, obeying a slight gesture of hers, moved aside and she introduced him to her niece, Miss Medwin. With the same winning grace, head courteously bowed, he stepped to Miss Medwin, and lightly raised the hand she held up to him. Maddock was greeting Mrs. Medwin.

"I think," said Gildea smiling slightly, "I think, Miss Medwin, that we are not quite strangers."

"And how is Mrs. Maddock?" asked Mrs. Medwin, "I hope she is quite well." Gildea sat down in a chair by Miss Medwin.

"No," answered Miss Medwin gravely, "I was careless enough to have almost ridden onto you."

"The carelessness was mine. I was dreaming. Day-dreamers should be awakened." Maddock was assuring Mrs. Medwin that Mrs. Maddock was in excellent health, and at this very moment enjoying herself quite satisfactorily without the society of her lord and master.

"Indeed," said Mrs. Medwin, "I hope we shall be able to see her before we leave Sydney. We are stopping at Winslow's."

"That," Miss Medwin said gravely again, "seems to me to depend a good deal on the day."

"Mr. Medwin is *with* you, Mrs. Medwin?" interrogated Alcock with his politest manner, "I understood that I should not have the pleasure of seeing him till monday or tuesday?"

"It is true," said Gildea, "that to-day the reality of things is so troubling to the peace and pleasure of many of us, that it is cruel to wake us from our dreams."

"Oh no!" said Mrs. Medwin with her usual unruffled serenity, "Mr. Medwin is not coming up till tuesday or perhaps wednesday."

A swift sense of the humour of a social scene like this, where the tendency of things is for the dramatis personæ to beat unlimited time with musical voices, graceful gestures, and a charming expression of countenance, dawned upon Gildea as a memory of almost distant days. The poetry of society is mostly expended in its common-places. To be able to do this is an art, an art of which provincial and colonial society is ignorant. Hence Gildea's sense of the humour of the present scene was as an almost distant memory. "Here," he thought, "we have four excellent musicians who would make the most charmingly meaningless quartet possible, Alcock being reduced to the part of accidental audience." It was not, of course, that Gildea's talk with Miss Medwin was social time-beating : it was, rather, spiritual time-beating, rendered in a manner that partook of the social. Miss Medwin had not recovered from the to her strange sensations of this second sudden meeting with him : she was neither as consummate a master of her emotions as he was, nor careful of becoming one, nor yet was she prepared, as he was, for their meeting : she was left by it as one is who has had some swift revelation of good or evil in himself—considering himself if he really was this, is that, and will be something that contains them both. The individualities of other men she had known had touched her as much, or almost as much, as his had on that day in the Domain, but none had ever entered into her and, as it were, "blown a thrilling summons to her will" as his had, as he stood looking at her in the shadowy sunlit doorway there. And her

will had answered that summons, and instantaneously. To him
that sight of her, sitting upright, looking almost proudly before
her, was ever to be as the sight of an Antigone, one who felt
" it was better not to be than not be noble,"·the depth of
whose scorn for unworthiness was equal to her love, high as
the everlasting hills, deep as the unplumbed sea.

" Yes," she said, " it is sometimes cruel to wake us from our
dreams, and yet it is best, I think."

" —You think it is best to modify our poetry with prose?
Was it better to have awakened Shelley, and given us his
' Prometheus ' with wooden limbs of a day's social dogmatism,
than to have let him make delicate music in the italian woods
and by the italian shores, for ever sweet and fair ?"

"So he told me," said Alcock, " and I was very glad to hear
it. The interests of all wealth, whether in land or in money, is
identic. But we have no organization.—And Labour," he
added with a look to Maddock, "as Mr. Hawkesbury just told
us, is organizing, if it is not already organized."

If it had been possible for Mrs. Medwin to be amazed at
anything, she would have been amazed at this. Hawkesbury
had a few years ago been an employé on one of Medwin's
stations, the very station to which she was now on her road.
This was a reflection which was positively annoying to her.
"It would," she had once simply remarked, "have been as
well perhaps, if he had eaten some poisoned meat when he was
there, as they used to say the troublesome blacks did. He is
a danger to society." Sydney Medwin, who liked to do his
best to ruffle his mother's serenity now and then, used
not unfrequently to speak in praise of Hawkesbury (his
friend Hawkesbury, a clever fellow too, and who would
make his mark out here yet !) and had once even, as Gildea
told Maddock, offered to introduce him to her. " You know,
Sydney," said Mrs. Medwin simply, " I am not interested in
Mr. Hawkesbury. If you like to make up a shooting-party at
Lathong," (a station of Medwin's in Victoria), "with all the
men on the station, I daresay he would be pleased to join
you."—What, then, was the meaning of Mr. Alcock's remark
that this firebrand socialist, this impertinent journalist and
pamphleteer, had been *just telling* something to Mr. Alcock,
Dr. Maddock, and presumably Sir Horace ?

" I'm sure," said Alcock with his politest manner again,
" that we all of us cannot be too—too pleased to have found a

lady who realized this, and could help us to what we so much want—a . . a sort of general rallying-point.—Nothing," he proceeded, "struck me so much in England as the use that the political parties made of their social gatherings, and they tell me that this was much more the case once than it is at present." Alcock found a certain amount of difficulty in saying that he thought women might, after all, be made of some use in political life, in a manner that should be pleasing to *this* woman.

The talk progressed more or less easily, Maddock, with a humorous perception of the effect Alcock's innocent allusion to Hawkesbury had produced on Mrs. Medwin, playing the part of conversational mediator between the two.

"You are not, then," said Gildea, in answer to a remark of Miss Medwin's, "in sympathy with dreams and dreamers?"

"No," she answered shaking her head, "not if they take their dreams for realities. It is just, I think, because we have been dreaming so long and dreaming so much, that our waking is so miserable.—You speak of prose and poetry," she continued, turning her head a little and looking at him, "as if the prose had something disagreeable in it. Well, so it may have —to the dreamers. I too am a dreamer, of course, in my way; but I dream about the earth and the things of the earth, and so my dreams are real as the wind is real, or the sunlight, or the moonlight, or the light of the stars, none of which fear the contact of the earth or the water. But these people seem to me to dream of the things of heaven, filling all space with them. But space is empty—at any rate of things like theirs."

"You do not believe," he said, "as Taine does, that 'at bottom there is nothing truly sweet and beautiful in our life but our dreams?'"

"Yes," she said, "yes and no! But what does it matter *what* I believe? I have no opinion of my own in this way. You would make me dogmatic. Now I shall always try not to be dogmatic. I rebel against defining things, especially things that I like: they are never the same afterwards. But I am often doing this, and I have to suffer for it. This comes of being born in an age which can describe everything and do nothing.—You see, you make me petulant!"

It flashed across Gildea's mind as she finished speaking that there was a great difference between the manner of his talk with this girl and with that bright intelligent girl in Melbourne.

He perceived the difference, and the greatness of the difference, but not much farther. It was many years, and in point of spiritual time many ages, since Gildea had been blind to the fact that another nature was influencing and being influenced by his own with the force of fatality. It is the distinguishing mark of the moderns that they are not blind in this respect. None of Shakspere's men, not even the intellectual Hamlet, get beyond a suspicion that Fate is playing upon them. The chief cause of Hamlet's delay lies in this suspicion and his antagonism to it : the others submit blindly, and only recognise fatality when the "wheel has come full circle," but *the process* of fatality is all unknown to them, not even a mystery. Miss Medwin too was in the same state as Gildea but even deeper in it. She spoke to him as she had never spoken to anyone else in her life, as to a comrade, without leaning, without supporting, with complete simplicity. The spell that compels a mutual truthfulness is the perception that you understand and are understood.

"I see," he said, "that *you* complain of your age because its senses are deranged, and idlers like me because the gifts that it assigns to the doers, as opposed to the thinkers, are not gold but tinsel."

"No, no," she said, "I do not complain of my age ! If I complained of anything, it would be of myself who am unfit for my age. And I do not think that the gifts of our actions are tinsel."

"Perhaps you are right, and the fault is mine because *my* senses are deranged ?"

"There is great room for action now, as it seems to me. If a man appeared to-morrow with the secret of attraction in him —the secret that Napoleon had or Byron—he would control us as much as they did. They are ours too, these men."

"But we think too much ? we can describe everything, and do nothing ?"

"I do not know," she said, "I have no opinion !"

"Alice," said Mrs. Medwin.

"Yes, aunt," answered Miss Medwin.

"Will you please make the tea ?" she said.

Miss Medwin rose at once, Gildea rising too, smiling. It was Mrs. Medwin's peculiar charm that, at certain apparently eccentric moments, she would speak and act with the pretty spontaneous sweetness of a young girl. This was the scent this wonderful flower had retained, despite all the terrible heats of the noontide and frosts of the dawn that had fallen upon its life. She had spoken in this manner now.

Miss Medwin went behind the tea-table which Edgar had just brought in and on which he was placing the bright silver tea-urn, and the water-can with its blue-violet-flamed spirit-lamp; then, at a nod from Gildea, disappeared. Miss Medwin poured out a cup of tea which Gildea took to Mrs. Medwin, returning for the milk and sugar, while Miss Medwin took the second cup to Maddock, who received it with suave and charming thanks. Mrs. Medwin thanked Gildea, who passed on with the milk and sugar to Maddock, and, as he returned to the tea-table for the cakes and biscuits, passed Miss Medwin with the third cup on her way to Alcock. Alcock received her with thanks profuse and jocular.

"Do you take milk and sugar?" asked Miss Medwin.

"No, no, thank you, Miss Medwin," returned Alcock, "I take neither!"

Gildea arrived, with a plate of cakes in one hand and a plate of biscuits in the other. Mrs. Medwin recognised in the biscuits those of a sort to which she was somewhat addicted, and divined that Gildea had noticed the fact.

"Thank you, Sir Horace," she said, with her manner of pretty spontaneous sweetness, "And presently Alice shall play for you. I know you will find her style of playing a treat."

Sir Horace made a suitable reply and passed on with the cakes and biscuits. Mrs. Medwin and Maddock began to talk together, Alcock playing the part of silent member.

"There is your tea," Miss Medwin said to Gildea as he came back to the tea-table. She was standing with her own cup in her hand as if about to move away to a seat. Gildea proffered the biscuits. She took one. He put down the plates and took up his cup.

"You are an epicure in tea," she said, sipping a little of hers from her tea-spoon, "are you not?"

"I do not know," he answered with a slightly amused look, "but I believe that the Russians are the only people in Europe who understand it."

"They take neither sugar nor milk, do they? and a slice of lemon floating in the tea?"

They were moving back to their places. He assented.

"And who are the only people in Europe who understand coffee?" she asked.

"Undoubtedly the French."

"Ah, you mean the café au lait—with the milk and coffee both boiling and poured in together? I like it that way, but not with too much milk. We had a french cook once who used to make it for us, and, as I liked it, of course I found out how to make it myself."

"Yes," he said, "certainly coffee with cold milk is a barbarism; but the shape in which I like coffee best is as, what the French call, café noir."

Miss Medwin said she had never seen it in that way, and, in answer to Gildea's slight expression of surprise, explained that she had never been in France. Gildea described the café noir and the proper manner in which to drink it.

"You fill the spoon with cognac," he said, "into which you put a lump of sugar—In France the sugar is in little thin slabs, not, as with us, in squares—and then you set the cognac alight. This melts down the sugar and, when all the spirit is burnt up, except that which saturates the sugar, and goes out, you put in your spoon. The flavour of burnt sugar and cognac is pleasant."

"It is indeed, Sir Horace," said Alcock, tired of playing the part of silent member in the other conversation, "I drank it that way myself in Paris. A friend of mine, an American told me of it. Paris is a very pleasant place. You have a treat in store for you, going there, Miss Medwin."

"Yes," she answered, "I should like to go to Paris; the Louvre is there."

"A very fine collection," said Alcock, "I was much struck with it! Unfortunately all the best works of art are now either in collections, or so expensive that they are out of the reach of us Australians who have claims upon us more pressing. You saw the Picture Gallery in Melbourne?"

"Yes, I saw it. I think it is rather painful. I liked the Library better."

"The building—the room, you mean?"

"No, I meant the books. I used to go and sit there and read."

"Oh indeed?" said Alcock. "And what now do you think of the Picture Gallery here?"

"Alice," said Mrs. Medwin, "you are not to say! I won't have you say that the things in Sydney are better than in Melbourne!"

"Very well, aunt," said Alice, "then I will not say it."

"And now," said Mrs. Medwin, "I want you to play for us."

Miss Medwin rose at once with a look for the piano, which was on the other side of the curtains. Both she and Gildea were amused and delighted by Mrs. Medwin's characteristic interruption and command: Maddock was amused: even Alcock, who did not yet know her ways, was too much influenced by the charm of this her happiest manner to think it rude or imperious. "She is such an invalid," he said, recounting this incident as an anecdote to a friend of his at the Melbourne Club, "and rules everyone about her like a little empress. But her manner is irresistible, really irresistible ; and it doesn't offend you in the least—in fact you rather like it. There is no woman in Melbourne who could help us to consolidate a party in the english social manner as *she* could. And I really attach—I really do !—considerable importance to the idea." Such was the subsequent expression of the thoughts which were passing through the mind of Alcock as Gildea, having held back the curtain for Miss Medwin to pass, was opening the piano for her. Mrs. Medwin sat in serene unconsciousness of the possibility of her manners being considered as otherwise than her own, and would have been surprised if she had heard that anyone thought they were open to question.

"Is there any piece, aunt," asked Miss Medwin, bending back so as to see Mrs. Medwin through the curtains, "that you would like me to play ?"

"Oh no !" Mrs. Medwin said, "Why, I wanted you to play for Sir Horace, not for me !"

Miss Medwin smiled assent, and, after a few moments' pause to consider what piece she would play and to collect her thoughts, began. The piece was the one which she considered would most please her audience, and which of course she knew. It was Chopin's Eleventh Nocturne. It suited her humour at many times, but particularly at the present. The Nocturne is divided into two parts : passionate and half-weary wandering, and rest in which passion is merged in peace. To her it conjured up the vision of a twilight road winding up between woody rolling fields and a plantation. The dark figure of the man, whose passionate and half-weary wandering is here expressing itself, is coming slowly up the road. Low down and far away behind the close straight stems of the plantation lie a few pallid veins of sunset light. The shadows are stealing swiftly around him. He is near to hopelessness, near to the wish to

> lie down like a tired child,
> and weep away the life of care
> which he has borne and yet must bear :

but passion and yearning are still too strong in him for self-abandonment. Then he hears sounds—a strain of music and voices—the nuns or monks perhaps, singing an evening hymn to the blessèd Mary, mother of passion and of peace ! He moves on slowly and softly, listening. His hopelessness, his weariness are soothed into rest : trust enters into him, trust in the aims of life, that general life in which his own is now merged, even as the yearning of passion is lost in the sweetness of peace. . . .

When she had finished, there was a long pause, and then Gildea thanked her for the pleasure she had given him. Mrs. Medwin and Maddock began to speak of the piece, Maddock expressing his pleasure at it and his admiration for Miss Medwin's playing.

"You are, then, a lover of this Chopin ?" said Gildea to Miss Medwin, "But he is not your Master, as you would say ?"

"No," she answered, "he is not my Master.—I suppose you mean Beethoven by that ?" she added, looking up at him. He assented.

"And yet," she said, "I cannot somehow call even him Master. I do not love music as I ought to do—especially Beethoven and Wagner. They are great, these men, very great, but I cannot lose myself in their spirit as I should do. I often feel this."

"It was one of Heine's few fantastic sayings," said Gildea, "that Chopin was the Raphael of the piano, and indeed a piece like this, or the stately opening of the Thirteenth Nocturne —You remember it ?" (She assented)—"or the Marche Funèbre, help to see what he meant ; but to call him a Raphael seems to me inapt. No Raphael, for instance, would have dreamed of so entirely giving himself up to the influence of his passion as Chopin does. Surely it is not in *his* spirit that you can lose yourself ?"

"No," she said, "less than in Beethoven's. But perhaps Heine only meant his expression about Chopin comparatively. Chopin, you remember, is the only great composer who devoted himself to the piano. Certainly he is a master of it, but his style of art is not like Raphael's—at least so far as I know of Raphael."

They came back talking into the other room, where Gildea, from a glance at Mrs. Medwin's face, perceived that she now wished them to go down to the yacht. In a few minutes he brought the conversation round to the subject and, having asked and she having expressed her wish, the party was presently crossing the lawn on its way down to the small landing-stage, close to which the "Petrel" had now been brought in. Mrs. Medwin, between Maddock and Alcock, was some yards ahead of Gildea and Miss Medwin who were following them.

"You did not know," Gildea was saying to her, "that Mr. Hawkesbury was a friend of mine? He has been having lunch with us, and only just went away before you arrived. He, and another friend of mine whom you perhaps have met in Melbourne, Mr. Fitzgerald—No?—were unable to stay."

"So I supposed," said Miss Medwin, "or something like that.—You do not perhaps know," she added, "that my aunt has a dislike for him that really almost amounts to antipathy?"

"Yes," said Gildea, "I was aware of it: his social opinions are too much for her, and Sydney Medwin annoys her by constantly mentioning both them and him. A meeting would have been awkward indeed, but I made my calculations carefully, and I should have regretted not giving my friend Fitzgerald the opportunity of making Hawkesbury's acquaintance. In a few days one will be going due north and the other due south, but I hope they will meet again later on. Two more charming examples of the two species of enthusiast it would be hard to find."

"What do you call the two species?"

"The enthusiast of heat and the enthusiast of light: both are to me equally beautiful, equally charming!"

"Mr. Hawkesbury, then," she said, "is the enthusiast of heat? I have never known any man so much in earnest as he is. He seems to understand nothing but devotion or abhorrence; and yet how well he generally conceals this from those whom he thinks unworthy of the knowledge of it! His patience and courtesy have often astonished and filled me with admiration. I have heard him arguing with a stupid opponent, and I have heard him addressing a crowd. His self-restraint, his clearness, were simply wonderful. Has he ever spoken to you of his friend and Master, as he says,—James Holden?"

"No," answered Gildea, "but I happen to have seen Holden myself.—But here we are!"

Alcock from the deck and Maddock from the shore had assisted Mrs. Medwin over the plank into the "Petrel," and now Miss Medwin, after shaking hands, expressing her regrets that he could not come, and saying good-bye to Maddock, followed.

Mrs. Medwin, Miss Medwin, Alcock and Gildea gathered opposite Maddock, with whom they talked while the ropes were being cast loose and the yacht got ready for starting. Then, as she glided away, bending slightly as the wind caught and filled her sails, Maddock took off his hat and stood bareheaded, bowing and waving farewell.

A more charming day for such a trip, it would have been hard to choose. The air was warmer than in the morning, but the breeze was still strong enough to prevent the volumes of foul smoke which issued from the funnels of the harbour steamers from polluting the air and spoiling the view. The "Petrel" made straight for the main channel of the harbour in the direction of the Heads.

While Gildea was away talking with his skipper about the arrangements that had been made for the trip, the other three passengers moved about looking at the yacht, praising and admiring its neatness and cleanness. And it was worthy too both of the praise and admiration which they bestowed on its general completeness, that namely of silence, and of the praise and admiration which they who were skilled in such matters bestowed on its sailing-powers.

Presently Gildea rejoined them, and the conversation flowed on lightly and pleasantly.

"I notice," said Miss Medwin, "that you carry very little gear up aloft. Your masts too are unusually tall, are they not?"

Gildea gave a pleased smile.

"Yes," he said, "they call her the ghost yacht at Cowes. I use as little hempen rope as I can. When the great point is speed, every extra inch that you give to the prise of the wind is of importance. The steel, you see, does not offer half as much resistance as the ordinary hempen rope. Besides which, I have in several cases done away with a rope altogether where I believed one, if properly handled, could do for two."

Miss Medwin, who knew the rigging and handling of a sailing-ship fairly well, asked for an explanation of how one or two things were done, which he gave her with a certain pleasure.

"And what," she said, "do your sailors think of your altera-tions?"

He laughed.

"They say the Old Man—that is my name with them—"

"It is the name of all skippers with their sailors, is it not?" she asked smiling.

He assented.

"—They say, or rather used to say, that I had a twist that way. The conservatism of sailors and builders as regards ships is quite wonderful. Imagine that, when they came to build iron sailing ships instead of wood, they actually had and have the stupidity to put up masts of the same circumference as the old wooden ones, although thereby they gain no extra strength, and expose square yards on yards needlessly to the prise of the wind! I would venture to say that this alone makes a difference of three for four knots per hour in a head wind to the speed of the vessel."

Miss Medwin thought Gildea more charming in his capacity of intelligent amateur captain than as consummate master of things social. They moved down together towards the stern, and stood there talking and looking forward. Mrs. Medwin and Alcock were standing together talking a little way in front of them. Then Edgar appeared with seats and rugs, which he offered to Mrs. Medwin and Alcock, who sat down, Mrs. Medwin with a rug over her knees, and then came aft to the other two, who accepted two chairs, but for the present remained standing as they talked.

Presently there came a pause in the conversation and Miss Medwin sat down, Gildea following suit. The pause became a silence. At last he broke it.

"You have noticed," he said, "how different is the effect on you of the sea, in a steamer and in a boat?"

"Yes," she said, "I have noticed it. The steamer goes its own determined way, breaking its sympathy with winds and waters, and you—you are so high up that you cannot mingle in the being of the spirits, the breathings of their lips, the wavings of their hands, the tossings of their hair."

"*Where,*" he said smiling,

> "*where the wild white horses play,*
> *champ and chafe and toss in the spray.*"

She smiled in turn. She was looking before her across the sunny rolling billows to where, against some high brown jagged rocks, the foam-mantle of the breakers rose ever silently and fell. She was breathing in gently and serenely the delight of the sea, the bright breeze, the movement of the yacht, the divine blue free expansion of the clouds and skies. There was a silence.

"You are not fond of steamers, then?" he asked with a side-look.

"No," she said, "except in rough weather, and then I too feel the elation of my kind,—the frail race of men which can yet dominate the winds and waters and make their paths along the neck of the untameable sea.—You do not know," she added, leaving her extraneous delight for a moment and looking at him with a touch of self-amusement, "you do not know how I swell with pride when I watch a great man-of-war sailing on and on with such serene confidence, dominating the expanse of water like a thing of self-evident strength and beauty. I remember once making sand-forts with some children in England in a little rock-girt cove, and suddenly I looked up and there, almost filling our narrow horizon, was a great white troop-ship passing close to the shore. It struck me quite dumb for a moment; and then I began to applaud and shout like a Bacchant, the children following suit." She turned her face away again, laughing, looking here and there, delighting again in what she felt and saw.

"You are a true daughter of kindly men," he said, laughing too, all suspicion of mockery passed away from look and tone. There was another silence. Gildea was beginning to perceive in himself a feeling he had never felt before, the feeling that he was in the presence and even in the influence of a girl-woman, (Such was the idea presented to him), of a spiritual force as consummate as, but wholly differing from, his own. In a few moments he had recognized this, and by a wonderful stroke of intuition divined the meaning of it. It partook of the nature of a revelation. He seemed to see all his past life in a new light. He felt that she—she, this woman, this girl, this child here—had, by some unknown wonderful means, won the true talisman of life, that talisman whose omnipotence is perpetuity. It was, then, possible, after all, to combine perfect knowledge of life with the radiant joy and peace of perfect trust in it!—It partook of the nature of a revelation and, to second thoughts, of a delusion. His lip curled : he almost despised himself for the swift speed with which a suddenly begotten hope had leaped to a birth whose form and pressure was but the mask of credulity. "There has been no man," he said to himself, "save Goethe, who knew what life was and yet could have a weariless joy in it. Carlyle well said that this man was to have no imitators or successors.—*Nostra vita a che val? solo a spregiarla.*" And yet the idea of a new life, a life wherein might be found something more than sweet resignation, hedonistic merely or even optimistic, but supplying thought, action, and speech with a motive-power whose strength should be in its truth—the idea would not be shaken off by mere self-contempt at credulity in it.

"To tell you the truth," he said to her, "I could almost envy you your pure free joy in things."

She looked at him, surprise passing swiftly into serene observation.

"What troubles you," she said, "that you should not have it yourself?"

He smiled slightly as he answered her.

"Pleasure, however sweet, however clear, is not joy.—And yet," he added quickly, "I would not change my pleasure for your joy."

"No?"

"A child has joy, a man has pleasure: joy, then, is a step backward. It may excel in height, as we should say, but breadth is the finer quality. The mountains are noble, but the sea, encompassing all lands, is great."

"The sea also is deep, it has its valleys whose shadow is nadir to the zenith peaks and light. I will not grant you your simile. You must not mock at joy, for joy is the gift not only of childhood which precedes, but of maturity which follows, manhood. I would sooner be a Christian and have joy than a Heathen with only pleasure."

"Christianity," said Gildea, "is spiritual opium. You do not eat it?"

"No," she said, "I see no use in drugs. But, as I said, I would sooner take drugs that give me joy than live on meats and wines that only gave me pleasure. Joy is mine, but pleasure is every one's."

"You had, then, once the temptation of drugs?"

"Yes," she assented a little dreamily, "I had the temptation.—And yet," she added with a sudden return of interest, "it is wonderful how little of *these* drugs you can take, and live with energy and joy. Are the lips of Monica pallid or her eyes stony? Theresa has a clear mind : she can set her house in order. The songs and glories of the Creatures, do they not pass purely and freely, as you say, through the lips of Saint Francis ? "

" True, but for us this aspect of the thing is past. The central trust in the Christ-God is a skeletoned shadow, that the grate holds up a moment beyond its time of falling in. You see it lying, a pile of shapeless ash, and wonder it ever stood. The Mother of Love and Grief appears no more save in the brilliant burning of distorted vision. It is a case of opium or nothing ! "

" You are right," she said, " and so I saw it."

" What, then, remains," he asked, " but resignation ? There is no joy in patience. Nay, worse, there is little pleasure. I too take drugs, and I have more than once thought that, if Fate had not kindly given me the wherewithal to buy them, I should have ended the dreary business for ever. What is the good of our life except to despise it ? says Leopardi. It is just bearable with drugs, but, without, I cannot think it worth the bearing. Pure indifference keeps more of its high souls alive now than the world wots of. They are careless of life, but they are equally careless of death. They live merely waiting for chance to kill them, or for life to become unendurable enough for them to care to kill themselves Such men are not miserable. Sometimes, it is true, they suffer disgust ; but they know nothing of despair, for despair means illusion, and they have the truth. Sometimes, again they have pleasure. But how, tell me, is it possible to have at once both truth and joy ? "

" All this," she said, " I too felt, and not so long ago— although I could not have put it to myself so clearly. You, I think, have learned your belief more by living than by reading : with me it was different. Before I began properly to live,—to be free, that is, to examine and try everything for myself,—I had arrived at my belief, and all my living has only confirmed me in it."

" *What* is your belief?" he asked.

She smiled and shook her head.

" I will not try to tell it you explicitly," she said, " for fear of harming it. Analysis is a mistake, and now I have so long known this, that I have little temptation to give way to it.

You, it seems, have tried to be a Heathen. You gave yourself up to the natural joy of your youth and fortune, your health and strength and riches and powers, until the joy turned to pleasure and the pleasure to almost pain. Then you went for interest to the spiritual life of those about you, and again joy turned to pleasure and pleasure to almost pain. But *you*—you were not one that knew how to be resigned! You could not, as your great Master could, add to the 'Vanity of Vanities, all is vanity' the 'Fear God and keep his commandments; for this is the whole duty of man.' Far otherwise with *you*, as you have told me, was 'the conclusion of the whole matter.'"

"And you?" he said with the tone of comrade to comrade, "and you?"

"I had a revelation. It took place in a London fog in front of a fire in a little backroom where I had my books. And, as it were, scales fell from my eyes, and I saw men as trees walking." Gildea, the true arch-mocker, for the first time in his life had to undergo the sensation of doubt whether or no he was being mocked at.

"Well?" he said.

"Well, I was in a rather miserable state at the time. Someone to whom I was attached had had to leave me. I was sick of trying to satisfy myself with the life of pleasure as pleasure, and I had the temptation to take spiritual drugs, for I felt an appalling loneliness of soul. I thought that no one had ever looked at things as I felt I should like to look at them, and I was at times almost afraid that I was suffering under a delusion that might end in something very like madness. Then I had my revelation. I found out that there had been a whole race whose central belief was the one I was stretching out my arms to."

"Greece?" said Gildea, "Greece?"

"Yes, Greece! Here I found were men who realized the secret of life, who knew what Truth was. They looked at life as it was, and they saw calmly and clearly that the butterfly's life is enough for the butterfly, and the man's for the man. They took no spiritual opium as the Christians do: they have no yearning love. They have not resignation as the Heathens have, resignation that sullenly accepts the evil, or that brightly determines to make the best of the good in things. They have better; they have truth and light and joy! Take, then, your Christian Faith and Love: your Heathen Trust and Hope: *I* am a Pagan, and my care is Truth and Light!—And I found," she went on, " I found, after a time, that there had been others in these later days that had looked, or striven to look at things, as I did. Such was Goethe, such was Keats. With Goethe the freedom of his Paganism was bought at a great price, but Keats was born free. When Goethe recognised what it was to have been a Christian, to be a Heathen, and to wish to be a Pagan, he renounced his past and present with all the strength of his soul, and fixed his eyes resolutely on his future. But he never won it—that is to say, as he had won the others. He was never a Pagan as he was a Heathen or a Christian. The Second Part of Faust is not like the First. It is not with impunity that we have passed through the Christianity of Catholicism and the Heathenism of the Renascence. A Dante or a Shakspere could not be shaken off by a Goethe, and a Sophokles wholly put on. Is a great pagan soul possible yet? How shall we say no with what Keats might have become before us?—Sometimes I think," she said a little dreamily, " that I am the only one of my time who understood these great men; Goethe, the god of the Transition, Keats, the Herakles of Modernity, strangled in his cradle by the serpents of Hera! And, for either of them, I would readily have given my life." . . .

Mrs. Medwin turned round towards them, Alcock turning too, as if they had reached a point in their conversation in which a break was expedient. Then Mrs. Medwin and Alcock rose and came up to them.

"Is not the water exquisitely clear?" she said to Gildea, " It reminds me of Capreae. It only wants the beautiful coral rocks."

Gildea smilingly assented. He remembered a remark of Mrs. Medwin's to the effect that, as you approached Melbourne from the north, it was like the bay of Naples with Vesuvius.

"Miss Medwin," he said, with the smile changing on his face and becoming sweet and radiant, "Miss Medwin has just been explaining to me a passage from Goethe which I never understood."

"Indeed?" said Mrs. Medwin, "I did not know you read German, Alice. Was it a passage from Faust? I think Faust is very difficult, and I do not understand the Second Part in the least."

"No," answered Gildea, "It was not from Faust.—

> Vom Halben zu entwöhnen;
> im Ganzen, Guten, Schönen
> resolut zu leben."

"That is not very difficult, Sir Horace," said Mrs. Medwin.

Gildea, in answer to the dumb look on Alcock's face, who did not happen to know German, translated it with courtesy:

"'I resolved to wean myself,'" he said, "'from halves, and to live for the Whole, the Good, the Beautiful.'"

"And what does it *mean?*" asked Alcock.

"Ah," answered Gildea smiling, "Miss Medwin must tell you that!"

April, 1885.

THE END.

MELBOURNE :

WILLIAM INGLIS AND CO., PRINTERS,

FLINDERS STREET EAST.

www.ingramcontent.com/pod-product-compliance
Lightning Source LLC
Chambersburg PA
CBHW030613040726
47497CB00008B/2957